THE WORLD'S CLASSICS

# THE FIXED PERIOD

ANTHONY TROLLOPE (1815–82), the son of a failing London barrister, was brought up an awkward and unhappy youth amidst debt and privation. His mother maintained the family by writing, but Anthony's own first novel did not appear until 1847, when he had at length established a successful Civil Service career in the Post Office, from which he retired in 1867. After a slow start, he achieved fame, with 47 novels and some 16 other books, and sales sometimes topping 100,000. He was acclaimed an unsurpassed portraitist of the lives of the professional and landed classes, especially in his perennially popular *Chronicles of Barsetshire* (1855–67), and his six brilliant Palliser novels (1864–80). His fascinating *Autobiography* (1883) recounts his successes with an enthusiasm which stems from memories of a miserable youth. Throughout the 1870s he developed new styles of fiction, but was losing critical favour by the time of his death.

DAVID SKILTON is the Head of the School of English Studies, Journalism, and Philosophy at the University of Wales, Cardiff. He is general editor of the Trollope Society/Folio Society edition of the novels of Anthony Trollope, and author of *Anthony Trollope and His Contemporaries* (Harlow, 1972) and *Defoe to the Victorians: Two Centuries of the English Novel* (Harmondsworth, 1985). He has edited numerous Victorian novels for Penguin, Pan, and the World's Classics series.

THE WORLD'S CLASSICS

ANTHONY TROLLOPE

*The Fixed Period*

*Edited with an Introduction by*
DAVID SKILTON

Oxford   New York
OXFORD UNIVERSITY PRESS
1993

Oxford University Press, Walton Street, Oxford OX2 6DP

Oxford  New York  Toronto
Delhi  Bombay  Calcutta  Madras  Karachi
Kuala Lumpur  Singapore  Hong Kong  Tokyo
Nairobi  Dar es Salaam  Cape Town
Melbourne  Auckland  Madrid
and associated companies in
Berlin  Ibadan

Oxford is a trade mark of Oxford University Press

First published as a World's Classics paperback 1993

British Library Cataloguing in Publication Data
Data available

Library of Congress Cataloging in Publication Data
Trollope, Anthony, 1815–1882.
The fixed period/Anthony Trollope: edited with an introduction
by David Skilton.
p.   cm. — (The World's classics)
Includes bibliographical references.
I. Skilton, David.  II. Title.  III. Series.
PR5684.F5  1993  823'.8—dc20  92-18982
ISBN 0-19-282842-8

1 3 5 7 9 10 8 6 4 2

Typeset by Best-set Typesetter Ltd., Hong Kong
Printed in Great Britain by
BPCC Hazells Ltd.
Aylesbury, Bucks

# CONTENTS

# CONTENTS

# INTRODUCTION

FOR many novels one can write an introduction in such a way as to conceal some crucial secret of the narrative which would damage readers' enjoyment if they knew it in advance. Introductions to other novels have to carry a warning that they of necessity let some cat out of some bag, and should not be read until the novel is finished. The present introductory essay is rather of this second kind. Although *The Fixed Period* is innocent of suspense, it is none the less so unlike any other of Trollope's works that it cannot be discussed without disclosing things which—certainly for the first chapter or so—it should be left to the text itself to surprise the reader with. Please therefore postpone your reading of these pages at least until the curious nature of the succeeding narrative has become apparent to you, and Trollope's only exercise in extended Swiftian irony has revealed itself to you in its own terms.

As any reader will know who has taken the editor's advice, *The Fixed Period* is based on the idea that in the second half of the twentieth century a British colony will have success-fully sought independence and then used its new legislative freedom to introduce compulsory euthanasia at the age of 66, in order to relieve itself of the burden of an ageing population—and the aged themselves of the burden of their continuing lives. Despite a web of personal and topical references such as we usually find in a Victorian novel, what most immediately strikes the reader is Trollope's unusual detachment from his subject. In general, while reading a Trollopian fiction, the reader is prepared to treat what it presents as paralleling the 'real' world. There is abundant evidence in the fictional world of the working of familiar socio-economic laws and other forces which shape people's lives, and those readers with a taste for the grander con-

viii                    *Introduction*

structions of humanist thought see the characters of the
novels as representative examples of 'human nature' in
action. Moreover, many of the frequent discussions within
the fiction, of the fiction itself, its world and its workings,
can be shown to coincide with the author's own opinions or
experience as he expresses them elsewhere. We are therefore lulled into a sense of security, based on the assumption
that we are in some sort of contact with the author's mind,
and that the narrator, whether an omniscient narrator or a
protagonist, is in some degree Trollope himself. But his
story-line is not always so straightforward. One of his *Tales
of All Countries*, 'A Ride across Palestine', so disturbs our
usual Trollopian assumptions as to induce us to contemplate
a situation in which a Victorian gentleman offers to rub
a young lady's saddle-sores with brandy—but even this
narrator-protagonist resembles Anthony Trollope on his
travels. There are more extreme cases. The unattractive
narrator of 'George Walker at Suez', for example, is one of
the few cases of Trollope successfully assuming an alien
persona and forcing us temporarily to change the reading
habits we usually bring to his work. *The Fixed Period* goes
much further. The narrator of this novel is the most thoroughly unreliable voice Trollope ever assumed, and the
novel itself is the most complex exercise in irony by this
great Victorian prose realist.

     Much of the irony in *The Fixed Period* is easy enough to
reconcile with sound Victorian morality and common sense.
In espousing the cause of compulsory euthanasia, President
Neverbend is running directly counter to the accepted
standards of Western civilization, and the irony consists in
what a literary critic writing in the 1870s defined as 'a mode
of speech which in derision says the very opposite of what it
really means; which praises what it wishes to blame, and
blames what it wishes to praise'.[1] Analysed in these terms,

---

[1] From a summary of the ideas of the German Romantics in 'A Smoking
Satirist', a review of Samuel Butler's *Erewhon*, in *Cope's Tobacco Plant*, 1
(July, 1872), 336.

much of the 'meaning' of the *The Fixed Period* is easy to locate. The political scheme the narrator advocates 'consists altogether of the abolition of the miseries, weakness, and *fainéant* imbecility of old age, by the prearranged ceasing to live of those who would otherwise become old' (p. 6). By simple reversal, we discover that readers are meant to understand that such legalized killing is wicked, that human life is always to be respected, that the old are to be cherished by the young, and so on. Along the way we take note of the fact that Mr Neverbend views himself as a benefactor of the human race, but that we take him to be a dangerous extremist, whose fanaticism has taken on resonances which Trollope could not have foreseen, since it deforms the language in a way which has become frighteningly familiar from our experience of authoritarian regimes in the twentieth century. In Neverbend's final solution to the problems of an ageing population, the words 'killing', 'victim', and 'execution' are outlawed. Forcible imprisonment becomes 'deposition', while death at the hands of the agents of the state becomes a 'mode of transition' (p. 21) and 'an act of grace' (p. 33), to be achieved in a 'gracious and alluring' ceremony (pp. 55–6). A chilling pseudo-reasonableness, characteristic of certain types of political and bureaucratic utterance, informs such expressions as 'the prearranged ceasing to live of those who would otherwise become old' (p. 6). It appears that the verb 'to Fix-Period' someone has developed (p. 156)—a usage which highlights the strangeness of this futuristic land far more effectively than Trollope's imagined technology of steam-tricycles and hair-telephones.

Thus far there is no difficulty in the interpretation. And at the same time it is even possible to produce a plausible biographical explanation: on reaching his 'Fixed Period' Trollope, overweight, asthmatic, and suffering from angina, was still actively writing, and by 'blaming what he wished to praise' was demonstrating how valuable life was after 65, and how tenaciously it was to be clung to. Besides, had he remained a Civil Servant, he would now have been compulsorily retired as one presumed too enfeebled by age to do

useful work. The whole thing might therefore be fuelled by
personal feelings about ageing, and, through its irony, be a
celebration of the continuing value of life after the government's official retirement age.

The text 'praises what it wishes to blame', and creates its
effects by exposing the rhetoric of fanaticism. The following
passage is a fine example:

Two mistakes have been made by mankind in reference to their
own race,—first, in allowing the world to be burdened with the
continued maintenance of those whose cares should have been
made to cease, and whose troubles should be at an end. . . . And the
second, in requiring those who remain to live a useless and painful
life. (p. 6)

The chief proponent of the Fixed Period reports that for
him 'the politico-economic view of the subject was always
very strong', and, like many other extremists, he is convinced
that people can be 'educated' to accept his views:

In fact, there was not a word to be said against us except that which
referred to the feelings of the young and old. Feelings are
changeable . . . (p. 8)

I had known from the beginning that the fear of death was a human
weakness. To obliterate that fear from the human heart, and to
build up a perfect manhood that should be liberated from so vile a
thraldom, had been one of the chief objects of my scheme. (p. 34)

All this—chilling as it may be in its reverberations for
readers familiar with the history of the twentieth century—is
easily accepted as a straightforward reversal of the views of
the author and his society. Similarly, it is not difficult to
accommodate the series of calculated shocks which Trollope
administers to his contemporary readers, who learn among
other things that only the 'scum of the population' adheres
to the British cause in this ex-colony (p. 116). The general
effect of strangeness is bolstered by references to an Anglo-
French naval war against Russia and the United States, the
violent struggle by New Zealand for independence, and the
secession of the western states of America. The situation,

however, is complicated by the fact that Neverbend believes in a number of things which later readers may find perfectly acceptable, and to at least one of which the author himself is known to have subscribed. In Britannula, for example, the study of modern languages is universal in schools, cremation is legal, and capital punishment has been abolished. These things serve both to create a fictional world and to characterize President Neverbend, but the irony of the book is more subtle than this suggests. Further striking deformations of the language come not from the mistaken idealism or fanaticism of Neverbend, but from the British, who put an end to the Fixed Period by force. The benefits to be derived from killing the aged are listed with an effect most easily likened to Swift's 'Modest Proposal' to cure Ireland's overpopulation and food shortage by cooking and eating human young. Another great political satirist, Orwell, is the comparison that springs to mind for the 'Secretary of Benevolence', who has replaced the Secretary for War in Britain, and who sends a gunboat, HMS *John Bright*, to subdue the ex-colony. The ship is mounted with a huge gun, a '250-ton swiveller': an ultimate weapon so powerful that it could destroy a city with one shot and so devastating that it need never be used. (The idea of a weapon too powerful to be used may have come from Bulwer Lytton's science fiction novel *The Coming Race* (1871), in which individuals control a force, the 'vril', which has enormous potential for good or ill, and has developed their sense of moral responsibility because of the lethal effect of ever unleashing it.) Britain comes off rather badly, even though its attitude to longevity may be unimpeachable: it is the newly imposed British governor who 'makes flowery speeches, and thinks that they will stand in lieu of independence' (p. 15).

There is a twist, then, to the irony. The representatives of that which the author is supposed to 'wish to praise' stand morally condemned. Moreover, the system which he 'wishes to blame' includes one of Trollope's pet projects: cremation. It is worth pursuing this. When Trollope wrote *The Fixed Period*, cremation was not legal in Britain, and indeed did not become so until 1884, two years after his death, when a Welsh general practitioner, Dr William Price, was acquitted of the charge of cremating an infant. It was an emotionally charged subject, and Neverbend recalls reading 'how feelings had been allowed in England to stand in the way of the great work of cremation' (p. 9). This reference may indicate ways in which the subject was more deeply involved in the conception of *The Fixed Period* than might at first appear. Resistance to Neverbend's system is aimed to a surprising degree not only against compulsory euthanasia but against cremation too and, though the two issues seem to us to be totally different in kind, the violent public reaction against people like Trollope himself, who advocated cremation in the England of the 1870s, may have suggested to the author in 1880 the idea of the lone (though in this case misguided) philanthropist standing up for his ideals in Britannula in 1980.

When examined further this idea is not so fanciful. Trollope, together with his friend Millais and others, was one of the signatories of a document which brought the Cremation Society of England into existence in 1874, under the leadership of the Queen's surgeon, Sir Henry Thompson. In January and March 1874, Thompson published two articles in the *Contemporary Review*, which were republished as a pamphlet in March of the same year under the title *Cremation: The Treatment of the Body after Death*. The aims of the cremationists were largely hygienic, but partly social and partly economic—for example, to ease the pressure on land around their cities. One aspect that must have appealed particularly to Trollope—with his distaste for extravagant funerals and extended mourning, which celebrated the dead at the cost of the living—was the possibility that a change in funerary customs would eventually bring about a revolution in social attitudes towards death. For Sir Henry Thompson cremation offered

the opportunity . . . of escape from the ghastly but costly ceremonial which mostly awaits our remains after death. How often have the slender shares of the widow and orphan been diminished in order to testify, and so unnecessarily, their loving memory of the deceased, by display of plumes and silken scarves about the unconscious clay.[2]

The cremationists had literary and philosophical support for their views. In *Utopia* (1515–16), Sir Thomas More describes joyful celebrations at Utopian cremations; in *Erewhon* (1872) Samuel Butler sees cremation and the scattering of ashes as part of a healthy attitude towards death among Erewhonians (1872); and in *The Coming Race* (1871) Bulwer Lytton, too, associates cremation with a healthy lack of excessive public mourning—though his view, unlike Trollope's or Thompson's, is religious at bottom, not worldly commonsensical. But in all these cases the object is, in Bulwer Lytton's words, not to 'invest death with gloomy and hideous associations'.[3] Neverbend's methods are more extreme, but he too wishes to effect a change to 'healthier' public attitudes to dying through a victory of reason over inherited feelings.

There is a close similarity between the methods of argument of Neverbend and the Queen's surgeon. When the President of Britannula computes the net yearly financial saving through the disposal of all 67-year-olds (p. 8), he may be less attractive but he is no more ridiculous than Thompson when the latter calculates a national saving on bone imports of 'much more than half a million pounds sterling per annum' through the scattering of human ashes as fertilizer.[4] Something in this very Victorian way of arguing in simple monetary terms seems to have struck Trollope as either absurd or unpleasant, and the ponderous solemnity of Neverbend's grisly calculations strangely resembles Thompson's. The final similarity between the real-life philanthropist and the ironic fiction is that each has abuse heaped on him when his opponents accuse him of 'savagery

[2] Sir Henry Thompson, *The Treatment of the Body after Death*, 2nd edn. (London, 1874), 19.

[3] Bulwer Lytton, *The Coming Race* (Edinburgh, 1871), 200.

[4] Thompson, *Treatment*, 11.

and cannibalism' in the case of Thompson,[5] or of being 'a bloody-minded cannibal' in the case of Mr Neverbend (pp. 179–80).

What Trollope has done is to take a complex of public and personal reactions towards a scheme for reform in which he believed, and transfer it ironically on to a proposal which the reader must find repellent, while all the time retaining a narrative closeness with the monomaniac who advocates the reform. Of course, if Trollope was hoping to further the cause of cremation, he was wildly misguided, for the worst thing he could have done was to associate it in the public mind with a greater horror, like compulsory euthanasia; but then Trollope did not write crusading fiction. What *The Fixed Period* presents is a study of what it means to be a fanatical advocate of a reform which meets with great public resistance, and yet steadfastly to believe that the feelings of one's opponents will 'be taught to comply with reason' (pp. 8–9). Some of Trollope's contemporaries thought the book a mere *jeu d'esprit*, but closer examination reveals it to be a work of complex irony and, at the very least, a presentation of the moral and political problems that face those who try to implement bold reforms.

Clearly *The Fixed Period* is not ironic in the simple, everyday sense which implies a reversal of all views expressed in order to arrive at the 'truth' of the author's own opinions—a kind of mathematical 'change of sign' throughout. Moreover, like all good ironists, Trollope further obscured the question in real life. As we have seen, his attitude to age was mixed. He was not a young 65, and his asthma and his angina troubled him increasingly. But he continued to write with undiminished energy, and he is reported to have angrily told an enquirer, an 'intimate friend', that he *meant* 'every word' of *The Fixed Period*.[6] His retort is grandly unhelpful, and leads us to turn to another concept of irony as 'not merely a

[5] Ibid. 43.
[6] Anon. (W. Lucas Collins), 'The Autobiography of Anthony Trollope', *Blackwood's Magazine*, 134 (Nov. 1883), 577–96.

clear survey of [the thoughts under examination] but ... the necessary counterpart or complement of artistic inspiration; the floating of the artist above the matter he treats, his free play therewith'.[7] Biographers and critics of Trollope do well to remember that, however beguiling the invitation to inhabit his texts as unproblematic extensions of the world, it is accepted at their peril.

The idea of compulsory euthanasia was probably suggested by Massinger's play *The Old Law*, which, as Bradford A. Booth points out in this context, Trollope is known to have read a few years before, on 8 July 1876.[8] *The Old Law* is not one of the great dramas of the language, and there are few close textual connections between the two works, but Massinger's play concerns the revival of an 'old law' which enables sons of old fathers to have them put to death so that their property may be passed on. The topics of avarice and impiety to the old are thus present in both texts, as is the conflict between written laws and morality. Booth is surely right to regard the play in the light of a kind of 'Jamesian *donnée*' rather than a source of detailed inspiration for *The Fixed Period*. The materialism of Massinger's characters is brought up to date by Neverbend's use of statistical evidence: 'Statistics have told us that the sufficient sustenance of an old man is more costly than the feeding of a young one' and the contrary view is 'an ill-judged and thoughtless tenderness ... no better than unpardonable weakness' (pp. 6–7)—arguments which again chillingly anticipate the rhetoric of reasonableness of twentieth-century totalitarian regimes.

Yet (and here the danger of 'interpreting' complex ironies becomes apparent) this same application of reason to Britannulan affairs has introduced issues about which the late-twentieth-century reader will probably feel quite differently from the author and his public. For example, the

[7] 'A Smoking Satirist'.
[8] Bradford A. Booth, *Anthony Trollope: Aspects of his Life and Art* (London: Edward Hulton, 1958), 129.

abolition of capital punishment (p. 67) and the practice of cremation might not have been taken by the majority of Trollope's original readers as a sign of the progress of civilization. And, not knowing whether these things stand in the text as instances of humane, reasonable reform, or as examples of misguided idealism, we are left uncertain as to how the text was read when it first appeared, and are thrown back on our own resources in our negotiations with the text. On some matters we know Trollope's personal opinions— for example, his insistence on bicameralism as a constitutional safeguard is apparent from the political discussions in *Australia and New Zealand* (1873), and from his admiration of the strengths of the American Constitution. We can imagine, too, an easy, or perhaps uneasy, acceptance, nine years after the Education Act, of Neverbend's comment that although 'not a man or a woman in the British Isles is now ignorant of his letters . . . the knowledge seldom approaches to any literary taste' (p. 15).

Of course Trollope is also having fun. His relations with Gladstone were troubled at about this time, and so he returns to his earlier attack in *Australia and New Zealand* on the grotesque impropriety (by 'gentlemanly' standards) of naming the proposed capital of Queensland after the Grand Old Man, by having the capital of this prosperous but ideologically uncomfortable ex-colony of Britannula named after his descendant. (Regrettably Trollope does not invent a term for 'the cult of personality'!) And how much fun he must have had inventing the story of a descendant of John Bright quelling a mutiny by sitting on a powder-keg! The overweight author must also have enjoyed putting William Banting, author of *A Letter on Corpulence* (1863) and the popularizer of weight-reduction by diet, on a par with Harvey, Wilberforce, and Cobden as a benefactor of the human race. We know that Trollope had followed Banting's recommendations, because we find George Eliot reporting it in a letter of 15 December 1864: 'I have seen people much changed by the Banting system. Mr A. Trollope is thinner by means of it, and is otherwise the better for the self-denial.'[9] In this minor respect, though perhaps in few others, Trollope appears in *The Fixed Period* in his familiar role of the voice of the mid-Victorian period.

The basic story-line of *The Fixed Period* is elaborated by Trollope's usual compulsory love interest, an affair between Craswellers's daughter and the President's son, on which characteristically the narrator places little importance, since it feeds off human emotions rather than principles and calculation. Though not in itself very gripping, the love plot is formally well integrated into the story. President Neverbend, of course, fails not only to understand what happens in the emotional lives of his own domestic circle, but also to grasp why its members do not follow his political theories in their everyday lives.

The other elaborations are more or less adequate for their purposes. Futuristic technology was not Trollope's forte. On the other hand he shows his usual flair for social and political invention. Even a matter so apparently silly as the mechanical cricket match has comic relevance to Trollope's own time. The age of the Test Match had just begun and, at the time Trollope was writing, London was buzzing with the preparations for the match with Australia which was to end in the humiliation of England, and the invention of the term 'the Ashes' (coined 2 September 1882). Trollope was no lover of ball-games—indeed he probably could not see the ball well enough to play or to watch. At this key moment in the history of cricket, *The Fixed Period* touches on the question of professional and amateur status in sport, and it is worth noting that the Britannulans field a side of 'gentlemen', while the English rely on the skills of their professional players. The obsession of Britannulan youth—and especially of Jack Neverbend—with cricket parallels his father's *idée fixe* of euthanasia: 'It astonished me to find that the boy was quite as eager about his cricket as I was about my Fixed Period' (p. 74). Sport may be in the process of becoming a distraction from serious politics, in a world where an international sporting engagement relegates politics to second place, as the President puts off his favourite scheme and the British government stays its hand until the end of a cricket match (p. 59). The match is also made relevant to the question of ageing when a cricketer of 35 is described as already old, 'having advanced nearer to his Fixed Period than any other of the cricketers' (p. 76).

If Trollope did mean 'every word' of *The Fixed Period*, it is far from clear in what way he meant it. We have the poignant opinion of his elder brother, Thomas Adolphus, that Anthony would not have wished to survive if he had lost his mental powers. Writing from Rome on 6 December 1882, a month after Anthony's paralytic stroke, Thomas Adolphus says

This I can say, not only from my own feelings on the subject, but from many conversations with him on the subject, that I am very sure that it would be better for him to go, than to live with the consciousness that his mental powers were gone. I can conceive no unhappiness greater than his would be under such circumstances; and am very sure that he would consider himself fortunate to escape it by quitting the scene.[10]

This, of course, does nothing to provide an interpretation of the text. It is the danger and the privilege of ironists to be misinterpreted, and that most humane of physicians Sir William Osler, in a retirement address at Johns Hopkins University in 1905, drew down upon himself a bitter stream of vilification from the Press by humorously approving Mr Neverbend's scheme. So great was the uproar that the verb 'to oslerize' was coined to carry the meaning 'to chloroform old people'.[11] Such is the fate of those who expect their audiences to understand them when they use irony. Trollope

[9] R. C. Terry (ed.), *Trollope: Interviews and Recollections* (London: Macmillan, 1987), 164.

[10] N. John Hall (ed.), *The Letters of Anthony Trollope* (Stanford, Calif.: Stanford University Press, 1983), 1037.

[11] See the preface to the 2nd edn. of W. Osler, *Aequanimitas* (London: H. K. Lewis, 1906), and H. Cushing, *The Life of Sir William Osler*, 2 vols. (Oxford: Clarendon Press, 1925), i. 664–72.

may well have been speaking the truth when he told the 'intimate friend' that he *meant* every word of it. But did the friend, any more than Sir William Osler's critics, know what those words meant?

D.S.

# NOTE ON THE TEXT

TROLLOPE started work on *The Fixed Period* on 17 December 1880, immediately after completing *Kept in the Dark*, writing to his son, Henry, on the twenty-first of the month: 'I finished on Thursday the novel I was writing, and on Friday I began another. Nothing really frightens me but the idea of enforced idleness. As long as I can write books, even though they be not published, I think that I can be happy.'[1] Having completed the manuscript on 28 February 1881, he offered it to William Blackwood by a letter of the same date, describing it as 'a tale, the same length as Dr Wortle, very unlike that in structure and method'.[2] By an agreement dated 1 July 1881, Blackwood was to pay £100 on the commencement of serialization in *Blackwood's Magazine*, and £100 on completion. £250 was to be paid by a note at three months when the first book edition was published.[3]

On 7 September 1881 William Blackwood wrote to Trollope, 'would you see if you could dispense with the phrases of a religious character—mention of "God" & "The Lord" which strike me as rather unnecessary & do not heighten the effect whilst they may wound the feelings of strict people & bring down upon us a religious storm'. Trollope obliged: 'I return the first number of the Fixed Period corrected, and as I go on will endeavour to put out all the profanities.'[4] The novel thus appeared in a slightly censored version in *Blackwood's Magazine*, but Trollope restored most of the cuts for the two-volume edition.[5] A

---

[1] N. John Hall (ed.), *The Letters of Anthony Trollope* (Stanford, Calif., 1983), 886.
[2] Ibid. 904.
[3] Ibid. 913 n.
[4] Ibid. 923-4.
[5] See R. H. Super (ed.), *The Fixed Period* (Ann Arbor: University of Michigan Press, 1990), 175.

notable unrestored cut which occurs in Chapter One of the manscript, when Neverbend is recounting the arguments used for and against the Fixed Period, is indicated in the Explanatory Notes.

The novel was serialized from October 1881 to March 1882, and was published at 12s. in two volumes early in 1882—Michael Sadleir conjectures February,[6] but reviews did not appear in the *Athenaeum* and the *Spectator*, which were usually prompt in noticing Trollope's books, until 11 and 18 March. The volume division falls between Chapters six and seven. The first edition was set from the magazine text on Trollope's recommendation: 'I think you should print the Fixed Period from your own pages, and let me have them to give a final revise. I have observed no blunders in the Maga.'[7]

The authority on variants between the manuscript, the serial version and the two-volume first edition is R. H. Super's edition of the novel, published by University of Michigan Press, 1990. The present edition follows the first edition of 1882, with 'Gideon' changed to 'Gibeon' on page 45, and on page 32 a sentence changed which, as it occurs in the serial text and in the first edition, is confused. The insertion of 'not' is the present editor's conjectural emendation: 'It won't teach any one [not] to think it better to live than to die while he is fit to perform all the functions of life.'

---

[6] M. Sadleir, *Trollope: A Bibliography* (London, 1964), 189.
[7] Letter of 28 January 1882, in Hall (ed.), *Letters*, 943–4.

# SELECT BIBLIOGRAPHY

THERE are few extensive treatments of *The Fixed Period*. A definitive comparison of the serial version, the first edition text and the manuscript is found in R. H. Super's edition (Ann Arbor, Mich., 1990). All significant points about the novel in David Skilton, 'Trollope's futuristic novel: The Fixed Period', *Studies in the Literary Imagination*, 6 (1973), 39–50 are repeated in the introductory material and notes to the present edition. Otherwise brief treatments or mentions of the novel occur in a number of general works on Trollope, including Bradford A. Booth, *Anthony Trollope: Aspects of His Life and Art* (London, 1958), A. O. J. Cockshut, *Anthony Trollope* (London, 1955), P. D. Edwards, *Anthony Trollope: His Art and Scope* (St Lucia, Queensland, 1977), John Halperin, *Trollope and Politics: A Study of the Pallisers and Others* (London, 1977), Geoffrey Harvey, *The Art of Anthony Trollope* (London, 1980), James R. Kincaid, *The Novels of Anthony Trollope* (Oxford, 1977), Coral Lansbury, *The Reasonable Man: Trollope's Legal Fiction* (Princeton, NJ, 1981), Arthur Pollard, *Anthony Trollope* (London, 1978), Michael Sadleir, *Trollope: A Commentary* (London, 1927), L. P. and R. P. Stebbins, *The Trollopes: The Chronicle of a Writing Family* (London, 1946), R. C. Terry, *Anthony Trollope: The Artist in Hiding* (London, 1977), Robert Tracy, *Trollope's Later Novels* (Berkeley, Calif., 1978). Lists of articles on Sir William Osler and *The Fixed Period* controversy are found in R. H. Super's edition and in M. L. Irwin, *Trollope: A Bibliography* (New York, 1926).

Donald Smalley (ed.), *Anthony Trollope: The Critical Heritage* (London, 1969), despite a number of serious bibliographical errors, contains a useful collection of Victorian criticism of Trollope's fiction. Trollope's contemporary reception is analysed in David Skilton, *Anthony Trollope and His Contemporaries: A Study in the Theory and Conventions of Mid-Victorian Fiction* (London, 1972). An annotated bibliography of more recent criticism is found in J. C. Olmsted and J. E. Welch, *The Reputation of Trollope: An Annotated Bibliography 1925–1975* (New York, 1978), and a fuller listing of Trollope editions as well as secondary works is forthcoming in 1992 from the Trollope Society. The standard descriptive bibliography of Trollope's works in their original editions is Michael Sadleir, *Trollope: A Bibliography* (London, 1928).

The best studies of Trollope's Life are N. John Hall, *Trollope: A Biography* (Oxford, 1991), R. H. Super, *The Chronicler of Barsetshire: A Life of Anthony Trollope* (Ann Arbor, Mich., 1988) and Richard Mullen, *Anthony Trollope: A Victorian in His World* (London, 1990). His letters are admirably collected in N. John Hall (ed.), *The Letters of Anthony Trollope* (Stanford, Calif., 1983). Also useful in the study of Trollope as a public and private figure is R. C. Terry (ed.), *Trollope: Interviews and Recollections* (London, 1987).

# A CHRONOLOGY OF ANTHONY TROLLOPE

Virtually all Trollope's fiction after *Framley Parsonage* (1860–1) appeared first in serial form, with book publication usually coming just prior to the final instalment of the serial.

1815 (24 Apr.) Born at 16 Keppel Street, Bloomsbury, the fourth son of Thomas and Frances Trollope.
(Summer?) Family moves to Harrow-on-the-Hill.

1823 To Harrow School as a day-boy.

1825 To a private school at Sunbury.

1827 To school at Winchester College.

1830 Removed from Winchester and returned to Harrow.

1834 (Apr.) The family flees to Bruges to escape creditors.
(Nov.) Accepts a junior clerkship in the General Post Office, London.

1841 (Sept.) Made Postal Surveyor's Clerk at Banagher, King's County, Ireland.

1843 (mid-Sept.) Begins work on his first novel, *The Macdermots of Ballycloran*.

1844 (11 June) Marries Rose Heseltine.
(Aug.) Transferred to Clonmel, County Tipperary.

1846 (13 Mar.) Son, Henry Merivale Trollope, born.

1847 *The Macdermots of Ballycloran*, published in 3 vols. (Newby).
(27 Sept.) Son, Frederic James Anthony Trollope, born.

1848 *The Kellys and the O'Kellys; Or, Landlords and Tenants*, 3 vols. (Colburn).
(Autumn) Moves to Mallow, County Cork.

1850 *La Vendée. An Historical Romance*, 3 vols. (Colburn).
Writes *The Noble Jilt* (a play, published 1923).

1851 (1 Aug.) Sent to south-west of England on special postal mission.

1853 (29 July) Begins *The Warden* (the first of the Barsetshire novels).

(29 Aug.) Moves to Belfast as Acting Surveyor.

1854 (9 Oct.) Appointed Surveyor of Northern District of Ireland.

1855 *The Warden*, 1 vol. (Longman).

Writes *The New Zealander*.

(June) Moves to Donnybrook, Dublin.

1857 *Barchester Towers*, 3 vols. (Longman).

1858 *The Three Clerks*, 3 vols. (Bentley).

*Doctor Thorne*, 3 vols. (Chapman & Hall).

(Jan.) Departs for Egypt on Post Office business.

(Mar.) Visits Holy Land.

(Apr.–May) Returns via Malta, Gibraltar and Spain.

(May–Sept.) Visits Scotland and north of England on postal business.

(16 Nov.) Leaves for the West Indies on postal mission.

1859 *The Bertrams*, 3 vols. (Chapman & Hall).

*The West Indies and the Spanish Main*, 1 vol. (Chapman & Hall).

(3 July) Arrives home.

(Nov.) Leaves Ireland; settles at Waltham Cross, Hertfordshire, after being appointed surveyor of the Eastern District of England.

1860 *Castle Richmond*, 3 vols. (Chapman & Hall).

First serialized fiction, *Framley Parsonage*, published in the *Cornhill Magazine*.

(Oct.) Visits, with his wife, his mother and brother in Florence; makes the acquaintance of Kate Field, a 22-year-old American for whom he forms a romantic attachment.

1861 *Framley Parsonage*, 3 vols. (Smith, Elder).

*Tales of All Countries*, 1 vol. (Chapman & Hall).

(24 Aug.) Leaves for America to write a travel book.

1862 *Orley Farm*, 2 vols. (Chapman & Hall).

*North America*, 2 vols. (Chapman & Hall).

*The Struggles of Brown, Jones, and Robinson: By One of the Firm*, 1 vol.

(New York, Harper—an American piracy; first English edition 1870, Smith, Elder).

       (25 Mar.) Arrives home from America.
       (5 Apr.) Elected to the Garrick Club.

1863   *Tales of All Countries*, Second Series, 1 vol. (Chapman & Hall).
       *Rachel Ray*, 2 vols. (Chapman & Hall).
       (6 Oct.) Death of his mother, Mrs Frances Trollope.

1864   *The Small House at Allington*, 2 vols. (Smith, Elder).
       (12 Apr.) Elected a member of the Athenaeum Club.

1865   *Can You Forgive Her?*, 2 vols. (Chapman & Hall).
       *Miss Mackenzie*, 2 vols. (Chapman & Hall).
       *Hunting Sketches*, 1 vol. (Chapman & Hall).

1866   *The Belton Estate*, 3 vols. (Chapman & Hall).
       *Travelling Sketches*, 1 vol. (Chapman & Hall).
       *Clergymen of the Church of England*, 1 vol. (Chapman & Hall).

1867   *Nina Balatka*, 2 vols. (Blackwood).
       *The Claverings*, 2 vols. (Smith, Elder).
       *The Last Chronicle of Barset*, 2 vols. (Smith, Elder).
       *Lotta Schmidt and Other Stories*, 1 vol. (Strahan).
       (1 Sept.) Resigns from the Post Office.
       Assumes editorship of *Saint Pauls Magazine*.

1868   *Linda Tressel*, 2 vols. (Blackwood).
       (11 Apr.) Leaves London for the United States on postal mission.
       (26 July) Returns from America.
       (Nov.) Stands unsuccessfully as Liberal candidate for Beverley, Yorkshire.

1869   *Phineas Finn, The Irish Member*, 2 vols. (Virtue & Co).
       *He Knew He was Right*, 2 vols. (Strahan).
       *Did He Steal It? A Comedy in Three Acts* (a version of *The Last Chronicle of Barset*, privately printed by Virtue & Co).

1870   *The Vicar of Bullhampton*, 1 vol. (Bradbury, Evans).
       *An Editor's Tales*, 1 vol. (Strahan).
       *The Commentaries of Caesar*, 1 vol. (Blackwood).
       (Jan.–July) Eased out of *Saint Pauls Magazine*.

1871   *Sir Harry Hotspur of Humblethwaite*, 1 vol. (Hurst & Blackett).
       *Ralph the Heir*, 3 vols. (Hurst & Blackett).
       (Apr.) Gives up house at Waltham Cross.
       (24 May) Sails to Australia to visit his son Frederic.
       (27 July) Arrives at Melbourne.

1872 *The Golden Lion of Granpere*, 1 vol. (Tinsley).
(Jan.–Oct.) Travelling in Australia and New Zealand.
(Dec.) Returns via the United States.

1873 *The Eustace Diamonds*, 3 vols. (Chapman & Hall).
*Australia and New Zealand*, 2 vols. (Chapman & Hall).
(Apr.) Settles in Montagu Square, London.

1874 *Phineas Redux*, 2 vols. (Chapman & Hall).
*Lady Anna*, 2 vols. (Chapman & Hall).
*Harry Heathcote of Gangoil. A Tale of Australian Bush Life*, 1 vol. (Sampson Low).

1875 *The Way We Live Now*, 2 vols. (Chapman & Hall).
(1 Mar.) Leaves for Australia via Brindisi, the Suez Canal, and Ceylon.
(4 May) Arrives in Australia.
(Aug.–Oct.) Sailing homewards.
(Oct.) Begins *An Autobiography*.

1876 *The Prime Minister*, 4 vols. (Chapman & Hall).

1877 *The American Senator*, 3 vols. (Chapman & Hall).
(29 June) Leaves for South Africa.
(11 Dec.) Sails for home.

1878 *South Africa*, 2 vols. (Chapman & Hall).
*Is He Popenjoy?*, 3 vols. (Chapman & Hall).
*How the 'Mastiffs' Went to Iceland*, 1 vol. (privately printed, Virtue & Co.).
(June–July) Travels to Iceland in the yacht 'Mastiff'.

1879 *An Eye for an Eye*, 2 vols. (Chapman & Hall).
*Thackeray*, 1 vol. (Macmillan).
*John Candigate*, 3 vols. (Chapman & Hall).
*Cousin Henry*, 2 vols. (Chapman & Hall).

1880 *The Duke's Children*, 3 vols. (Chapman & Hall).
*The Life of Cicero*, 2 vols. (Chapman & Hall).
(July) Settles at South Harting, Sussex, near Petersfield.

1881 *Dr Wortle's School*, 2 vols. (Chapman & Hall).
*Ayala's Angel*, 3 vols. (Chapman & Hall).

1882 *Why Frau Frohmann Raised Her Prices; and Other Stories*, 1 vol. (Isbister).
*The Fixed Period*, 2 vols. (Blackwood).
*Marion Fay*, 3 vols. (Chapman & Hall).

*Lord Palmerston*, 1 vol. (Isbister).

*Kept in the Dark*, 2 vols. (Chatto & Windus).

(May) Visits Ireland to collect material for a new Irish novel.

(Aug.) Returns to Ireland a second time.

(2 Oct.) Takes rooms for the winter at Garlant's Hotel, Suffolk Street, London.

(3 Nov.) Suffers paralytic stroke.

(6 Dec.) Dies in nursing home, 34 Welbeck Street, London.

1883   *Mr Scarborough's Family*, 3 vols. (Chatto & Windus).

      *The Landleaguers* (unfinished), 3 vols. (Chatto & Windus).

      *An Autobiography*, 2 vols. (Blackwood).

1884   *An Old Man's Love*, 2 vols. (Blackwood).

1923   *The Noble Jilt*, 1 vol. (Constable).

1927   *London Tradesmen*, 1 vol. (Elkin Mathews and Marrat).

1972   *The New Zealander*, 1 vol. (Oxford University Press).

*The Fixed Period*

# CONTENTS

# CONTENTS

# CHAPTER I

## Introduction

IT may be doubted whether a brighter, more prosperous, and specially a more orderly colony than Britannula was ever settled by British colonists. But it had its period of separation from the mother country, though never of rebellion,—like its elder sister New Zealand. Indeed, in that respect it simply followed the lead given her by the Australias, which, when they set up for themselves, did so with the full co-operation of England. There was, no doubt, a special cause with us which did not exist in Australia, and which was only, in part, understood by the British Government when we Britannulists were allowed to stand by ourselves. The great doctrine of a 'Fixed Period' was received by them at first with ridicule, and then with dismay; but it was undoubtedly the strong faith which we of Britannula had in that doctrine which induced our separation. Nothing could have been more successful than our efforts to live alone during the thirty years that we remained our own masters. We repudiated no debt,—as have done some of our neighbours; and no attempts have been made towards communism,—as has been the case with others. We have been laborious, contented, and prosperous; and if we have been reabsorbed by the mother country, in accordance with what I cannot but call the pusillanimous conduct of certain of our elder Britannulists, it has not been from any failure on the part of the island, but from the opposition with which the Fixed Period has been regarded.

I think I must begin my story by explaining in moderate language a few of the manifest advantages which would attend the adoption of the Fixed Period in all countries. As far as the law went it was adopted in Britannula. Its adoption was the first thing discussed by our young Assembly, when we found ourselves alone; and though there were disputes on the subject, in none of them was opposition made to the system. I myself, at the age of thirty, had been elected Speaker of that Parliament. But I was, nevertheless, able to discuss the merits of the bills in committee, and I did so with some enthusiasm. Thirty years have passed since, and my 'period' is drawing nigh. But I am still as energetic as ever, and as assured that the doctrine will ultimately prevail over the face of the civilised world, though I will acknowledge that men are not as yet ripe for it.

The Fixed Period has been so far discussed as to make it almost unnecessary for me to explain its tenets, though its advantages may require a few words of argument in a world that is at present dead to its charms. It consists altogether of the abolition of the miseries, weakness, and *fainéant* imbecility of old age, by the prearranged ceasing to live of those who would otherwise become old. Need I explain to the inhabitants of England, for whom I chiefly write, how extreme are those sufferings, and how great the costliness of that old age which is unable in any degree to supply its own wants? Such old age should not, we Britannulists maintain, be allowed to be. This should be prevented, in the interests both of the young and of those who do become old when obliged to linger on after their 'period' of work is over. Two mistakes have been made by mankind in reference to their own race,—first, in allowing the world to be burdened with the continued maintenance of those whose cares should have been made to cease, and whose troubles should be at an end. Does not the Psalmist say the same?—'If by reason of strength they be fourscore years, yet is their strength labour and sorrow.'* And the second, in requiring those who remain to live a useless and painful life. Both these errors have come from an ill-judged and a thoughtless tenderness,—a tenderness to the young in not calling upon them to provide for the decent and comfortable departure of their progenitors; and a tenderness to the old lest the man, when uninstructed and unconscious of good and evil, should be unwilling to leave the world for which he is not fitted. But such tenderness is no better than unpardonable weakness. Statistics have told us that the sufficient sustenance of an old man is more costly than the feeding of a young one,—as is also the care, nourishment, and education of the as yet unprofitable child. Statistics also have told us that the unprofitable young and the no less unprofitable old form a third of the population. Let the reader think of the burden with which the labour of the world is thus saddled. To these are to be added all who, because of illness cannot work, and because of idleness will not. How are a people to thrive when so weighted? And for what good? As for the children, they are clearly necessary. They have to be nourished in order that they may do good work as their time shall come. But for whose good are the old and effete to be maintained amid all these troubles and miseries? Had there been any one in our Parliament capable of showing that they could reasonably desire it, the bill would not have been passed. Though to me the politico-economical view of the subject was always very strong, the relief to be brought to the aged was the one argument to which no reply could be given.

It was put forward by some who opposed the movement, that the old themselves would not like it. I never felt sure of that, nor do I now. When the colony had become used to the Fixed Period system, the old would become accustomed as well as the young. It is to be understood that a euthanasia was to be prepared for them;—and how many, as men now are, does a euthanasia await? And they would depart with the full respect of all their fellow-citizens. To how many does that lot now fall? During the last years of their lives they were to be saved from any of the horrors of poverty. How many now lack the comforts they cannot earn for themselves? And to them there would be no degraded feeling that they were the recipients of charity. They would be prepared for their departure, for the benefit of their country, surrounded by all the comforts to which, at their time of life, they would be susceptible, in a college maintained at the public expense; and each, as he drew nearer to the happy day, would be treated with still increasing honour. I myself had gone most closely into the question of expense, and had found that by the use of machinery the college could almost be made self-supporting. But we should save on an average £50 for each man and woman who had departed. When our population should have become a million, presuming that one only in fifty would have reached the desired age, the sum actually saved to the colony would amount to £1,000,000 a-year. It would keep us out of debt, make for us our railways, render all our rivers navigable, construct our bridges, and leave us shortly the richest people on God's earth! And this would be effected by a measure doing more good to the aged than to any other class of the community!

Many arguments were used against us, but were vain and futile in their conception. In it religion was brought to bear; and in talking of this the terrible word 'murder' was brought into common use. I remember startling the House by forbidding any member to use a phrase so revolting to the majesty of the people. Murder! Did any one who attempted to deter us by the use of foul language, bethink himself that murder, to be murder, must be opposed to the law? This thing was to be done by the law. There can be no other murder. If a murderer be hanged,—in England, I mean, for in Britannula we have no capital punishment,—is that murder? It is not so, only because the law enacts it. I and a few others did succeed at last in stopping the use of that word.* Then they talked to us of Methuselah, and endeavoured to draw an argument from the age of the patriarchs. I asked them in committee whether they were prepared to prove that the 969 years, as spoken of in Genesis,* were the same measure of time as 969 years now, and told them that if the sanitary arrangements of the world would again permit men to live as long as the patriarchs, we would gladly change the Fixed Period.

In fact, there was not a word to be said against us except that which referred to the feelings of the young and old. Feelings are changeable, I told them at that great and glorious meeting which we had at Gladstonopolis, and though naturally governed only by instinct, would be taught at last to comply with reason. I had lately read how feelings had been allowed in England to stand in the way of the great work of cremation.* A son will not like, you say, to lead his father into the college. But ought he not to like to do so? and if so, will not reason teach him to like to do what he ought? I can conceive with rapture the pride, the honour, the affection with which, when the Fixed Period had come, I could have led my father into the college, there to enjoy for twelve months that preparation for euthanasia which no cares for this world would be allowed to disturb. All the existing ideas of the grave would be absent. There would be no further struggles to prolong the time of misery which nature had herself produced. That temptation to the young to begrudge to the old the costly comforts which they could not earn would be no longer fostered. It would be a pride for the young man to feel that his parent's name had been enrolled to all coming time in the bright books of the college which was to be established for the Fixed Period. I have a son of my own, and I have carefully educated him to look forward to the day in which he shall deposit me there as the proudest of his life. Circumstances, as I shall relate in this story, have somewhat interfered with him; but he will, I trust, yet come back to the right way of thinking. That I shall never spend that last happy year within the walls of the college, is to me, from a selfish point of view, the saddest part of England's reassuming our island as a colony.

My readers will perceive that I am an enthusiast. But there are reforms so great that a man cannot but be enthusiastic when he has received into his very soul the truth of any human improvement. Alas me! I shall never live to see carried out the glory of this measure to which I have devoted the best years of my existence. The college, which has been built under my auspices as a preparation for the happy departure, is to be made a Chamber of Commerce. Those aged men who were awaiting, as I verily believe, in impatience the coming day of their perfected dignity, have been turned loose in the world, and allowed to grovel again with mundane thoughts amidst the idleness of years that are useless. Our bridges, our railways, our Government are not provided for. Our young men are again becoming torpid beneath the weight imposed upon them. I was, in truth, wrong to think that so great a reform could be brought to perfection within the days of the first reformers. A divine idea has to be made common to men's minds by frequent ventilation before it will be seen to be fit for humanity. Did not the first Christians all suffer affliction, poverty, and martyrdom? How many centuries has it taken in the history of the world to induce it to denounce the not yet abolished theory of slavery? A throne, a lord, and a bishop still remain to encumber the earth! What right had I, then, as the first of the Fixed-Periodists, to hope that I might live to see my scheme carried out, or that I might be allowed to depart as among the first glorious recipients of its advantages?

It would appear absurd to say that had there been such a law in force in England, England would not have prevented its adoption in Britannula. That is a matter of course. But it has been because the old men are still alive in England that the young in Britannula are to be afflicted,—the young and the old as well. The Prime Minister in Downing Street was seventy-two when we were debarred from carrying out our project, and the Secretary for the Colonies was sixty-nine. Had they been among us, and had we been allowed to use our wisdom without interference from effete old age, where would they have been? I wish to speak with all respect of Sir William Gladstone. When we named our metropolis after him,* we were aware of his good qualities. He has not the eloquence of his great-grandfather, but he is, they tell us, a safe man. As to the Minister for the Crown Colonies,—of which, alas! Britannula has again become one,—I do not, I own, look upon him as a great statesman. The present Duke of Hatfield has none of the dash, if he has more than the prudence, of his grandfather.* He was elected to the present Upper Chamber as a strong anti-Church Liberal, but he never has had the spirit to be a true reformer. It is now due to the 'feelings' which fill no doubt the bosoms of these two anti-Fixed-Period seniors, that the doctrine of the Fixed

Period has for a time been quenched in Britannula. It is sad to think that the strength and intellect and spirit of manhood should thus be conquered by that very imbecility which it is their desire to banish from the world.

Two years since I had become the President of that which we gloried to call the rising Empire of the South Pacific. And in spite of all internal opposition, the college of the Fixed Period was already completed. I then received violent notice from the British Government that Britannula had ceased to be independent, and had again been absorbed by the mother country among the Crown Colonies. How that information was received, and with what weakness on the part of the Britannulists, I now proceed to tell.

I confess that I for one was not at first prepared to obey. We were small, but we were independent, and owed no more of submission to Great Britain than we do to the Salomon Islands or to Otaheite. It was for us to make our own laws, and we had hitherto made them in conformity with the institutions, and, I must say, with the prejudices of so-called civilisation. We had now made a first attempt at progress beyond these limits, and we were immediately stopped by the fatuous darkness of the old men whom, had Great Britain known her own interest, she would already have silenced by a Fixed Period law on her own account. No greater instance of uncalled-for tyranny is told of in the history of the world as already written. But my brother Britannulists did not agree with me that, in the interest of the coming races,* it was our duty rather to die at our posts than yield to the menaces of the Duke of Hatfield. One British gunboat, they declared, in the harbour of Gladstonopolis, would reduce us—to order. What order? A 250-ton steam-swiveller could no doubt crush us, and bring our Fixed Period college in premature ruin about our ears. But, as was said, the captain of the gunboat would never dare to touch the wire that should commit so wide a destruction. An Englishman would hesitate to fire a shot that would send perhaps five thousand of his fellow-creatures to destruction before their Fixed Period. But even in Britannula fear still remains. It was decided, I will confess by the common voice of the island, that we should admit this Governor, and swear fealty again to the British Crown. Sir Ferdinando Brown was allowed to land, and by the rejoicing made at the first Government House ball, as I have already learned since I left the island, it appeared that the Britannulists rejoiced rather than otherwise at their thraldom.

Two months have passed since that time, and I, being a worn-out old man, and fitted only for the glory of the college, have nothing left me but to write this story, so that coming ages may see how noble were our efforts. But in truth, the difficulties which lay in our way were very stern. The philosophical truth on which the system is founded was too strong, too mighty, too divine, to be adopted by man in the immediate age of its first appearance. But it has appeared; and I perhaps should be contented and gratified, during the years which I am doomed to linger through impotent imbecility, to think that I have been the first reformer of my time, though I shall be doomed to perish without having enjoyed its fruits.

I must now explain before I begin my story certain details of our plan, which created much schism among ourselves. In the first place, what should be the Fixed Period? When a party of us, three or four hundred in number, first emigrated from New Zealand to Britannula, we were, almost all of us, young people. We would not consent to measures in regard to their public debt which the Houses in New Zealand threatened to take; and as this island had been discovered, and a part of it cultivated, thither we determined to go. Our resolution was very popular, not only with certain parties in New Zealand, but also in the mother country. Others followed us, and we settled ourselves with great prosperity. But we were essentially a young community. There were not above ten among us who had then reached any Fixed Period; and not above twenty others who could be said to be approaching it. There never could arrive a time or a people when, or among whom, the system could be tried with so good a hope of success. It was so long before we had been allowed to stand on our bottom, that the Fixed Period became a matter of common conversation in Britannula. There were many who looked forward to it as the creator of a new idea of wealth and comfort; and it was in those days that the calculation was made as to the rivers and railways. I think that in England they thought that a few, and but a few, among us were dreamers of a dream. Had they believed that the Fixed Period would ever have become law, they would not have permitted us to be law-makers. I acknowledge that. But when we were once independent, then again to reduce us to submission by a 250-ton steam-swiveller was an act of gross tyranny.

What should be the Fixed Period? That was the first question which demanded an immediate answer. Years were named absurd in their intended leniency;—eighty and even eighty-five! Let us say a hundred, said I, aloud, turning upon them all the battery of my ridicule. I suggested sixty; but the term was received with silence. I pointed out that the few old men now on the island might be exempted, and that even those above fifty-five might be allowed to drag out their existences if they were weak enough to select for themselves so degrading a position. This latter proposition was accepted at once, and the exempt showed no repugnance even when it was proved to them that they would be left alone in the community and entitled to no honour, and never allowed even to enter the pleasant gardens of the college. I think now that sixty was too early an age, and that sixty-five, to which I gracefully yielded, is the proper Fixed Period for the human race. Let any man look among his friends and see whether men of sixty-five are not in the way of those who are still aspiring to rise in the world. A judge shall be deaf on the bench when younger men below him can hear with accuracy. His voice shall have descended to a poor treble, or his eyesight shall be dim and failing. At any rate, his limbs will have lost all that robust agility which is needed for the adequate performance of the work of the world. It is self-evident that at sixty-five a man has done all that he is fit to do. He should be troubled no longer with labour, and therefore should be troubled no longer with life. 'It is all vanity and vexation of spirit,' such a one would say, if still brave, and still desirous of honour. 'Lead me into the college, and there let me prepare myself for that brighter life which will require no mortal strength.' My words did avail with many, and then they demanded that seventy should be the Fixed Period.

How long we fought over this point need not now be told. But we decided at last to divide the interval. Sixty-seven and a half was named by a majority of the Assembly as the Fixed Period. Surely the colony was determined to grow in truth old before it could go into the college. But then there came a further dispute. On which side of the Fixed Period should the year of grace be taken? Our debates even on this subject were long and animated. It was said that the seclusion within the college would be tantamount to penal departure, and that the old men should thus have the last lingering drops of breath allowed them, without, in the world at large. It was at last decided that men and women should be brought into the college at sixty-seven, and that before their sixty-eighth birthday they should have departed. Then the bells were rung, and the whole community rejoiced, and banquets were eaten, and the young men and women called each other brother and sister, and it was felt that a great reform had been inaugurated among us for the benefit of mankind at large.

Little was thought about it at home in England when the bill was passed. There was, I suppose, in the estimation of Englishmen, time enough to think about it. The idea was so strange to them that it was considered impossible that we should carry it out. They heard of the bill, no doubt; but I maintain that, as we had been allowed to separate ourselves and stand alone, it was no more their concern than if it had been done in Arizona or Idaho, or any of those Western States of America which have lately formed themselves into a new union. It was from them, no doubt, that we chiefly expected that sympathy which, however, we did not receive. The world was clearly not yet alive to the grand things in store for it. We received, indeed, a violent remonstrance from the old-fashioned Government at Washington; but in answer to that we stated that we were prepared to stand and fall by the new system—that we expected glory rather than ignominy, and to be followed by mankind rather than repudiated. We had a lengthened correspondence also with New Zealand and with Australia; but England at first did not believe us; and when she was given to understand that we were in earnest, she brought to bear upon us the one argument that could have force, and sent to our harbour her 250-ton steam-swiveller. The 250-ton swiveller, no doubt, was unanswerable—unless we were prepared to die for our system. I was prepared, but I could not carry the people of my country with me.

I have now given the necessary prelude to the story which I have to tell. I cannot but think that, in spite of the isolated manners of Great Britain, readers in that country generally must have become acquainted with the views of the Fixed-Periodists. It cannot but be that a scheme with such power to change,—and, I may say, to improve,—the manners and habits of mankind, should be known in a country in which a portion of the inhabitants do, at any rate, read and write. They boast, indeed, that not a man or a woman in the British Islands is now ignorant of his letters; but I am informed that the knowledge seldom approaches to any literary taste. It may be that a portion of the masses should have been ignorant of what was being done within the empire of the South Pacific. I have therefore written this preliminary chapter to explain to them what was the condition of Britannula in regard to the Fixed Period just twelve months before England had taken possession of us, and once more made us her own. Sir Ferdinando Brown now rules us, I must say, not with a rod of iron, but very much after his own good will. He makes us flowery speeches, and thinks that they will stand in lieu of independence. He collects his revenue, and informs us that to be taxed is the highest privilege of an ornate civilisation. He pointed to the gunboat in the bay when it came, and called it the divine depository of beneficent power. For a time, no doubt, British 'tenderness' will prevail. But I shall have wasted my thoughts, and in vain poured out my eloquence as to the Fixed Period, if, in the course of years, it does not again spring to the front, and prove itself to be necessary before man can accomplish all that he is destined to achieve.

## CHAPTER II
## Gabriel Crasweller

I WILL now begin my tale. It is above thirty years since I commenced my agitation in Britannula. We were a small people, and had not then been blessed by separation; but we were, I think, peculiarly intelligent. We were the very cream, as it were, that had been skimmed from the milk-pail of the people of a wider colony, themselves gifted with more than ordinary intelligence. We were the *élite* of the selected population of New Zealand. I think I may say that no race so well informed ever before set itself down to form a new nation. I am now nearly sixty years old,—very nearly fit for the college which, alas! will never be open for me,—and I was nearly thirty when I began to be in earnest as to the Fixed Period. At that time my dearest friend and most trusted coadjutor was Gabriel Crasweller. He was ten years my senior then, and is now therefore fit for deposition in the college were the college there to receive him. He was one of those who brought with them merino sheep into the colony. At great labour and expense he exported from New Zealand a small flock of choice animals, with which he was successful from the first. He took possession of the lands of Little Christchurch, five or six miles from Gladstonopolis, and showed great judgment in the selection. A prettier spot, as it turned out, for the fattening of both beef and mutton and for the growth of wool, it would have been impossible to have found. Everything that human nature wants was there at

Little Christchurch. The streams which watered the land were bright and rapid, and always running. The grasses were peculiarly rich, and the old English fruit-trees, which we had brought with us from New Zealand, throve there with an exuberant fertility, of which the mother country, I am told, knows nothing. He had imported pheasants' eggs, and salmon-spawn, and young deer, and black-cock and grouse, and those beautiful little Alderney cows no bigger than good-sized dogs, which, when milked, give nothing but cream. All these things throve with him uncommonly, so that it may be declared of him that his lines had fallen in pleasant places.* But he had no son; and therefore in discussing with him, as I did daily, the question of the Fixed Period, I promised him that it should be my lot to deposit him in the sacred college when the day of his withdrawal should have come. He had been married before we left New Zealand, and was childless when he made for himself and his wife his homestead at Little Christchurch. But there, after a few years, a daughter was born to him, and I ought to have remembered, when I promised to him that last act of friendship, that it might become the duty of that child's husband to do for him with filial reverence the loving work which I had undertaken to perform.

Many and most interesting were the conversations held between Crasweller and myself on the great subject which filled our hearts. He undoubtedly was sympathetic, and took delight in expatiating on all those benefits that would come to the world from the race of mankind which knew nothing of the debility of old age. He saw the beauty of the theory as well as did I myself, and would speak often of the weakness of that pretended tenderness which would fear to commence a new operation in regard to the feelings of the men and women of the old world. 'Can any man love another better than I do you?' I would say to him with energy; 'and yet would I scruple for a moment to deposit you in the college when the day had come? I should lead you in with that perfect reverence which it is impossible that the young should feel for the old when they become feeble and incapable.' I doubt now whether he relished these allusions to his own seclusion. He would run away from his own individual case, and generalise widely about some future time. And when the time for voting came, he certainly did vote for seventy-five. But I took no offence at his vote. Gabriel Crasweller was almost my dearest friend, and as his girl grew up it was a matter of regret to me that my only son was not quite old enough to be her husband.

Eva Crasweller was, I think, the most perfect piece I ever beheld of youthful feminine beauty. I have not yet seen those English beauties of which so much is said in their own romances, but whom the young men from New York and San Francisco who make their way to Gladstonopolis do not seem to admire very much. Eva was perfect in symmetry, in features, in complexion, and in simplicity of manners. All languages are the same to her; but that accomplishment has become so common in Britannula that but little is thought of it. I do not know whether she ravished our ears most with the old-fashioned piano and the nearly obsolete violin, or with the modern mousometor, or the more perfect melpomeneon.* It was wonderful to hear the way with which she expressed herself at the meeting held about the rising buildings of the college when she was only sixteen. But I think she touched me most with just a roly-poly pudding which she made with her own fair hands for our dinner one Sunday at Little Christchurch. And once when I saw her by chance take a kiss from her lover behind the door, I felt that it was a pity indeed that a man should ever become old. Perhaps, however, in the eyes of some her brightest charm lay in the wealth which her father possessed. His sheep had greatly increased in number; the valleys were filled with his cattle; and he could always sell his salmon for half-a-crown a pound and his pheasants for seven-and-six-pence a brace. Everything had thriven with Crasweller, and everything must belong to Eva as soon as he should have been led into the college. Eva's mother was now dead, and no other child had been born. Crasweller had also embarked his money largely in the wool trade, and had become a sleeping-partner in the house of Grundle & Grabbe. He was an older man by ten years than either of his partners, but yet Grundle's eldest son Abraham was older than Eva when Crasweller lent his money to the firm. It was soon known who was to be the happiest man in the empire. It was young Abraham, by whom Eva was kissed behind the door that Sunday when we ate the roly-poly pudding. Then she came into the room, and, with her eyes raised to heaven; and with a halo of glory almost round her head as she poured forth her voice, she touched the mousometor, and gave us the Old Hundredth psalm.

She was a fine girl at all points, and had been quite alive to the dawn of the Fixed Period system. But at this time, on the memorable occasion of the eating of that dinner, it first began to strike me that my friend Crasweller was getting very near his Fixed Period, and it occurred to me to ask myself questions as to what might be the daughter's wishes. It was the state of her feelings rather that would push itself into my mind. Quite lately he had said nothing about it,— nor had she. On that Sunday morning when he and his girl were at church,—for Crasweller had stuck to the old habit of saying his prayers in a special place on a special day,—I had discussed the matter with young Grundle. Nobody had been into the college as yet. Three or four had died naturally, but Crasweller was about to be the first. We were arranging that he should be attended by pleasant visitors till within the last week or two, and I was making special allusion to the law which required that he should abandon all control of his property immediately on his entering the college. 'I suppose he would do that,' said Grundle, expressing considerable interest by the tone of his voice.

'Oh, certainly,' said I; 'he must do that in accordance with the law. But he can make his will up to the very moment in which he is deposited.' He had then about twelve months to run. I suppose there was not a man or woman in the community who was not accurately aware of the very day of Crasweller's birth. We had already introduced the habit of tattooing on the backs of the babies the day on which they were born; and we had succeeded in operating also on many of the children who had come into the world before the great law. Some there were who would not submit on behalf of themselves or their children; and we did look forward to some little confusion in this matter. A register had of course been commenced, and there were already those who refused to state their exact ages; but I had been long on the look-out for this, and had a little book of my own in which were inscribed the 'periods' of all those who had come to Britannula with us; and since I had first thought of the Fixed Period I had been very careful to note faithfully the births as they occurred. The reader will see how important, as time went on, it would become to have an accurate record, and I already then feared that there might be some want of fidelity after I myself had been deposited. But my friend Crasweller was the first on the list, and there was no doubt in the empire as to the exact day on which he was born. All Britannula knew that he would be the first, and that he was to be deposited on the 13th of June 1980. In conversation with my friend I had frequently alluded to the very day,—to the happy day, as I used to call it before I became acquainted with his actual feelings,—and he never ventured to deny that on that day he would become sixty-seven.

I have attempted to describe his daughter Eva, and I must say a word as to the personal qualities of her father. He too was a remarkably handsome man, and though his hair was beautifully white, had fewer of the symptoms of age than any old man I had before known. He was tall, robust, and broad, and there was no beginning even of a stoop about him. He spoke always clearly and audibly, and he was known for the firm voice with which he would perform occasionally at some of our decimal readings. We had fixed our price at a decimal in order that the sum so raised might be used for the ornamentation of the college. Our population at Gladstonopolis was so thriving that we found it as easy to collect ten pennies as one. At these readings Gabriel Crasweller was the favourite performer, and it had begun to be whispered by some caitiffs who would willingly disarrange the whole starry system for their own immediate gratification, that Crasweller should not be deposited because of the beauty of his voice. And then the difficulty was somewhat increased by the care and precision with which he attended to his own business. He was as careful as ever about his flocks, and at shearing-time would stand all day in the wool-shed to see to the packing of his wool and the marking of his bales.

'It would be a pity,' said to me a Britannulist one day,—a man younger than myself,—'to lock up old Crasweller, and let the business go into the hands of young Grundle. Young Grundle will never know half as much about sheep, in spite of his conceit; and Crasweller is a deal fitter for his work than for living idle in the college till you shall put an end to him.'

There was much in these words which made me very angry. According to this man's feelings, the whole system was to be made to suit itself to the peculiarities of one individual constitution. A man who so spoke could have known nothing of the general beauty of the Fixed Period. And he had alluded to the manner of depositing in most disrespectful terms. I had felt it to be essentially necessary so to maintain the dignity of the ceremony as to make it appear as unlike an execution as possible. And this depositing of Crasweller was to be the first, and should—according to my own intentions—be attended with a peculiar grace and reverence. 'I don't know what you call locking up,' said I, angrily. 'Had Mr Crasweller been about to be dragged to a felon's prison, you could not have used more opprobrious language; and as to putting an end to him, you must, I think, be ignorant of the method proposed for adding honour and glory to the last moments in this world of those dear friends whose happy lot it will be to be withdrawn from the world's troubles amidst the love and veneration of their fellow-subjects.' As to the actual mode of transition, there had been many discussions held by the executive in President Square, and it had at last been decided that certain veins should be opened while the departing one should, under the influence of morphine, be gently entranced within a warm bath. I, as president of the empire, had agreed to use the lancet in the first two or three cases, thereby intending to increase the honours conferred. Under these circumstances I did feel the sting bitterly when he spoke of my putting 'an end' to him. 'But you have not,' I said, 'at all realised the feeling of the ceremony. A few ill-spoken words, such as these you have just uttered, will do us more harm in the minds of many than all your voting will have done good.' In answer to this he merely repeated his observation that Crasweller was a very bad specimen to begin with. 'He has got ten years of work in him,' said my friend, 'and yet you intend to make away with him without the slightest compunction.'

Make away with him! What an expression to use,—and this from the mouth of one who had been a determined Fixed-Periodist! It angered me to think that men should be so little reasonable as to draw deductions as to an entire system from a single instance. Crasweller might in truth be strong and hearty at the Fixed Period. But that period had been chosen with reference to the community at large; and what though he might have to depart a year or two before he was worn out, still he would do so with everything around him to make him happy, and would depart before he had ever known the agony of a headache. Looking at the entire question with the eyes of reason, I could not but tell myself that a better example of a triumphant beginning to our system could not have been found. But yet there was in it something unfortunate. Had our first hero been compelled to abandon his business by old age—had he become doting over its details—parsimonious, or extravagant, or even short-sighted in his speculations—public feeling, than which nothing is more ignorant, would have risen in favour of the Fixed Period. 'How true is the president's reasoning,' the people would have said. 'Look at Crasweller; he would have ruined Little Christchurch had he stayed there much longer.' But everything he did seemed to prosper; and it occurred to me at last that he forced himself into abnormal sprightliness, with a view of bringing disgrace upon the law

of the Fixed Period. If there were any such feeling, I regard
it as certainly mean.

On the day after the dinner at which Eva's pudding was
eaten, Abraham Grundle came to me at the Executive Hall,
and said that he had a few things to discuss with me of
importance. Abraham was a good-looking young man, with
black hair and bright eyes, and a remarkably handsome
mounstache; and he was one well inclined to business, in
whose hands the firm of Grundle, Grabbe, & Crasweller was
likely to thrive; but I myself had never liked him much. I had
thought him to be a little wanting in that reverence which he
owed to his elders, and to be, moreover, somewhat over-
fond of money. It had leaked out that though he was no
doubt attached to Eva Crasweller, he had thought quite as
much of Little Christchurch; and though he could kiss Eva
behind the door, after the ways of young men, still he was
more intent on the fleeces than on her lips. 'I want to say a
word to you, Mr President,' he began, 'upon a subject that
disturbs my conscience very much.'

'Your conscience?' said I.

'Yes, Mr President. I believe you're aware that I am
engaged to marry Miss Crasweller?'

It may be as well to explain here that my own eldest son,
as fine a boy as ever delighted a mother's eye, was only two
years younger than Eva, and that my wife, Mrs Neverbend,
had of late got it into her head that he was quite old enough
to marry the girl. It was in vain that I told her that all that
had been settled while Jack was still at the didascalion.* He
had been Colonel of the Curriculum, as they now call the
head boy; but Eva had not then cared for Colonels of
Curriculums, but had thought more of young Grundle's
moustache. My wife declared that all that was altered,—that
Jack was, in fact, a much more manly fellow than Abraham
with his shiny bit of beard; and that if one could get at a
maiden's heart, we should find that Eva thought so. In
answer to this I bade her hold her tongue, and remember
that in Britannula a promise was always held to be as good as
a bond. 'I suppose a young woman may change her mind in

Britannula as well as elsewhere,' said my wife. I turned all this over in my mind, because the slopes of Little Christchurch are very alluring, and they would all belong to Eva so soon. And then it would be well, as I was about to perform for Crasweller so important a portion of his final ceremony, our close intimacy should be drawn still nearer by a family connection. I did think of it; but then it occurred to me that the girl's engagement to young Grundle was an established fact, and it did not behove me to sanction the breach of a contract. 'Oh yes,' said I to the young man, 'I am aware that there is an understanding to that effect between you and Eva's father.'

'And between me and Eva, I can assure you.'

Having observed the kiss behind the door on the previous day, I could not deny the truth of this assertion.

'It is quite understood,' continued Abraham, 'and I had always thought that it was to take place at once, so that Eva might get used to her new life before her papa was deposited.'

To this I merely bowed my head, as though to signify that it was a matter with which I was not personally concerned. 'I had taken it for granted that my old friend would like to see his daughter settled, and Little Christchurch put into his daughter's hands before he should bid adieu to his own sublunary affairs,' I remarked, when I found that he paused.

'We all thought so up at the warehouse,' said he,—'I and father, and Grabbe, and Postlecott, our chief clerk. Postlecott is the next but three on the books, and is getting very melancholy. But he is especially anxious just at present to see how Crasweller bears it.'

'What has all that to do with Eva's marriage?'

'I suppose I might marry her. But he hasn't made any will.'

'What does that matter? There is nobody to interfere with Eva.'

'But he might go off, Mr Neverbend,' whispered Grundle; 'and where should I be then? If he was to get across to Auckland, or to Sydney, and to leave some one to manage the property for him, what could you do? That's what I want to know. The law says that he shall be deposited on a certain day.'

'He will become as nobody in the eye of the law,' said I, with all the authority of a President.

'But if he and his daughter have understood each other; and if some deed be forthcoming by which Little Christchurch shall have been left to trustees; and if he goes on living at Sydney, let us say, on the fat of the land,—drawing all the income, and leaving the trustees as legal owners,—where should I be then?'

'In that case,' said I, having taken two or three minutes for consideration,—'in that case, I presume the property would be confiscated by law, and would go to his natural heir. Now if his natural heir be then your wife, it will be just the same as though the property were yours.' Young Grundle shook his head. 'I don't know what more you would want. At any rate, there is no more for you to get.' I confess that at that moment the idea of my boy's chance of succeeding with the heiress did present itself to my mind. According to what my wife had said, Jack would have jumped at the girl with just what she stood up in; and had sworn to his mother, when he had been told that moring about the kiss behind the door, that he would knock that brute's head off his shoulders before many days were gone by. Looking at the matter merely on behalf of Jack, it appeared to me that Little Christchurch would, in that case, be quite safe, let Crasweller be deposited,—or run away to Sydney.

'You do not know for certain about the confiscation of the property,' said Abraham.

'I've told you as much, Mr Grundle, as it is fit that you should know,' I replied, with severity. 'For the absolute condition of the law you must look in the statute-book, and not come to the President of the empire.'

Abraham Grundle then departed. I had assumed an angry air, as though I were offended with him, for troubling me on a matter by referring simply to an individual. But he had in truth given rise to very serious and solemn thoughts. Could it be that Crasweller, my own confidential friend—the man to whom I had trusted the very secrets of my soul on this important matter,—could it be that he should be unwilling to be deposited when the day had come? Could it be that he should be anxious to fly from his country and her laws, just as the time had arrived when those laws might operate upon him for the benefit of that country? I could not think that he was so vain, so greedy, so selfish, and so unpatriotic. But this was not all. Should he attempt to fly, could we prevent his flying? And if he did fly, what step should we take next? The Government of New South Wales was hostile to us on the very matter of the Fixed Period, and certainly would not surrender him in obedience to any law of extradition. And he might leave his property to trustees who would manage it on his behalf; although, as far as Britannula was concerned, he would be beyond the reach of law, and regarded even as being without the pale of life. And if he, the first of the Fixed-Periodists, were to run away, the fashion of so running would become common. We should thus be rid of our old men, and our object would be so far attained. But looking forward, I could see at a glance that if one or two wealthy members of our community were thus to escape, it would be almost impossible to carry out the law with reference to those who should have no such means. But that which vexed me most was that Gabriel Crasweller should desire to escape,—that he should be anxious to throw over the whole system to preserve the poor remnant of his life. If he would do so, who could be expected to abstain? If he should prove false when the moment came, who would prove true? And he, the first, the very first on our list! Young Grundle had now left me, and as I sat thinking of it I was for a moment tempted to abandon the Fixed Period altogether. But as I remained there in silent meditation, better thoughts came to me. Had I dared to regard myself as the foremost spirit of my age, and should I thus be turned back by the human weakness of one poor creature who had not sufficiently collected the strength of his heart to be able to look death in the face and to laugh him down. It was a difficulty—a difficulty the more. It might be the crushing difficulty which would put an end to the system as far as my existence was concerned. But I bethought me how many early reformers had perished in their efforts, and how seldom it had been given to the first man to scale the walls of prejudice, and force himself into the citadel of reason. But they had not yielded when things had gone against them; and though they had not brought their visions down to the palpable touch of humanity, still they had persevered, and their efforts had not been altogether lost to the world.

'So it shall be with me,' said I. 'Though I may never live to deposit a human being within that sanctuary, and though I may be doomed by the foolish prejudice of men to drag out a miserable existence amidst the sorrows and weakness of old age; though it may never be given to me to feel the ineffable comforts of a triumphant deposition,—still my name will be handed down to coming ages, and I shall be spoken of as the first who endeavoured to save grey hairs from being brought with sorrow to the grave.'*

I am now writing on board HM gunboat John Bright,— for the tyrannical slaves of a modern monarch have taken me in the flesh and are carrying me off to England, so that, as they say, all that nonsense of a Fixed Period may die away in Britannula. They think,—poor ignorant fighting men,—that such a theory can be made to perish because one individual shall have been mastered. But no! The idea will still live, and in ages to come men will prosper and be strong, and thrive, unpolluted by the greed and cowardice of second childhood, because John Neverbend was at one time President of Britannula.

It occurred to me then, as I sat meditating over the tidings conveyed to me by Abraham Grundle, that it would be well that I should see Crasweller, and talk to him freely on the subject. It had sometimes been that by my strength I had reinvigorated his halting courage. This suggestion that he might run away as the day of his deposition drew nigh,—or rather, that others might run away,—had been the subject of some conversation between him and me. 'How will it be,' he had said. 'if they mizzle?'* He had intended to allude to the possible premature departure of those who were about to be deposited.

'Men will never be so weak,' I said.

'I suppose you'd take all their property?'

'Every stick of it.'

'But property is a thing which can be conveyed away.'

'We should keep a sharp look-out upon themselves. There might be a writ, you know, *ne exeant regno*.* If we are driven to a pinch, that will be the last thing to do. But I should be sorry to be driven to express my fear of human weakness by any general measure of that kind. It would be tantamount to an accusation of cowardice against the whole empire.'

Craswell had only shaken his head. But I had understood him to shake it on the part of the human race generally, and not on his own behalf.

# CHAPTER III
## The First Break-down

IT was now mid-winter, and it wanted just twelve months to that 30th of June on which, in accordance with all our plans, Craswell was to be deposited. A full year would, no doubt, suffice for him to arrange his worldly affairs, and to see his daughter married; but it would not more than suffice. He still went about his business with an alacrity marvellous in one who was so soon about to withdraw himself from the world. The fleeces for bearing which he was preparing his flocks, though they might be shorn by him, would never return their prices to his account. They would do so for his daughter and his son-in-law; but in these circumstances, it would have been well for him to have left the flocks to his son-in-law, and to have turned his mind to the consideration of other matters. 'There should be a year devoted to that final year to be passed within the college, so that, by degrees, the mind may be weaned from the ignoble art of money-making.' I had once so spoken to him; but there he was, as intent as ever, with his mind fixed on the records of the price of wool as they came back to him from the English and American markets. 'It is all for his daughter,' I had said to myself. 'Had he been blessed with a son, it would have been otherwise with him.' So I got on to my steam-tricycle, and in a few minutes I was at Little Christchurch. He was coming in after a hard day's work among the flocks, and seemed to be triumphant and careful at the same time.

'I tell you what it is, Neverbend,' said he; 'we shall have the fluke over here if we don't look after ourselves.'

'Have you found symptoms of it?'

'Well; not exactly among my own sheep; but I know the signs of it so well. My grasses are peculiarly dry, and my flocks are remarkably well looked after; but I can see indications of it. Only fancy where we should all be if fluke showed itself in Britannula! If it once got ahead we should be no better off than the Australians.'

This might be anxiety for his daughter; but it looked strangely like that personal feeling which would have been expected in him twenty years ago. 'Crasweller,' said I, 'do you mind coming into the house, and having a little chat?' and so I got off my tricycle.

'I was going to be very busy,' he said, showing an unwillingness. 'I have fifty young foals in that meadow there; and I like to see that they get their suppers served to them warm.'

'Bother the young foals!' said I. 'As if you had not men enough about the place to see to feeding your stock without troubling yourself. I have come out from Gladstonopolis, because I want to see you; and now I am to be sent back in order that you might attend to the administration of hot mashes! Come into the house.' Then I entered in under the verandah, and he followed. 'You certainly have got the best-furnished house in the empire,' said I, as I threw myself on to a double arm-chair, and lighted my cigar in the inner verandah.

'Yes, yes,' said he; 'it is pretty comfortable.'

He was evidently melancholy, and knew the purpose for which I had come. 'I don't suppose any girl in the old country was ever better provided for than will be Eva.' This I said wishing to comfort him, and at the same time to prepare for what was to be said.

'Eva is a good girl,—a dear girl. But I am not at all so sure about that young fellow Abraham Grundle. It's a pity, President, your son had not been born a few years sooner.' At this moment my boy was half a head taller than young Grundle, and a much better specimen of a Britannulist. 'But it is too late now, I suppose, to talk of that. It seems to me that Jack never even thinks of looking at Eva.'

This was a view of the case which certainly was strange to me, and seemed to indicate that Crasweller was gradually becoming fit for the college. If he could not see that Jack was madly in love with Eva, he could see nothing at all. But I had not come out to Little Christchurch at the present moment to talk to him about the love matters of the two children. I was intent on something of infinitely greater importance. 'Crasweller,' said I, 'you and I have always agreed to the letter on this great matter of the Fixed Period.' He looked into my face with supplicating, weak eyes, but he said nothing. 'Your period now will soon have been reached, and I think it well that we, as dear loving friends, should learn to discuss the matter closely as it draws nearer. I do not think that it becomes either of us to be afraid of it.'

'That's all very well for you,' he replied. 'I am your senior.'

'Ten years, I believe.'

'About nine, I think.'

This might have come from a mistake of his as to my exact age; and though I was surprised at the error, I did not notice it on this occasion. 'You have no objection to the law as it stands now?' I said.

'It might have been seventy.'

'That has all been discussed fully, and you have given your assent. Look round on the men whom you can re-

member, and tell me, on how many of them life has not sat
as a burden at seventy years of age?'

'Men are so different,' said he. 'As far as one can judge of
his own capacities, I was never better able to manage my
business than I am at present. It is more than I can say for
that young fellow Grundle, who is so anxious to step into my
shoes.'

'My dear Craswell,' I rejoined, 'it was out of the
question so to arrange the law as to vary the term to suit the
peculiarities of one man or another.'

'But in a change of such terrible severity you should have
suited the eldest.'

This was dreadful to me,—that he, the first to receive at
the hands of his country the great honour intended for
him,—that he should have already allowed his mind to have
rebelled against it! If he, who had once been so keen a
supporter of the Fixed Period, now turned round and
opposed it, how could others who should follow be expected
to yield themselves up in a fitting frame of mind? And then I
spoke my thoughts freely to him. 'Are you afraid of
departure?' I said,—'afraid of that which must come; afraid
to meet as a friend that which you must meet so soon as
friend or enemy?' I paused; but he sat looking at me without
reply. 'To fear departure;—must it not be the greatest evil of
all our life, if it be necessary? Can God have brought us into
the world, intending us so to leave it that the very act of
doing so shall be regarded by us as a curse so terrible as to
neutralise all the blessings of our existence? Can it be that
He who created us should have intended that we should so
regard our dismissal from the world? The teachers of
religion have endeavoured to reconcile us to it, and have, in
their vain zeal, endeavoured to effect it by picturing to our
imaginations a hell-fire into which ninety-nine must fall;
while one shall be allowed to escape to a heaven, which is
hardly made more alluring to us! Is that the way to make a
man comfortable at the prospect of leaving this world? But it
is necessary to our dignity as men that we shall find the
mode of doing so. To lie quivering and quaking on my bed

at the expectation of the Black Angel of Death, does not suit my manhood,—which would fear nothing;—which does not, and shall not, stand in awe of aught but my own sins. How best shall we prepare ourselves for the day which we know cannot be avoided? That is the question which I have ever been asking myself,—which you and I have asked ourselves, and which I thought we had answered. Let us turn the inevitable into that which shall in itself be esteemed a glory to us. Let us teach the world so to look forward with longing eyes, and not with a faint heart. I had thought to have touched some few, not by the eloquence of my words, but by the energy of my thoughts; and you, oh my friend, have ever been he whom it has been my greatest joy to have had with me as the sharer of my aspirations.'

'But I am nine years older than you are.'

I again passed by the one year added to my age. There was nothing now in so trifling an error. 'But you still agree with me as to the fundamental truth of our doctrine.'

'I suppose so,' said Crasweller.

'I suppose so!' repeated I. 'Is that all that can be said for the philosophy to which we have devoted ourselves, and in which nothing false can be found?'

'It won't teach any one not to think it better to live than to die while he is fit to perform all the functions of life.* It might be very well if you could arrange that a man should be deposited as soon as he becomes absolutely infirm.'

'Some men are infirm at forty.'

'Then deposit them,' said Crasweller.

'Yes; but they will not own that they are infirm. If a man be weak at that age, he thinks that with advancing years he will resume the strength of his youth. There must, in fact, be a Fixed Period. We have discussed that fifty times, and have always arrived at the same conclusion.'

He sat still, silent, unhappy, and confused. I saw that there was something on his mind to which he hardly dared to give words. Wishing to encourage him, I went on. 'After all, you have a full twelve months yet before the day shall have come.'

'Two years,' he said, doggedly.

'Exactly; two years before your departure, but twelve months before deposition.'

'Two years before deposition,' said Craswseller.

At this I own I was astonished. Nothing was better known in the empire than the ages of the two or three first inhabitants to be deposited. I would have undertaken to declare that not a man or a woman in Britannula was in doubt as to Mr Craswseller's exact age. It had been written in the records, and upon the stones belonging to the college. There was no doubt that within twelve months of the present date he was due to be detained there as the first inhabitant. And now I was astounded to hear him claim another year, which could not be allowed him.

'That impudent fellow Grundle has been with me,' he continued, 'and wishes to make me believe that he can get rid of me in one year. I have, at any rate, two years left of my out-of-door existence, and I do not mean to give up a day of it for Grundle or any one else.'

It was something to see that he still recognised the law, though he was so meanly anxious to evade it. There had been some whisperings in the empire among the elderly men and women of a desire to obtain the assistance of Great Britain in setting it aside. Peter Grundle, for instance, Craswseller's senior partner, had been heard to say that England would not allow a deposited man to be slaughtered. There was much in that which had angered me. The word slaughter was in itself peculiarly objectionable to my ears,— to me who had undertaken to perform the first ceremony as an act of grace. And what had England to do with our laws? It was as though Russia were to turn upon the United States and declare that their Congress should be put down. What would avail the loudest voice of Great Britain against the smallest spark of a law passed by our Assembly?—unless, indeed, Great Britain should condescend to avail herself of her great power, and thus to crush the free voice of those whom she had already recognised as independent. As I now write, this is what she has already done, and history will have to tell the story. But it was especially sad to have to think that there should be a Britannulist so base, such a coward, such a traitor, as himself to propose this expedient for adding a few years to his own wretched life.

But Crasweller did not, as it seemed, intend to avail himself of these whispers. His mind was intent on devising some falsehood by which he should obtain for himself just one other year of life, and his expectant son-in-law purposed to prevent him. I hardly knew as I turned it all in my mind, which of the two was the more sordid; but I think that my sympathies were rather in accord with the cowardice of the old man than with the greed of the young. After all, I had known from the beginning that the fear of death was a human weakness. To obliterate that fear from the human heart, and to build up a perfect manhood that should be liberated from so vile a thraldom, had been one of the chief objects of my scheme. I had no right to be angry with Crasweller, because Crasweller, when tried, proved himself to be no stronger than the world at large. It was a matter to me of infinite regret that it should be so. He was the very man, the very friend, on whom I had relied with confidence! But his weakness was only a proof that I myself had been mistaken. In all that Assembly by which the law had been passed, consisting chiefly of young men, was there one on whom I could rest with confidence to carry out the purpose of the law when his own time should come? Ought I not so to have arranged matters that I myself should have been the first,—to have postponed the use of the college till such time as I might myself have been deposited? This had occured to me often throughout the whole agitation; but then it had occurred also that none might perhaps follow me, when under such circumstances I should have departed!

But in my heart I could forgive Crasweller. For Grundle I felt nothing but personal dislike. He was anxious to hurry on the deposition of his father-in-law, in order that the entire possession of Little Christchurch might come into his own hands just one year the earlier! No doubt he knew the exact age of the man as well as I did, but it was not for him to have hastened his deposition. And then I could not but think, even in this moment of public misery, how willing Jack would have been to have assisted old Crasweller in his little fraud, so that Eva might have been the reward. My belief is that he would have sworn against his own father, perjured himself in the very teeth of truth, to have obtained from Eva that little privilege which I had once seen Grundle enjoying.

I was sitting there silent in Crasweller's verandah as all this passed through my mind. But before I spoke again I was enabled to see clearly what duty required of me. Eva and Little Christchurch, with Jack's feelings and interests, and all my wife's longings, must be laid on one side, and my whole energy must be devoted to the literal carrying out of the law. It was a great world's movement that had been projected, and if it were to fail now, just at its commencement, when everything had been arranged for the work, when again would there be hope? It was a matter which required legislative sanction in whatever country might adopt it. No despot could attempt it, let his power be ever so confirmed. The whole country would rise against him when informed, in its ignorance, of the contemplated intention. Nor could it be effected by any congress of which the large majority were not at any rate under forty years of age. I had seen enough of human nature to understand its weakness in this respect. All circumstances had combined to make it practicable in Britannula, but all these circumstances might never be combined again. And it seemed to me to depend now entirely on the power which I might exert in creating courage in the heart of the poor timid creature who sat before me. I did know that were Britannula to appeal aloud to England, England, with that desire for interference which has always characterised her, would interfere. But if the empire allowed the working of the law to be commenced in silence, then the Fixed Period might perhaps be regarded as a thing settled. How much, then, depended on the words which I might use!

'Crasweller,' I said, 'my friend, my brother!'

'I don't know much about that. A man ought not to be so anxious to kill his brother.'

'If I could take your place, as God will be my judge, I would do so with as ready a step as a young man to the arms of his beloved. And if for myself, why not for my brother?'

'You do not know,' he said. 'You have not, in truth, been tried.'

'Would that you could try me!'

'And we are not all made of such stuff as you. You have talked about this till you have come to be in love with deposition and departure. But such is not the natural condition of a man. Look back upon all the centuries, and you will perceive that life has ever been dear to the best of men. And you will perceive also that they who have brought themselves to suicide have encountered the contempt of their fellow-creatures.'

I would not tell him of Cato and Brutus,* feeling that I could not stir him to grandeur of heart by Roman instances. He would have told me that in those days, as far as the Romans knew,

> 'the Everlasting had not fixed
> His canon 'gainst self-slaughter.'*

I must reach him by other methods than these, if at all. 'Who can be more alive than you,' I said, 'to the fact that man, by the fear of death, is degraded below the level of the brutes?'

'If so, he is degraded,' said Crasweller. 'It is his condition.'

'But need he remain so? Is it not for you and me to raise him to a higher level?'

'Not for me—not for me, certainly. I own that I am no more than man. Little Christchurch is so pleasant to me, and Eva's smiles and happiness; and the lowing of my flocks and the bleating of my sheep are so gracious in my ears, and it is so sweet to my eyes to see how fairly I have turned this wilderness into a paradise, that I own that I would fain stay here a little longer.'

'But the law, my friend, the law,—the law which you yourself have been so active in creating.'

'The law allows me two years yet,' said he; that look of stubbornness which I had before observed again spreading itself over his face.

Now this was a lie; an absolute, undoubted, demonstrable lie. And yet it was a lie which, by its mere telling, might be made available for its intended purpose. If it were known through the capital that Crasweller was anxious to obtain a year's grace by means of so foul a lie, the year's grace would be accorded to him. And then the Fixed Period would be at an end.

'I will tell you what it is,' said he, anxious to represent his wishes to me in another light. 'Grundle wants to get rid of me.'

'Grundle, I fear, has truth on his side,' said I, determined to show him that I, at any rate, would not consent to lend myself to the furtherance of a falsehood.

'Grundle wants to get rid of me,' he repeated in the same tone. 'But he shan't find that I am so easy to deal with. Eva already does not above half like him. Eva thinks that this depositing plan is abominable. She says that no good Christians ever thought of it.'

'A child—a sweet child—but still only a child; and brought up by her mother with all the old prejudices.'

'I don't know much about that. I never knew a decent woman who wasn't an Episcopalian. Eva is at any rate a good girl, to endeavour to save her father; and I'll tell you what—it is not too late yet. As far as my opinion goes, Jack Neverbend is ten to one a better sort of fellow than Abraham Grundle. Of course a promise has been made; but promises are like pie-crusts. Don't you think that Jack Neverbend is quite old enough to marry a wife, and that he only needs be told to make up his mind to do it? Little Christchurch would do just as well for him as for Grundle. If he don't think much of the girl he must think something of the sheep.'

Not think much of the girl! Just at this time Jack was talking to his mother, morning, noon, and night, about Eva, and threatening young Grundle with all kinds of schoolboy punishments if he should persevere in his suit. Only yesterday he had insulted Abraham grossly, and, as I had reason to suspect, had been more than once out to Christchurch on some clandestine object, as to which it was necessary, he thought, to keep old Crasweller in the dark. And then to be told in this manner that Jack didn't think much of Eva, and should be encouraged in preference to look after the sheep! He would have sacrificed every sheep on the place for the sake of half an hour with Eva alone in the woods. But he was afraid of Crasweller, whom he knew to have sanctioned an engagement with Abraham Grundle.

'I don't think that we need bring Jack and his love into this dispute,' said I.

'Only that it isn't too late, you know. Do you think that Jack could be brought to lend an ear to it?'

Perish Jack! perish Eva! perish Jack's mother, before I would allow myself to be bribed in this manner, to abandon the great object of all my life! This was evidently Crasweller's purpose. He was endeavouring to tempt me with his flocks and herds.* The temptation, had he known it, would have been with Eva,—with Eva and the genuine, downright, honest love of my gallant boy. I knew, too, that at home I should not dare to tell my wife that the offer had been made to me and had been refused. My wife could not understand,—Crasweller could not underestand,—how strong may be the passion founded on the conviction of a life. And honesty, simple honesty, would forbid it. For me to strike a bargain with one already destined for deposition,— that he should be withdrawn from his glorious, his almost immortal state, on the payment of a bribe to me and my family! I had called this man my friend and brother, but how little had the man known me! Could I have saved all Gladstonopolis from imminent flames by yielding an inch in my convictions, I would not have done so in my then frame of mind; and yet this man,—my friend and brother,—had supposed that I could be bought to change my purpose by the pretty slopes and fat flocks of Little Christchurch!

'Crasweller,' said I, 'let us keep these two things separate; or rather, in discussing the momentous question of the Fixed Period, let us forget the loves of a boy and a girl.'

'But the sheep, and the oxen, and the pastures! I can still make my will.'

'The sheep, and the oxen, and the pastures must also be forgotten. They can have nothing to do with the settlement of this matter. My boy is dear to me, and Eva is dear also, but not to save even their young lives could I consent to a falsehood in this matter.'

'Falsehood! There is no falsehood intended.'

'Then there need be no bargain as to Eva, and no need for discussing the flocks and herds on this occasion. Crasweller, you are sixty-six now, and will be sixty-seven this time next year. Then the period of your deposition will have arrived, and in the year following,—two years hence, mind,—the Fixed Period of your departure will have come.'

'No.'

'Is not such the truth?'

'No; you put it all on a year too far. I was never more than nine years older than you. I remember it all as well as though it were yesterday when we first agreed to come away from New Zealand. When will you have to be deposited?'

'In 1989,' I said carefully. 'My Fixed Period is 1990.'

'Exactly; and mine is nine years earlier. It always was nine years earlier.'

It was all manifestly untrue. He knew it to be untrue. For the sake of one poor year he was imploring my assent to a base falsehood, and was endeavouring to add strength to his prayer by a bribe. How could I talk to a man who would so far descend from the dignity of manhood? The law was there to support me, and the definition of the law was in this instance supported by ample evidence. I need only go before the executive of which I myself was the chief, desire that the established documents should be searched, and demand the body of Gabriel Crasweller to be deposited in accordance with the law as enacted. But there was no one else to whom I could leave the performance of this invidious task, as a matter of course. There were aldermen in Gladstonopolis and magistrates in the country whose duty it would no doubt be to see that the law was carried out. Arrangements to this effect had been studiously made by myself. Such arrangements would no doubt be carried out when the working of the Fixed Period had become a thing established. But I had long foreseen that the first deposition should be effected with some *éclat* of voluntary glory. It would be very detrimental to the cause to see my special friend Crasweller hauled away to the college by constables through the streets of Gladstonopolis, protesting that he was forced to his doom twelve months before the appointed time. Crasweller was a popular man in Britannula, and the people around would not be so conversant with the fact as was I, nor would they have the same reasons to be anxious that the law should be accurately followed. And yet how much depended upon the accuracy of following the law! A willing obedience was especially desired in the first instance, and a willing obedience I had expected from my friend Crasweller.

'Crasweller,' I said, addressing him with great solemnity; 'it is not so.'

'It is—it is; I say it is.'

'It is not so. The books that have been printed and sworn to, which have had your own assent with that of others, are all against you.'

'It was a mistake. I have got a letter from my old aunt in Hampshire, written to my mother when I was born, which proves the mistake.'

'I remember the letter well,' I said,—for we had all gone through such documents in performing the important task of settling the Period. 'You were born in New South Wales, and the old lady in England did not write till the following year.'

'Who says so? How can you prove it? She wasn't at all the woman to let a year go by before she congratulated her sister.'

'We have your own signature affirming the date.'

'How was I to know when I was born? All that goes for nothing.'

'And unfortunately,' said I, as though clenching the matter, 'the Bible exists in which your father entered the date with his usual exemplary accuracy.' Then he was silent for a moment as though having no further evidence to offer. 'Crasweller,' said I, 'are you not man enough to do this thing in a straightforward, manly manner?'

'One year!' he exclaimed. 'I only ask for one year. I do think that, as the first victim, I have a right to expect that one year should be granted me. Then Jack Neverbend shall have Little Christchurch, and the sheep, and the cattle, and Eva also, as his own for ever and ever,—or at any rate till he too shall be led away to execution!'

A victim; and execution! What language in which to speak of the great system! For myself I was determined that though I would be gentle with him I would not yield an inch. The law at any rate was with me, and I did not think as yet that Crasweller would lend himself to those who spoke of inviting the interference of England. The law was on my side, and so must still be all those who in the Assembly had voted for the Fixed Period. There had been enthusiasm then, and the different clauses had been carried by large majorities. A dozen different clauses had been carried, each referring to various branches of the question. Not only had the period been fixed, but money had been voted for the college; and the mode of life at the college had been settled; the very amusements of the old men had been sanctioned; and last, but not least, the very manner of departure had been fixed. There was the college now, a graceful building surrounded by growing shrubs and broad pleasant walks for the old men, endowed with a kitchen in which their taste should be consulted, and with a chapel for such of those who would require to pray in public; and all this would be made a laughing-stock to Britannula, if this old man Crasweller declined to enter the gates. 'It must be done,' I said in a tone of firm decision.

'No!' he exclaimed.

'Crasweller, it must be done. The law demands it.'

'No, no; not by me. You and young Grundle together are in a conspiracy to get rid of me. I am not going to be shut up a whole year before my time.'

With that he stalked into the inner house, leaving me alone on the verandah. I had nothing for it but to turn on the electric lamp of my tricycle and steam back to Government House at Gladstonopolis with a sad heart.

# CHAPTER IV
## Jack Neverbend

SIX months passed away, which, I must own, to me was a period of great doubt and unhappiness, though it was relieved by certain moments of triumph. Of course, as the time drew nearer, the question of Crasweller's deposition became generally discussed by the public of Gladstonopolis. And so also did the loves of Abraham Grundle and Eva Crasweller. There were 'Evaites' and 'Abrahamites' in the community; for though the match had not yet been altogether broken, it was known that the two young people differed altogether on the question of the old man's deposition. It was said by the defendents of Grundle, who were to be found for the most part among the young men and young women, that Abraham was simply anxious to carry out the laws of his country. It happened that, during this period, he was elected to a vacant seat in the Assembly, so that, when the matter came on for discussion there, he was able to explain publicly his motives; and it must be owned that he did so with good words and with a certain amount of youthful eloquence. As for Eva, she was simply intent on preserving the lees of her father's life, and had been heard to express an opinion that the college was 'all humbug,' and that people ought to be allowed to live as long as it pleased

God to let them. Of course she had with her the elderly ladies of the community, and among them my own wife as the foremost. Mrs Neverbend had never made herself prominent before in any public question; but on this she seemed to entertain a very warm opinion. Whether this arose entirely from her desire to promote Jack's welfare, or from a reflection that her own period of deposition was gradually becoming nearer, I never could quite make up my mind. She had, at any rate, ten years to run, and I never heard from her any expressed fear of,—departure. She was,—and is,—a brave, good woman, attached to her household duties, anxious for her husband's comfort, but beyond measure solicitous for all good things to befall that scapegrace Jack Neverbend, for whom she thinks that nothing is sufficiently rich or sufficiently grand. Jack is a handsome boy, I grant, but that is about all that can be said of him; and in this matter he has been diametrically opposed to his father from first to last.

It will be seen that, in such circumstances, none of these moments of triumph to which I have alluded can have come to me within my own home. There Mrs Neverbend and Jack, and after a while Eva, sat together in perpetual council against me. When these meetings first began, Eva still acknowledged herself to be the promised bride of Abraham Grundle. There were her own vows, and her parent's assent, and something perhaps of remaining love. But presently she whispered to my wife that she could not but feel horror for the man who was anxious to 'murder her father;' and by-and-by she began to own that she thought Jack a fine fellow. We had a wonderful cricket club in Gladstonopolis, and Britannula had challenged the English cricketers to come and play on the Little Christchurch ground, which they declared to be the only cricket ground as yet prepared on the face of the earth which had all the accomplishments possible for the due prosecution of the game. Now Jack, though very young, was captain of the club, and devoted much more of his time to that occupation than to his more legitimate business as a merchant. Eva, who had not hitherto paid much attention to cricket, became on a sudden passionately devoted to it; whereas Abraham Grundle, with a steadiness beyond his years, gave himself up more than ever to the business of the Assembly, and expressed some contempt for the game, though he was no mean player.

It had become necessary during this period to bring forward in the Assembly the whole question of the Fixed Period, as it was felt that, in the present state of public opinion, it would not be expedient to carry out the established law without the increased sanction which would be given to it by a further vote in the House. Public opinion would have forbidden us to deposit Crasweller without some such further authority. Therefore it was deemed necessary that a question should be asked, in which Crasweller's name was not mentioned, but which might lead to some general debate. Young Grundle demanded one morning whether it was the intention of the Government to see that the different clauses as to the new law respecting depositions were at once carried out. 'The House is aware, I believe,' he said, 'that the first operation will soon be needed.' I may as well state here that this was repeated to Eva, and that she pretended to take huff at such a question from her lover. It was most indecent, she said; and she, after such words, must drop him for ever. It was not for some months after that, that she allowed Jack's name to be mentioned with her own; but I was aware that it was partly settled between her and Jack and Mrs Neverbend. Grundle declared his intention of proceeding against old Crasweller in reference to the breach of contract, according to the laws of Britannula; but that Jack's party disregarded altogether. In telling this, however, I am advancing a little beyond the point in my story to which I have as yet carried my reader.

Then there arose a debate upon the whole principle of the measure, which was carried on with great warmth. I, as President, of course took no part in it; but, in accordance with our constitution, I heard it all from the chair which I usually occupied at the Speaker's right hand. The arguments on which the greatest stress was laid tended to show that the

Fixed Period had been carried chiefly with a view to relieving the miseries of the old. And it was conclusively shown that, in a very great majority of cases, life beyond sixty-eight was all vanity and vexation of spirit. That other argument as to the costliness of old men to the state was for the present dropped. Had you listened to young Grundle, insisting with all the vehemence of youth on the absolute wretchedness to which the aged had been condemned by the absence of any such law,—had you heard the miseries of rheumatism, gout, stone, and general debility pictured in the eloquent words of five-and-twenty,—you would have felt that all who could lend themselves to perpetuate such a state of things must be guilty of fiendish cruelty. He really rose to a grear height of parliamentary excellence, and altogether carried with him the younger, and luckily the greater, part of the House. There was really nothing to be said on the other side, except a repetition of the prejudices of the Old World. But, alas! so strong are the weaknesses of the world, that prejudice can always vanquish truth by the mere strength of its battalions. Not till it had been proved and re-proved ten times over, was it understood that the sun could not have stood still upon Gibeon.* Crasweller, who was a member, and who took his seat during these debates without venturing to speak, merely whispered to his neighbour that the heartless greedy fellow was unwilling to wait for the wools of Little Christchurch.

Three divisions were made on the debate, and thrice did the Fixed-Periodists beat the old party by a majority of fifteen in a House consisting of eighty-five members. So strong was the feeling in the empire, that only two members were absent, and the number remained the same during the whole week of the debate. This, I did think, was a triumph; and I felt that the old country, which had really nothing on earth to do with the matter, could not interfere with an opinion expressed so strongly. My heart throbbed with pleasurable emotion as I heard that old age, which I was myself approaching, depicted in terms which made its impotence truly conspicuous,—till I felt that, had it been proposed to deposit all of us who had reached the age of fifty-eight, I really think that I should joyfully have given my assent to such a measure, and have walked off at once and deposited myself in the college.

But it was only at such moments that I was allowed to experience this feeling of triumph. I was encountered not only in my own house but in society generally, and on the very streets of Gladstonopolis, by the expression of an opinion that Crasweller would not be made to retire to the college at his Fixed Period. 'What on earth is there to hinder it?' I said once to my old friend Ruggles. Ruggles was now somewhat over sixty, and was an agent in the town for country wool-growers. He took no part in politics; and though he had never agreed to the principle of the Fixed Period, had not interested himself in opposition to it. He was a man whom I regarded as indifferent to length of life, but one who would, upon the whole, rather face such lot as Nature might intend for him, than seek to improve it by any new reform.

'Eva Crasweller will hinder it,' said Ruggles.

'Eva is a mere child. Do you suppose that her opinion will be allowed to interrupt the laws of the whole community, and oppose the progress of civilisation?'

'Her feelings will,' said Ruggles. 'Who's to stand a daughter interceding for the life of her father?'

'One man cannot, but eighty-five can do so.'

'The eighty-five will be to the community just what the one would be to the eighty-five. I am not saying anything about your law. I am not expressing an opinion whether it would be good or bad. I should like to live out my own time, though I acknowledge that you Assembly men have on your shoulders the responsibility of deciding whether I shall do so or not. You could lead me away and deposit me without any trouble, because I am not popular. But the people are beginning to talk about Eva Crasweller and Abraham Grundle, and I tell you that all the volunteers you have in Britannula will not suffice to take the old man to the college, and to keep him there till you have polished him off. He would be deposited again at Little Christchurch in triumph, and the college would be left a wreck behind him.'

This view of the case was peculiarly distressing to me. As the chief magistrate of the community, nothing is so abhorrent to me as rebellion. Of a populace that are not law-abiding, nothing but evil can be predicted; whereas a people who will obey the laws cannot but be prosperous. It grieved me greatly to be told that the inhabitants of Gladstonopolis would rise in tumult and destroy the college merely to favour the views of a pretty girl. Was there any honour, or worse again, could there be any utility, in being the President of a republic in which such things could happen? I left my friend Ruggles in the street, and passed on to the executive hall in a very painful frame of mind.

When there, tidings reached me of a much sadder nature. At the very moment at which I had been talking with Ruggles in the street on the subject, a meeting had been held in the market-place with the express purpose of putting down the Fixed Period; and who had been the chief orator on the occasion but Jack Neverbend! My own son had taken upon himself this new work of public speechifying in direct opposition to his own father! And I had reason to believe that he was instigated to do so by my own wife! 'Your son, sir, has been addressing the multitude about the Fixed Period, and they say that it has been quite beautiful to hear him.' It was thus that the matter was told me by one of the clerks in my office, and I own that I did receive some slight pleasure at finding that Jack could do something beyond cricket. But it became immediately necessary to take steps to stop the evil, and I was the more bound to do so because the only delinquent named to me was my own son.

'If it be so,' I said aloud in the office, 'Jack Neverbend shall sleep this night in prison.' But it did not occur to me at the moment that it would be necessary I should have formal evidence that Jack was conspiring against the laws before I could send him to jail. I had no more power over him in that respect than on any one else. Had I declared that he should be sent to bed without his supper, I should have expressed myself better both as a father and a magistrate.

I went home, and on entering the house the first person that I saw was Eva. Now, as this matter went on, I became full of wrath with my son, and with my wife, and with poor old Crasweller; but I never could bring myself to be angry with Eva. There was a coaxing, sweet, feminine way with her which overcame all opposition. And I had already begun to regard her as my daughter-in-law, and to love her dearly in that position, although there were moments in which Jack's impudence and new spirit of opposition almost tempted me to disinherit him.

'Eva,' I said, 'what is this that I hear of a public meeting in the streets?'

'Oh, Mr Neverbend,' she said, taking me by the arm, 'there are only a few boys who are talking about papa.' Through all the noises and tumults of these times there was an evident determination to speak of Jack as a boy. Everything that he did and all that he said were merely the efflux of his high spirits as a schoolboy. Eva always spoke of him as a kind of younger brother. And yet I soon found that the one opponent whom I had most to fear in Britannula was my own son.

'But why,' I asked, 'should these foolish boys discuss the serious question respecting your dear father in the public street?'

'They don't want to have him—deposited,' she said, almost sobbing as she spoke.

'But, my dear,' I began, determined to teach her the whole theory of the Fixed Period with all its advantages from first to last.

But she interrupted me at once. 'Oh, Mr Neverbend, I know what a good thing it is—to talk about. I have no doubt the world will be a great deal the better for it. And if all the papas had been deposited for the last five hundred years, I don't suppose that I should care so much about it. But to be the first that ever it happened to in all the world! Why should papa be the first? You ought to begin with some weak, crotchety, poor old cripple, who would be a great deal better out of the way. But papa is in excellent health, and has all his wits about him a great deal better than Mr Grundle. He manages everything at Little Christchurch, and manages it very well.'

'But, my dear——' I was going to explain to her that in a question of such enormous public interest as this of the Fixed Period it was impossible to consider the merits of individual cases. But she interrupted me again before I could get out a word.

'Oh, Mr Neverbend, they'll never be able to do it, and I'm afraid that then you'll be vexed.'

'My dear, if the law be——'

'Oh yes, the law is a very beautiful thing; but what's the good of laws if they cannot be carried out? There's Jack there;—of course he is only a boy, but he swears that all the executive, and all the Assembly, and all the volunteers in Britannula, shan't lead my papa into that beastly college.'

'Beastly! My dear, you cannot have seen the college. It is perfectly beautiful.'

'That's only what Jack says. It's Jack that calls it beastly. Of course he's not much of a man as yet, but he is your own son. And I do think, that for an earnest spirit about a thing, Jack is a very fine fellow.'

'Abraham Grundle, you know, is just as warm on the other side.'

'I hate Abraham Grundle. I don't want ever to hear his name again. I understand very well what it is that Abraham Grundle is after. He never cared a straw for me; nor I much for him, if you come to that.'

'But you are contracted.'

'If you think that I am going to marry a man because our names have been written down in a book together, you are very much mistaken. He is a nasty mean fellow, and I will never speak to him again as long as I live. He would deposit papa this very moment if he had the power. Whereas Jack is determined to stand up for him as long as he has got a tongue to shout or hands to fight.' These were terrible words, but I had heard the same sentiment myself from

Jack's own lips. 'Of course Jack is nothing to me,' she continued, with that half sob which had become habitual to her whenever she was forced to speak of her father's deposition. 'He is only a boy, but we all know that he could thrash Abraham Grundle at once. And to my thinking he is much more fit to be a member of the Assembly.'

As she would not hear a word that I said to her, and was only intent on expressing the warmth of her own feelings, I allowed her to go her way, and retired to the privacy of my own library. There I endeavoured to console myself as best I might by thinking of the brilliant nature of Jack's prospects. He himself was over head and ears in love with Eva, and it was clear to me that Eva was nearly as fond of him. And then the sly rogue had found the certain way to obtain old Crasweller's consent. Grundle had thought that if he could once see his father-in-law deposited, he would have nothing to do but to walk into Little Christchurch as master. That was the accusation generally made against him in Gladstonopolis. But Jack, who did not, as far as I could see, care a straw for humanity in the matter, had vehemently taken the side of the Anti-Fixed-Periodists as the safest way to get the father's consent. There was a contract of marriage, no doubt, and Grundle would be entitled to take a quarter of the father's possessions if he could prove that the contract had been broken. Such was the law of Britannula on the subject. But not a shilling had as yet been claimed by any man under that law. And Crasweller no doubt concluded that Grundle would be unwilling to bear the odium of being the first. And there were clauses in the law which would make it very difficult for him to prove the validity of the contract. It had been already asserted by many that a girl could not be expected to marry the man who had endeavoured to destroy her father; and although in my mind there could be no doubt that Abraham Grundle had only done his duty as a senator, there was no knowing what view of the case a jury might take in Gladstonopolis. And then, if the worst came to the worst, Crasweller would resign a fourth of his property almost without a pang, and Jack would content himself in making the meanness of Grundle conspicuous to his fellow-citizens.

And now I must confess that, as I sat alone in my library, I did hesitate for an hour as to my future conduct. Might it not be better for me to abandon altogether the Fixed Period and all its glories? Even in Britannula the world might be too strong for me. Should I not take the good things that were offered, and allow Jack to marry his wife and be happy in his own way? In my very heart I loved him quite as well as did his mother, and thought that he was the finest young fellow that Britannula had produced. And if this kind of thing went on, it might be that I should be driven to quarrel with him altogether, and to have him punished under the law, like some old Roman of old. And I must confess that my relations with Mrs Neverbend made me very unfit to ape the Roman *paterfamilias*. She never interfered with public business, but she had a way of talking about household matters in which she was always victorious. Looking back as I did at this moment on the past, it seemed to me that she and Jack, who were the two persons I loved best in the world, had been the enemies who had always successfully conspired against me. 'Do have done with your Fixed Period and nonsense,' she had said to me only yesterday. 'It's all very well for the Assembly; but when you come to killing poor Mr Crasweller in real life, it is quite out of the question.' And then, when I began to explain to her at length the immense importance of the subject, she only remarked that that would do very well for the Assembly. Should I abandon it all, take the good things with which God had provided me, and retire into private life? I had two sides to my character, and could see myself sitting in luxurious comfort amidst the furniture of Crasweller's verandah while Eva and her children were around, and Jack was standing with a cigar in his mouth outside laying down the law for the cricketers at Gladstonopolis. 'Were not better done as others use,'* I said to myself over and over again as I sat there wearied with this contest, and thinking of the much more frightful agony I should be called upon to endure when the time had actually come for the departure of old Crasweller.

And then again if I should fail! For half an hour or so I did fear that I should fail. I had been always a most popular magistrate, but now, it seemed, had come the time in which all my popularity must be abandoned. Jack, who was quick enough at understanding the aspect of things, had already begun to ask the people whether they would see their old friend Crasweller murdered in cold blood. It was a dreadful word, but I was assured that he had used it. How would it be when the time even for depositing had come, and an attempt was made to lead the old man up through the streets of Gladstonopolis? Should I have strength of character to perform the task in opposition to the loudly expressed wishes of the inhabitants, and to march him along protected by a strong body of volunteers? And how would it be if the volunteers themselves refused to act on the side of law and order? Should I not absolutely fail; and would it not afterwards be told of me that, as President, I had broken down in an attempt to carry out the project with which my name had been so long associated?

As I sat there alone I had almost determined to yield. But suddenly there came upon me a memory of Socrates, of Galileo, of Hampden,* and of Washington. What great things had these men done by constancy, in opposition to the wills and prejudices of the outside world! How triumphant they now appeared to have been in fighting against the enormous odds which power had brought against them! And how pleasant now were the very sounds of their names to all who loved their fellow-creatures! In some moments of private thought, anxious as were now my own, they too must have doubted. They must have asked themselves the question, whether they were strong enough to carry their great reforms against the world. But in these very moments the necessary strength had been given to them. It must have been that, when almost despairing, they had been comforted by an inner truth, and had been all but inspired to trust with confidence in their cause. They, too, had been weak, and had trembled, and had almost feared. But they had found in their own hearts that on which they could rely. Had they been less sorely pressed than was I now at this present moment? Had not they believed and trusted and been confident? As I thought of it, I became aware that it was not only necessary for a man to imagine new truths, but to be able to endure, and to suffer, and to bring them to maturity. And how often before a truth was brought to maturity must it be necessary that he who had imagined it, and seen it, and planned it, must give his very life for it, and all in vain? But not perhaps all in vain as far as the world was concerned; but only in vain in regard to the feelings and knowledge of the man himself. In struggling for the welfare of his fellow-creatures, a man must dare to endure to be obliterated,—must be content to go down unheard of,—or, worse still, ridiculed, and perhaps abused by all,—in order that something afterwards may remain of those changes which he has been enabled to see, but not to carry out. How many things are requisite to true greatness! But, first of all, is required that self-negation which is able to plan new blessings, although certain that those blessings will be accounted as curses by the world at large.

Then I got up, and as I walked about the room I declared to myself aloud my purpose. Though I might perish in the attempt, I would certainly endeavour to carry out the doctrine of the Fixed Period. Though the people might be against me, and regard me as their enemy,—that people for whose welfare I had done it all,—still I would persevere, even though I might be destined to fall in the attempt. Though the wife of my bosom and the son of my loins should turn against me, and embitter my last moments by their enmity, still would I persevere. When they came to speak of the vices and the virtues of President Neverbend,—to tell of his weakness and his strength,—it should never be said of him that he had been deterred by fear of the people from carrying out the great measure which he had projected solely for their benefit.

Comforted by this resolve, I went into Mrs Neverbend's parlour, where I found her son Jack sitting with her. They had evidently been talking about Jack's speech in the market-place; and I could see that the young orator's brow was still flushed with the triumph of the moment. 'Father,' said he, immediately, 'you will never be able to deposit old Crasweller. People won't let you do it.'

'The people of Britannula,' I said, 'will never interfere to prevent their magistrate from acting in accordance with the law.'

'Bother!' said Mrs Neverbend. When my wife said 'bother,' it was, I was aware, of no use to argue with her. Indeed, Mrs Neverbend is a lady upon whom argument is for the most part thrown away. She forms her opinion from the things around her, and is, in regard to domestic life, and to her neighbours, and to the conduct of people with whom she lives, almost invariably right. She has a quick insight, and an affectionate heart, which together keep her from going astray. She knows how to do good, and when to do it. But to abstract argument, and to political truth, she is wilfully blind. I felt it to be necessary that I should select this opportunity for making Jack understand that I would not fear his opposition; but I own that I could have wished that Mrs Neverbend had not been present on the occasion.

'Won't they?' said Jack. 'That's just what I fancy they will do.'

'Do you mean to say that it is what you wish them to do,—that you think it right that they should do it?'

'I don't think Crasweller ought to be deposited, if you mean that, father.'

'Not though the law requires it?' This I said in a tone of authority. 'Have you formed any idea in your own mind of the subjection to the law which is demanded from all good citizens? Have you ever bethought yourself that the law should be in all things——'

'Oh, Mr President, pray do not make a speech here,' said my wife. 'I shall never understand it, and I do not think that Jack is much wiser than I am.'

'I do not know what you mean by a speech, Sarah.' My wife's name is Sarah. 'But it is necessary that Jack should be instructed that he, at any rate, must obey the law. He is my son, and, as such, it is essentially necessary that he should be amenable to it. The law demands——'

'You can't do it, and there's an end of it,' said Mrs Neverbend. 'You and all your laws will never be able to put an end to poor Mr Crasweller,—and it would be a great shame if you did. You don't see it; but the feeling here in the city is becoming very strong. The people won't have it; and I must say that it is only rational that Jack should be on the same side. He is a man now, and has a right to his own opinion as well as another.'

'Jack,' said I, with much solemnity, 'do you value your father's blessing?'

'Well; sir, yes,' said he. 'A blessing, I suppose, means something of an allowance paid quarterly.'

I turned away my face that he might not see the smile which I felt was involuntarily creeping across it. 'Sir,' said I, 'a father's blessing has much more than a pecuniary value. It includes that kind of relation between a parent and his son without which life would be a burden to me, and, I should think, very grievous to you also.'

'Of course I hope that you and I may always be on good terms.'

I was obliged to take this admission for what it was worth. 'If you wish to remain on good terms with me,' said I, 'you must not oppose me in public when I am acting as a public magistrate.'

'Is he to see Mr Crasweller murdered before his very eyes, and to say nothing about it?' said Mrs Neverbend.

Of all terms in the language there was none so offensive to me as that odious word when used in reference to the ceremony which I had intended to be so gracious and alluring. 'Sarah,' said I, turning upon her in my anger, 'that is a very improper word, and one which you should not tempt the boy to use, especially in my presence.'

'English is English, Mr President,' she said. She always called me 'Mr President' when she intended to oppose me.

'You might as well say that a man was murdered when he is—is—killed in battle.' I had been about to say 'executed,' but I stopped myself. Men are not executed in Britannula.

'No. He is fighting his country's battle and dies gloriously.'

'He has his leg shot off, or his arm, and is too frequently left to perish miserably on the ground. Here every comfort will be provided for him, so that he may depart from this world without a pang, when, in the course of years, he shall have lived beyond the period at which he can work and be useful.'

'But look at Mr Crasweller, father. Who is more useful than he is?'

Nothing had been more unlucky to me as the promoter of the Fixed Period than the peculiar healthiness and general sanity of him who was by chance to be our first martyr. It might have been possible to make Jack understand that a rule which had been found to be applicable to the world at large was not fitted for some peculiar individual, but it was quite impossible to bring this home to the mind of Mrs Neverbend. I must, I felt, choose some other opportunity for expounding that side of the argument. I would at the present moment take a leaf out of my wife's book and go straight to my purpose. 'I tell you what it is, young man,' said I; 'I do not intend to be thwarted by you in carrying on the great reform to which I have devoted my life. If you cannot hold your tongue at the present moment, and abstain from making public addresses in the market-place, you shall go out of Britannula. It is well that you should travel and see something of the world before you commence the trade of public orator. Now I think of it, the Alpine Club from Sydney are to be in New Zealand this summer, and it will suit you very well to go and climb up Mount Earnshawe and

see all the beauties of nature instead of talking nonsense
here in Gladstonopolis.'

'Oh, father, I should like nothing better,' cried Jack,
enthusiastically.

'Nonsense,' said Mrs Neverbend; 'are you going to send
the poor boy to break his neck among the glaciers? Don't
you remember that Dick Ardwinkle was lost there a year or
two ago, and came to his death in a most frightful manner?'

'That was before I was born,' said Jack, 'or at any rate very
shortly afterwards. And they hadn't then invented the new
patent steel climbing arms. Since they came up, no one has
ever been lost among the glaciers.'

'You had better prepare then to go,' said I, thinking that
the idea of getting rid of Jack in this manner was very happy.

'But, father,' said he, 'of course I can't stir a step till after
the great cricket-match.'

'You must give up cricket for this time. So good an
opportunity for visiting the New Zealand mountains may
never come again.'

'Give up the match!' he exclaimed. 'Why, the English
sixteen are coming here on purpose to play us, and swear
that they'll beat us by means of the new catapult. But I know
that our steam-bowler will beat their catapult hollow. At any
rate I cannot stir from here till after the match is over. I've
got to arrange everything myself. Besides, they do count
something on my spring-batting. I should be regarded as
absolutely a traitor to my country if I were to leave
Britannula while this is going on. The young Marquis of
Marylebone, their leader, is to stay at our house; and the
vessel bringing them will be due here about eleven o'clock
next Wednesday.'

'Eleven o'clock next Wednesday,' said I, in surprise. I had
not as yet heard of this match, nor of the coming of our
aristocratic visitor.

'They won't be above thirty minutes late at the outside.
They left the Land's End three weeks ago last Tuesday at
two, and London at half-past ten. We have had three or four

water telegrams from them since they started, and they hadn't then lost ten minutes on the journey. Of course I must be at home to receive the Marquis of Marylebone.'

All this set me thinking about many things. It was true that at such a moment I could not use my parental authority to send Jack out of the island. To such an extent had the childish amusements of youth been carried, as to give to them all the importance of politics and social science. What I had heard about this cricket-match had gone in at one ear and come out at the other; but now that it was brought home to me, I was aware that all my authority would not serve to banish Jack till it was over. Not only would he not obey me, but he would be supported in his disobedience by even the elders of the community. But perhaps the worst feature of it all was the arrival just now at Gladstonopolis of a crowd of educated Englishmen. When I say educated I mean prejudiced. They would be Englishmen with no ideas beyond those current in the last century, and would be altogether deaf to the wisdom of the Fixed Period. I saw at a glance that I must wait till they should have taken their departure, and postpone all further discussion on the subject as far as might be possible till Gladstonopolis should have been left to her natural quiescence after the disturbance of the cricket. 'Very well,' said I, leaving the room. 'Then it may come to pass that you will never be able to visit the wonderful glories of Mount Earnshawe.'

'Plenty of time for that,' said Jack, as I shut the door.

# CHAPTER V
## The Cricket-match

I HAD been of late so absorbed in the affairs of the Fixed Period, that I had altogether forgotten the cricket-match and the noble strangers who were about to come to our shores. Of course I had heard of it before, and had been informed that Lord Marylebone was to be our guest. I had probably also been told that Sir Lords Longstop and Sir Kennington Oval were to be entertained at Little Christchurch. But when I was reminded of this by Jack a few days later, it had quite gone out of my head. But I now at once began to recognise the importance of the occasion, and to see that for the next two months Crasweller, the college, and the Fixed Period must be banished, if not from my thoughts, at any rate from my tongue. Better could not be done in the matter than to have them banished from the tongue of all the world, as I certainly should not be anxious to have the subject ventilated within hearing and speaking of the crowd of thoroughly old-fashioned, prejudiced, aristocratic young Englishmen who were coming to us. The cricket-match sprang to the front so suddenly, that Jack seemed to have forgotten all his energy respecting the college, and to have transferred his entire attention to the various weapons, offensive and defensive, wherewith the London club was, if possible, to be beaten. We are never short of money in Britannula; but it seemed, as I watched the various preparations made for carrying on two or three days' play at Little Christchurch, that England must be sending out another army to take another Sebastopol. More paraphernalia were required to enable these thirty-two lads to play their game with propriety than would have been needed for the depositing of half Gladstonopolis. Every man from England had his attendant to look after his bats and balls, and shoes and greaves; and it was necessary, of course, that our boys should be equally well served. Each of them had two bicycles for his own use, and as they were all constructed with the new double-acting levers, they passed backwards and forwards along the bicycle track between the city and Crasweller's house with astonishing rapidity. I used to hear that the six miles had been done in fifteen minutes. Then there came a struggle with the English and the Britannulists, as to which would get the nearest to fourteen minutes; till it seemed that bicycle-racing and not cricket had been the purpose for which the English had sent out the

4000-ton steam-yacht at the expense of all the cricketers of the nation. It was on this occasion that the track was first divided for comers and goers, and that volunteers were set to prevent stragglers from crossing except by the regular bridges. I found that I, the President of the Republic, was actually forbidden to go down in my tricycle to my old friend's house, unless I would do so before noon. 'You'd be run over and made mincemeat of,' said Jack, speaking of such a catastrophe with less horror than I thought it ought to have engendered in his youthful mind. Poor Sir Lords was run down by our Jack,—collided as Jack called it. 'He hadn't quite impetus enough on to make the turning sharp as he ought,' said Jack, without the slightest apparent regret at what had occurred. 'Another inch and a half would have saved him. If he can touch a ball from our steam-bowler when I send it, I shall think more of his arms than I do of his legs, and more of his eyes than I do of his lungs. What a fellow to send out! Why, he's thirty, and has been eating soup, they tell me, all through the journey.' These young men had brought a doctor with them, Dr MacNuffery, to prescribe to them what to eat and drink at each meal; and the unfortunate baronet whom Jack had nearly slaughtered, had encountered the ill-will of the entire club because he had called for mutton-broth when he was sea-sick.

They were to be a month in Britannula before they would begin the match, so necessary was it that each man should be in the best possible physical condition. They had brought their Dr MacNuffery, and our lads immediately found the need of having a doctor of their own. There was, I think, a little pretence in this, as though Dr Bobbs had been a long-established officer of the Southern Cross cricket club, they had not in truth thought of it, and Bobbs was only appointed the night after MacNuffery's position and duties had been made known. Bobbs was a young man just getting into practice in Gladstonopolis, and understood measles, I fancy, better than the training of athletes. MacNuffery was the most disagreeable man of the English party, and soon began to turn up his nose at Bobbs. But Bobbs, I think, got

the better of him. 'Do you allow coffee to your club;
—coffee?' asked MacNuffery, in a voice mingling ridicule
and reproof with a touch of satire, as he had begun to guess
that Bobbs had not been long attending to his present work.
'You'll find,' said Bobbs, 'that young men in our air do not
need the restraints which are necessary to you English.
Their fathers and mothers were not soft and flabby before
them, as was the case with yours, I think.' Lord Marylebone
looked across the table, I am told, at Sir Kennington Oval,
and nothing afterwards was said about diet.

But a great trouble arose, which, however, rather assisted
Jack in his own prospects in the long-run,—though for a
time it seemed to have another effect. Sir Kennington Oval
was much struck by Eva's beauty, and, living as he did in
Crasweller's house, soon had an opportunity of so telling
her. Abraham Grundle was one of the cricketers, and, as
such, was frequently on the ground at Little Christchurch;
but he did not at present go into Crasweller's house, and
the whole fashionable community of Gladstonoplis was
beginning to entertain the opinion that that match was off.
Grundle had been heard to declare most authoritatively that
when the day came Crasweller should be deposited, and had
given it as his opinion that the power did not exist which
could withstand the law of Britannula. Whether in this he
preferred the law to Eva, or acted in anger against Crasweller
for interfering with his prospects, or had an idea that it
would not be worth his while to marry the girl while the
girl's father should be left alive, or had gradually fallen into
this bitterness of spirit from the opposition shown to him, I
could not quite tell. And he was quite as hostile to Jack as to
Crasweller. But he seemed to entertain no aversion at all
to Sir Kennington Oval; nor, I was informed, did Eva. I
had known that for the last month Jack's mother had been
instant with him to induce him to speak out to Eva; but he,
who hardly allowed me, his father, to open my mouth without contradicting me, and who in our house ordered everything about just as though he were the master, was so
bashful in the girl's presence that he had never as yet asked

her to be his wife. Now Sir Kennington had come in his way, and he by no means carried his modesty so far as to abstain from quarrelling with him. Sir Kennington was a good-looking young aristocrat, with plenty of words, but nothing special to say for himself. He was conspicuous for his cricketing finery, and when got up to take his place at the wicket, looked like a diver with his diving-armour all on; but Jack said that he was very little good at the game. Indeed, for mere cricket Jack swore that the English would be 'nowhere' but for eight professional players whom they had brought out with them. It must be explained that our club had no professionals. We had not come to that yet,—that a man should earn his bread by playing cricket. Lord Marylebone and his friend had brought with them eight professional 'slaves,' as our young men came to call them,—most ungraciously. But each 'slave' required as much looking after as did the masters, and they thought a great deal more of themselves than did the non-professionals.

Jack had in truth been attempting to pass Sir Kennington on the bicycle track when he had upset poor Sir Lords Longstop; and, according to his own showing, he had more than once allowed Sir Kennington to start in advance, and had run into Little Christchurch bicycle quay before him. This had not given rise to the best feeling, and I feared lest there might be an absolute quarrel before the match should have been played. 'I'll punch that fellow's head some of these days,' Jack said one evening when he came back from Little Christchurch.

'What's the matter now?' I asked.

'Impudent puppy! He thinks because he has got an unmeaning handle to his name, that everybody is to come to his whistle. They tell me that his father was made what they call a baronet because he set a broken arm for one of those twenty royal dukes that England has to pay for.'

'Who has had to come to his whistle now?' asked his mother.

'He went over with his steam curricle, and sent to ask Eva whether she would not take a drive with him on the cliffs.'

'She needn't have gone unless she wished it,' I said.

'But she did go; and there she was with him for a couple of hours. He's the most unmeaning upstart of a puppy I ever met. He has not three ideas in the world. I shall tell Eva what I think about him.'

The quarrel went on during the whole period of preparation, till it seemed as though Gladstonopolis had nothing else to talk about. Eva's name was in every one's mouth, till my wife was nearly beside herself with anger. 'A girl,' said she, 'shouldn't get herself talked about in that way by every one all round. I don't suppose the man intends to marry her.'

'I can't see why he shouldn't,' I replied.

'She's nothing more to him than a pretty provincial lass. What would she be in London?'

'Why should not Mr Crasweller's daughter be as much admired in London as here?' I answered. 'Beauty is the same all the world over, and her money will be thought of quite as much there as here.'

'But she will have such a spot upon her.'

'Spot! What spot?'

'As the daughter of the first deposited of the Fixed Period people,—if ever that comes off. Or if it don't, she'll be talked about as her who was to be. I don't suppose any Englishman will think of marrying her.'

This made me very angry. 'What!' I said. 'Do you, a Britannulist and my wife, intend to turn the special glory of Britannula to the disgrace of her people? That which we should be ready to claim as the highest honour,—as being an advance in progress and general civilisation never hitherto even thought of among other people,—to have conceived that, and to have prepared it, in every detail for perfect consummation,—that is to be accounted as an opprobrium to our children, by you, the Lady President of the Republic! Have you no love of country, no patriotism, no feeling at any rate of what has been done for the world's welfare by your own family?' I own I did feel vexed when she spoke of Eva as having been as it were contaminated by being a Britannulist, because of the law enacting the Fixed Period.

'She'd better face it out at home than go across the world to hear what other people say of us. It may be all very well as far as state wisdom goes; but the world isn't ripe for it, and we shall only be laughed at.'

There was truth in this, and a certain amount of concession had also been made. I can fancy that an easy-going butterfly should laugh at the painful industry of the ant; and I should think much of the butterfly who should own that he was only a butterfly because it was the age of butterflies. 'The few wise,' said I, 'have ever been the laughing-stock of silly crowds.'

'But Eva isn't one of the wise,' she replied, 'and would be laughed at without having any of your philosophy to support her. However, I don't suppose the man is thinking of it.'

But the young man was thinking of it; and had so far made up his mind before he went as to ask Eva to marry him out of hand and return with him to England. We heard of it when the time came, and heard also that Eva had declared that she could not make up her mind so quickly. That was what was said when the time drew near for the departure of the yacht. But we did not hear it direct from Eva, nor yet from Crasweller. All these tidings came to us from Jack, and Jack was in this instance somewhat led astray.

Time passed on, and the practice on the Little Christ-church ground was continued. Several accidents happened, but the cricketers took very little account of these. Jack had his cheek cut open by a ball running off his bat on to his face; and Eva, who saw the accident, was carried fainting into the house. Sir Kennington behaved admirably, and himself brought him home in his curricle. We were told afterwards that this was done at Eva's directions, because old Crasweller would have been uncomfortable with the boy in his house, seeing that he could not in his present circumstances receive me or my wife. Mrs Neverbend swore a solemn oath that Jack should be made to abandon his cricket; but Jack was playing again the next day, with his face strapped up athwart and across with republican black-silk adhesive. When I saw Bobbs at work over him I thought that one side of his face was gone, and that his eye would be dreadfully out of place. 'All his chance of marrying Eva is gone,' said I to my wife. 'The nasty little selfish slut!' said Mrs Neverbend. But at two the next day Jack had been patched up, and nothing could keep him from Little Christchurch. Bobbs was with him the whole morning, and assured his mother that if he could go out and take exercise his eye would be all right. His mother offered to take a walk with him in the city park; but Bobbs declared that violent exercise would be necessary to keep the eye in its right place, and Jack was at Little Christchurch manipulating his steam-bowler in the afternoon. Afterwards Littlebat, one of the English professionals, had his leg broken, and was necessarily laid on one side; and young Grundle was hurt on the lower part of the back, and never showed himself again on the scene of danger. 'My life is too precious in the Assembly just at present,' he said to me, excusing himself. He alluded to the Fixed Period debate, which he knew would be renewed as soon as the cricketers were gone. I no doubt depended very much on Abraham Grundle, and assented. The match was afterwards carried on with fifteen on each side; for though each party had spare players, they could not agree as to the use of them. Our next man was better then theirs, they said, and they were anxious that we should take our second best, to which our men would not agree. Therefore the game was ultimately played with thirty combatants.

'So one of our lot is to come back for a wife almost immediately,' said Lord Marylebone at our table the day before the match was to be played.

'Oh, indeed, my lord!' said Mrs Neverbend. 'I am glad to find that a Britannulan young lady has been so effective. Who is the gentleman?' It was easy to see by my wife's face, and to know by her tone of voice, that she was much disturbed by the news.

'Sir Kennington,' said Lord Marylebone. 'I supposed you had all heard of it.' Of course we had all heard of it;

but Lord Marylebone did not know what had been Mrs Neverbend's wishes for her own son.

'We did know that Sir Kennington had been very attentive, but there is no knowing what that means from you foreign gentlemen. It's a pity that poor Eva, who is a good girl in her way, should have her head turned.' This came from my wife.

'It's Oval's head that is turned,' continued his lordship; 'I never saw a man so bowled over in my life. He's awfully in love with her.'

'What will his friends say at home?' asked Mrs Neverbend.

'We understand that Miss Crasweller is to have a large fortune; eight or ten thousand a year at the least. I should imagine that she will be received with open arms by all the Ovals; and as for a foreigner,—we don't call you foreigners.'

'Why not?' said I, rather anxious to prove that we were foreigners. 'What makes a foreigner but a different allegiance? Do we not call the Americans foreigners?' Great Britain and France had been for years engaged in the great maritime contest with the united fleets of Russia and America, and had only just made that glorious peace by which, as politicians said, all the world was to be governed for the future; and after that, it need not be doubted but that the Americans were foreign to the English;—and if the Americans, why not the Britannulists? We had separated ourselves from Great Britain, without coming to blows indeed; but still our own flag, the Southern Cross, flew as proudly to our gentle breezes as ever had done the Union-jack amidst the inclemency of a British winter. It was the flag of Britannula, with which Great Britain had no concern. At the present moment I was specially anxious to hear a distinguished Englishman like Lord Marylebone acknowledge that we were foreigners. 'If we be not foreigners, what are we, my lord?'

'Englishmen, of course,' said he. 'What else? Don't you talk English?'

'So do the Americans, my lord,' said I, with a smile that was intended to be gracious. 'Our language is spreading itself over the world, and is no sign of nationality.'

'What laws do you obey?'

'English,—till we choose to repeal them. You are aware that we have already freed ourselves from the stain of capital punishment.'

'Those coins pass in your market-places?' Then he brought out a gold piece from his waistcoat-pocket, and slapped it down on the table. It was one of those pounds which the people will continue to call sovereigns, although the name has been made actually illegal for the rendering of all accounts. 'Whose is this image and superscription?' he asked. 'And yet this was paid to me to-day at one of your banks, and the lady cashier asked me whether I would take sovereigns. How will you get over that, Mr President?'

A small people,—numerically small,— cannot of course do everything at once. We have been a little slack perhaps in instituting a national mint. In fact there was a difficulty about the utensil by which we would have clapped a Southern Cross over the British arms, and put the portrait of the Britannulan President of the day,—mine for instance,—in the place where the face of the British monarch has hitherto held its own. I have never pushed the question much, lest I should seem, as have done some presidents, over anxious to exhibit myself. I have ever thought more of the glory of our race than of putting forward my own individual self,—as may be seen by the whole history of the college. 'I will not attempt to get over it,' I said; 'but according to my ideas, a nation does not depend on the small external accidents of its coin or its language.'

'But on the flag which it flies. After all, a bit of bunting is easy.'

'Nor on its flag, Lord Marylebone, but on the hearts of its people. We separated from the old mother country with no quarrel, with no ill-will; but with the mutual friendly wishes of both. If there be a trace of the feeling of antagonism in the word foreigners, I will not use it; but British subjects we are not, and never can be again.' This I said because I felt that there was creeping up, as it were in the very atmosphere, a feeling the England should be again asked to annex us, so as to save our old people from the wise decision to which our own Assembly had come. Oh for an adamantine law to protect the human race from the imbecility, the weakness, the discontent, and the extravagance of old age! Lord Marylebone, who saw that I was in earnest, and who was the most courteous of gentlemen, changed the conversation. I had already observed that he never spoke about the Fixed Period in our house, though, in the condition in which the community then was, he must have heard it discussed elsewhere.

The day for the match had come. Jack's face was so nearly healed that Mrs Neverbend had been brought to believe entirely in the efficacy of violent exercise for cuts and bruises. Grundle's back was still bad, and the poor fellow with the broken leg could only be wheeled out in front of the verandah to look at the proceedings through one of those wonderful little glasses which enable the critic to see every motion of the players at half-a-mile's distance. He assured me that the precision with which Jack set his steam-bowler was equal to that of one of those Shoeburyness gunners who can hit a sparrow as far as they can see him, on condition only that they know the precise age of the bird. I gave Jack great credit in my own mind, because I felt that at the moment he was much down at heart. On the preceding day Sir Kennington had been driving Eva about in his curricle, and Jack had returned home tearing his hair. 'They do it on purpose to put him off his play,' said his mother. But if so, they hadn't known Jack. Nor indeed had I quite known him up to this time.

I was bound myself to see the game, because a special tent and a special glass had been prepared for the President. Crasweller walked by as I took my place, but he only shook his head sadly and was silent. It now wanted but four months to his deposition. Though there was a strong party in his favour, I do not know that he meddled much with it. I did hear from different sources that he still continued to assert that he was only nine years my senior, by which he intended to gain the favour of a postponement of his term by twelve poor months; but I do not think that he ever lent himself to the other party. Under my auspices he had always voted for the Fixed Period, and he could hardly oppose it now in theory. They tossed for the first innings, and the English club won it. It was all England against Britannula! Think of the population of the two countries. We had, however, been taught to believe that no community ever played cricket as did the Britannulans. The English went in first, with the two baronets at the wickets. They looked like two stout Minervas with huge wicker helmets. I know a picture of the goddess, all helmet, spear, and petticoats, carrying her spear over her shoulder as she flies through the air over the cities of the earth. Sir Kennington did not fly, but in other respects he was very like the goddess, so completely enveloped was he in his indiarubber guards, and so wonderful was the machine upon his head, by which his brain and features were to be protected.

As he took his place upon the ground there was great cheering. Then the steam-bowler was ridden into its place by the attendant engineer, and Jack began his work. I could see the colour come and go in his face as he carefully placed the ball and peeped down to get its bearing. It seemed to me as though he were taking infinite care to level it straight and even at Sir Kennington's head. I was told afterwards that he never looked at Sir Kennington, but that, having calculated his distance by means of a quicksilver levelling-glass, his object was to throw the ball on a certain inch of turf, from which it might shoot into the wicket at such a degree as to make it very difficult for Sir Kennington to know what to do with it. It seemed to me to take a long time, during which the fourteen men around all looked as though each man were intending to hop off to some other spot than that on which he was standing. There used, I am told, to be only eleven of these men; but now, in a great match, the long-offs, and the long-ons, and the rest of them, are all doubled. The double long-off was at such a distance that, he being a small man, I could only just see him through the field-glass which I kept in my waistcoat-pocket. When I had been looking hard at them for what seemed to be a quarter of an hour, and the men were apparently becoming tired of their continual hop, and when Jack had stooped and kneeled and sprawled, with one eye shut, in every conceivable attitude, on a sudden there came a sharp snap, a little smoke, and lo, Sir Kennington Oval was———out!

There was no doubt about it. I myself saw the two bails fly away into infinite space, and at once there was a sound of kettle-drums, trumpets, fifes, and clarionets. It seemed as though all the loud music of the town band had struck up at the moment with their shrillest notes. And a huge gun was let off.

> 'And let the kettle to the trumpet speak,
> The trumpet to the cannoneer without,
> The cannons to the heavens, the heavens to earth.
> Now drinks the king to Hamlet.'*

I could not but fancy, at these great signs of success, that I was Hamlet's father.

Sir Kennington Oval was out,—out at the very first ball. There could be no doubt about it, and Jack's triumph was complete. It was melancholy to see the English Minerva, as he again shouldered his spear and walked back to his tent. In spite of Jack's good play, and the success on the part of my own countrymen, I could not but be sorry to think that the young baronet had come half round the world to be put out at the first ball. There was a cruelty in it,—an inhospitality,—which, in spite of the exigencies of the game, went against the grain. Then, when the shouting, and the holloaing, and the flinging up of the ball were still going on, I remembered that, after it, he would have his consolation with Eva. And poor Jack, when his short triumph was over, would have to reflect that, though fortunate in his cricket, he was unhappy in his love. As this occurred to me, I looked back towards the house, and there, from a little lattice window at the end of the verandah, I saw a lady's handkerchief waving. Could it be that Eva was waving it so as to comfort her vanquished British lover? In the meantime Minerva went to his tent, and hid himself among sympathetic friends; and I was told afterwards that he was allowed half a pint of bitter beer by Dr MacNuffery.

After twenty minutes spent in what seemed to me the very ostentation of success, another man was got to the wickets. This was Stumps, one of the professionals, who was not quite so much like a Minerva, though he, too, was prodigiously greaved. Jack again set his ball, snap went the machine, and Stumps wriggled his bat. He touched the ball, and away it flew behind the wicket. Five republican Minervas ran after it as fast as their legs could carry them; and I was told by a gentleman who sat next to me scoring, that a dozen runs had been made. He spent a great deal of time in explaining how, in the old times, more than six at a time were never scored. Now all this was altered. A slight tip counted ever so much more than a good forward blow, because the ball went behind the wicket. Up flew on all sides of the ground figures to show that Stumps had made a dozen, and two British clarionets were blown with a great deal of vigour. Stumps was a thick-set, solid, solemn-looking man, who had been ridiculed by our side as being much too old for the game; but he seemed to think very little of Jack's precise machine. He kept chopping at the ball, which always went behind, till he had made a great score. It was two hours before Jack had sorely lamed him in the hip, and the umpire had given it leg-before-wicket. Indeed it was leg-before-wicket, as the poor man felt when he was assisted back to his tent. However, he had scored 150. Sir Lords Longstop, too, had run up a good score before he was caught out by the middle long-off,—a marvellous catch they all said it was,— and our trumpets were blown for fully five minutes. But the big gun was only fired when a ball was hurled from the machine directly into the wicket.

At the end of three days the Britishers were all out, and the runs were numbered in four figures. I had my doubts, as I looked at the contest, whether any of them would be left to play out the match. I was informed that I was expected to take the President's seat every day; but when I heard that there were to be two innings for each set, I positively declined. But Crasweller took my place; and I was told that a gleam of joy shot across his worn, sorrowful face when Sir Kennington began the second innings with ten runs. Could he really wish, in his condition, to send his daughter away to England simply that she might be a baronet's wife?

When the Britannulists went in for the second time, they had 1500 runs to get; and it was said afterwards that Grundle had bet four to one against his own side. This was thought to be very shabby on his part, though if such was the betting, I don't see why he should lose his money by backing his friends. Jack declared in my hearing that he would not put a shilling on. He did not wish either to lose his money or to bet against himself. But he was considerably disheartened when he told me that he was not going in on the first day of their second innings. He had not done much when the Britannulists were in before,—had only made some thirty or forty runs; and, worse than that, Sir Kennington Oval had scored up to 300. They told me that his Pallas helmet was shaken with tremendous energy as he made his running. And again, that man Stumps had seemed to be invincible, though still lame, and had carried out his bat with a tremendous score. He trudged away without any sign of triumph; but Jack said that the professional was the best man they had.

On the second day of our party's second innings,—the last day but one of the match,—Jack went in. They had only made 150 runs on the previous day, and three wickets were down. Our kettle-drums had had but little opportunity for making themselves heard. Jack was very despondent, and had had some tiff with Eva. He had asked Eva whether she were not going to England, and Eva had said that perhaps she might do so if some Britannulists did not do their duty. Jack had chosen to take this as a bit of genuine imperti-nence, and had been very sore about it. Stumps was bowling from the British catapult, and very nearly gave Jack his quietus during the first over. He hit wildly, and four balls passed him without touching his wicket. Then came his turn again, and he caught the first ball with his Neverbend spring-bat,—for he had invented it himself,—such a swipe, as he called it, that nobody has ever yet been able to find the ball. The story goes that it went right up to the verandah, and that Eva picked it up, and has treasured it ever since.

Be that as it may, during the whole of that day, and the next, nobody was able to get him out. There was a continual banging of the kettle-drum, which seemed to give him renewed spirits. Every ball as it came to him was sent away into infinite space. All the Englishmen were made to retire to further distances from the wickets, and to stand about almost at the extremity of the ground. The management of the catapults was intrusted to one man after another,—but in vain. Then they sent the catapults away, and tried the old-fashioned slow bowling. It was all the same to Jack. He would not be tempted out of his ground, but stood there awaiting the ball, let it come ever so slowly. Through the first of the two days he stood before his wicket, hitting to the right and the left, till hope seemed to spring up again in the bosom of the Britannulists. And I could see that the Englishmen were becoming nervous and uneasy, although the odds were still much in their favour.

At the end of the first day Jack had scored above 500;—but eleven wickets had gone down, and only three of the most inferior players were left to stand up with him. It was considered that Jack must still make another 500 before the game would be won. This would allow only twenty each to the other three players. 'But,' said Eva to me that evening, 'they'll never get the twenty each.'

'And on which side are you, Eva?' I inquired with a smile. For in truth I did believe at that moment that she was engaged to the baronet.

'How dare you ask, Mr Neverbend?' she demanded, with indignation. 'Am not I a Britannulist as well as you?' And as she walked away I could see that there was a tear in her eye.

On the last day feelings were carried to a pitch which was more befitting the last battle of a great war,—some Waterloo of other ages,—than the finishing of a prolonged game of cricket. Men looked, and moved, and talked as though their all were at stake. I cannot say that the Englishmen seemed to hate us, or we them; but that the affair was too serious to admit of playful words between the parties. And those unfortunates who had to stand up with Jack were so afraid of themselves that they were like young country orators about to make their first speeches. Jack was silent, determined, and yet inwardly proud of himself, feeling that the whole future success of the republic was on his shoulders. He ordered himself to be called at a certain hour, and the assistants in our household listened to his words as though feeling that everything depended on their obedience. He would not go out on his bicycle, as fearing that some accident might occur. 'Although, ought I not to wish that I might be struck dead?' he said; 'as then all the world would know that though beaten, it had been by the hand of God, and not by our default.' It astonished me to find that the boy was quite as eager about his cricket as I was about my Fixed Period.

At eleven o'clock I was in my seat, and on looking round, I could see that all the rank and fashion of Britannula were at the ground. But all the rank and fashion were there for nothing, unless they had come armed with glasses. The spaces required by the cricketers were so enormous that otherwise they could not see anything of the play. Under my canopy there was room for five, of which I was supposed to be able to fill the middle thrones. On the two others sat those who officially scored the game. One seat had been demanded for Mrs Neverbend. 'I will see his fate,—whether it be his glory or his fall,'—said his mother, with true Roman feeling. For the other Eva had asked, and of course it had been awarded to her. When the play began, Sir Kennington was at the catapult and Jack at the opposite wicket, and I could hardly say for which she felt the extreme interest which she certainly did exhibit. I, as the day went on, found myself worked up to such excitement that I could hardly keep my hat on my head or behave myself with becoming presidential dignity. At one period, as I shall have to tell, I altogether disgraced myself.

There seemed to be an opinion that Jack would either show himself at once unequal to the occasion, and immediately be put out,—which opinion I think that all Gladstonopolis was inclined to hold,—or else that he would get his 'eye in' as he called it, and go on as long as the three others could keep their bats. I know that his own opinion was the same as that general in the city, and I feared that his very caution at the outset would be detrimental to him. The great object on our side was that Jack should, as nearly as possible, be always opposite to the bowler. He was to take the four first balls, making but one run off the last, and then beginning another over at the opposite end do the same thing again. It was impossible to manage this exactly; but something might be done towards effecting it. There were the three men with whom to work during the day. The first unfortunately was soon made to retire; but Jack, who had walked up to my chair during the time allowed for fetching down the next man, told me that he had 'got his eye,' and I could see a settled look of fixed purpose in his face. He bowed most gracefully to Eva, who was so stirred by emotion that she could not allow herself to speak a word. 'Oh Jack, I pray for you; I pray for you,' said his mother. Jack, I fancy, thought more of Eva's silence than of his mother's prayer.

Jack went back to his place, and hit the first ball with such energy that he drove it into the other stumps and smashed them to pieces. Everybody declared that such a thing had never been before achieved at cricket,—and the ball passed on, and eight or ten runs were scored. After that Jack seemed to be mad with cricketing power. He took off his greaves, declaring that they impeded his running, and threw away altogether his helmet. 'Oh, Eva, is he not handsome?' said his mother, in ecstasy, hanging across my chair. Eva sat quiet without a sign. It did not become me to say a word, but I did think that he was very handsome;—and I thought also how uncommonly hard it would be to hold him if he should chance to win the game. Let him make what orations he might against the Fixed Period, all Gladstonopolis would follow him if he won this game of cricket for them.

I cannot pretend to describe all the scenes of that day, nor the growing anxiety of the Englishmen as Jack went on with one hundred after another. He had already scored nearly 1000 when young Grabbe was caught out. Young Grabbe was very popular, because he was so altogether unlike his partner Grundle. He was a fine frank fellow, and was Jack's great friend. 'I don't mean to say that he can really play cricket,' Jack had said that morning, speaking with great authority; 'but he is the best fellow in the world, and will do exactly what you ask him.' But he was out now; and Jack, with over 200 still to make, declared that he gave up the battle almost as lost.

'Don't say that, Mr Neverbend,' whispered Eva.

'Ah yes; we're gone coons. Even your sympathy cannot bring us round now. If anything could do it that would!'

'In my opinion,' continued Eva, 'Britannula will never be beaten as long as Mr Neverbend is at the wicket.'

'Sir Kennington has been too much for us, I fear,' said Jack, with a forced smile, as he retired.

There was now but the one hope left. Mr Brittlereed remained, but he was all. Mr Brittlereed was a gentleman who had advanced nearer to his Fixed Period than any other of the cricketers. He was nearly thirty-five years of age, and was regarded by them all as quite an old man. He was supposed to know all the rules of the game, and to be rather quick in keeping the wicket. But Jack had declared that morning that he could not hit a ball in a week of Sundays. 'He oughtn't to be here,' Jack had whispered; 'but you know how those things are managed.' I did not know how those things were managed, but I was sorry that he should be there, as Jack did not seem to want him.

Mr Brittlereed now went to his wicket, and was bound to receive the first ball. This he did; made one run, whereas he might have made two, and then had to begin the war over. It certainly seemed as though he had done it on purpose. Jack in his passion broke the handle of his spring-bat, and then had half-a-dozen brought to him in order that he might choose another. 'It was his favourite bat,' said his mother, and buried her face in her handkerchief.

I never understood how it was that Mr Brittlereed lived through that over; but he did live, although he never once touched the ball. Then it came to be Jack's turn, and he at once scored thirty-nine during the over, leaving himself at the proper wicket for recommencing the operation. I think that this gave him new life. It added, at any rate, new fire to every Britannulist on the ground, and I must say that after that Mr Brittlereed managed the matter altogether to Jack's satisfaction. Over after over Jack went on, and received every ball that was bowled. They tried their catapult with single, double, and even treble action. Sir Kennington did his best, flinging the ball with his most tremendous impetus, and then just rolling it up with what seemed to me the most provoking languor. It was all the same to Jack. He had in truth got his 'eye in,' and as surely as the ball came to him, it was sent away to some most distant part of the ground. The Britishers were mad with dismay as Jack worked his way on through the last hundred. It was piteous to see the exertions which poor Mr Brittlereed made in running backwards and forwards across the ground. They tried, I think, to bustle him by the rapid succession of their bowling. But the only result was that the ball was sent still further off when it reached Jack's wicket. At last, just as every clock upon the ground struck six with that wonderful unanimity which our clocks have attained since they were all regulated by wires from Greenwich, Jack sent a ball flying up into the air, perfectly regardless whether it might be caught or not, knowing well that the one now needed would be scored before it could come down from the heavens into the hands of any Englishman. It did come down, and was caught by Stumps, but by that time Britannula had won her victory. Jack's total score during that innings was 1275. I doubt whether in the annals of cricket any record is made of a better innings than that. Then it was that, with an absence of that presence of mind which the President of a republic should always remember, I took off my hat and flung it into the air.

Jack's triumph would have been complete, only that it was

ludicrous to those who could not but think, as I did, of the very little matter as to which the contest had been raised;— just a game of cricket which two sets of boys had been playing, and which should have been regarded as no more than an amusement,—as a pastime, by which to refresh themselves between their work. But they regarded it as though a great national combat had been fought, and the Britannulists looked upon themselves as though they had been victorious against England. It was absurd to see Jack as he was carried back to Gladstonopolis as the hero of the occasion, and to hear him, as he made his speeches at the dinner which was given on the day, and at which he was called upon to take the chair. I was glad to see, however, that he was not quite so glib with his tongue as he had been when addressing the people. He hesitated a good deal, nay, almost broke down, when he gave the health of Sir Kennington Oval and the British sixteen; and I was quite pleased to hear Lord Marylebone declare to his mother that he was 'a wonderfully nice boy.' I think the English did try to turn it off a little, as though they had only come out there just for the amusement of the voyage. But Grundle, who had now become quite proud of his country, and who lamented loudly that he should have received so severe an injury in preparing for the game, would not let this pass. 'My lord,' he said, 'what is your population?' Lord Marylebone named sixty million. 'We are but two hundred and fifty thousand,' said Grundle, 'and see what we have done.' 'We are cocks fighting on our own dunghill,' said Jack, 'and that does make a deal of difference.'

But I was told that Jack had spoken a word to Eva in quite a different spirit before he had left Little Christchurch. 'After all, Eva, Sir Kennington has not quite trampled us under his feet,' he said.

'Who thought that he would?' said Eva. 'My heart has never fainted, whatever some others may have done.'

# CHAPTER VI
## The College

I WAS surprised to see that Jack, who was so bold in playing his match, and who had been so well able to hold his own against the Englishmen,—who had been made a hero, and had carried off his heroism so well,—should have been so shamefaced and bashful in regard to Eva. He was like a silly boy, hardly daring to look her in the face, instead of the gallant captain of the band who had triumphed over all obstacles. But I perceived, though it seemed that he did not, that she was quite prepared to give herself to him, and that there was no real obstacle between him and all the flocks and herds of Little Christchurch. Not much had been seen or heard of Grundle during the match, and as far as Eva was concerned, he had succumbed as soon as Sir Kennington Oval had appeared upon the scene. He had thought so much of the English baronet as to have been cowed and quenched by his grandeur. And Sir Kennington himself had, I think, been in earnest before the days of the cricket-match. But I could see now that Eva had merely played him off against Jack, thinking thereby to induce the younger swain to speak his mind. This had made Jack more than ever intent on beating Sir Kennington, but had not as yet had the effect which Eva had intended. 'It will all come right,' I said to myself, 'as soon as these Englishmen have left the island.' But then my mind reverted to the Fixed Period, and to the fast-approaching time for Crasweller's deposition. We were now nearly through March, and the thirtieth of June was the day on which he ought to be led to the college. It was my first anxiety to get rid of these Englishmen before the subject should be again ventilated. I own I was anxious that they should not return to their country with their prejudices strengthened by what they might hear at Gladstonopolis. If I could only get them to go before the matter was again debated, it might be that no strong public feeling would be excited in England till it was too late. That was my first desire; but then I was also anxious to get rid of Jack for a short time. The more I thought of Eva and the flocks, the more determined was I not to allow the personal interests of my boy,—and therefore my own,—to clash in any way with the performance of my public duties.

I heard that the Englishmen were not to go till another week had elapsed. A week was necessary to recruit their strength and to enable them to pack up their bats and bicycles. Neither, however, were packed up till the day before they started; for the track down to Little Christchurch was crowded with them, and they were still practising as though another match were contemplated. I was very glad to have Lord Marylebone as an inmate in our house, but I acknowledge that I was anxious for him to say something as to his departure. 'We have been very proud to have you here, my lord,' I remarked.

'I cannot say that we are very proud,' he replied, 'because we have been so awfully licked. Barring that, I never spent a pleasanter two months in my life, and should not be at all unwilling to stay for another. Your mode of life here seems to me to be quite delightful, and we have been thinking so much of our cricket, that I have hardly as yet had a moment to look at your institutions. What is all this about the Fixed Period?' Jack, who was present, put on a serious face, and assumed that air of determination which I was beginning to fear. Mrs Neverbend pursed up her lips, and said nothing; but I knew what was passing through her mind. I managed to turn the conversation, but I was aware that I did it very lamely.

'Jack,' I said to my son, 'I got a post-card from New Zealand yesterday.' The boats had just begun to run between the two islands six days a-week, and as their regular contract pace was twenty-five miles an hour, it was just an easy day's journey.

'What said the post-card?'

'There's plenty of time for Mount Earnshawe yet. They

all say the autumn is the best. The snow is now disappearing in great quantities.'

But an old bird is not to be caught with chaff. Jack was determined not to go to the Eastern Alps this year; and indeed, as I found, not to go till this question of the Fixed Period should be settled. I told him that he was a fool. Although he would have been wrong to assist in depositing his father-in-law for the sake of getting the herd and flocks himself, as Grundle would have done, nevertheless he was hardly bound by any feelings of honour or conscience to keep old Craswell at Little Christchurch in direct opposition to the laws of the land. But all this I could not explain to him, and was obliged simply to take it as a fact that he would not join an Alpine party for Mount Earnshawe this year. As I thought of all this, I almost feared Jack's presence in Gladstonopolis more than that of the young Englishmen.

It was clear, however, that nothing could be done till the Englishmen were gone, and as I had a day at my disposal I determined to walk up to the college and meditate there on the conduct which it would be my duty to follow during the next two months. The college was about five miles from the town, at the side opposite to you as you enter the town from Little Christchurch, and I had some time since made up my mind how, in the bright genial days of our pleasant winter, I would myself accompany Mr Craswell through the city in an open barouche as I took him to be deposited, through admiring crowds of his fellow-citizens. I had not then thought that he would be a recreant, or that he would be deterred by the fear of departure from enjoying the honours which would be paid to him. But how different now was his frame of mind from that glorious condition to which I had looked forward in my sanguine hopes! Had it been I, I myself, how proud should I have been of my country and its wisdom, had I been led along as a first hero, to anticipate the euthanasia prepared for me! As it was, I hired an inside cab, and hiding myself in the corner, was carried away to the college unseen by any.

The place was called Necropolis. The name had always been distasteful to me, as I had never wished to join with it the feeling of death. Various names had been proposed for the site. Young Grundle had suggested Cremation Hall, because such was the ultimate end to which the mere husks and hulls of the citizens were destined. But there was something undignified in the sound,—as though we were talking of a dancing saloon or a music hall,—and I would have none of it. My idea was to give to the mind some notion of an approach to good things to come, and I proposed to call the place 'Aditus.'* But men said that it was unmeaning, and declared that Britannulists should never be ashamed to own the truth. Necropolis sounded well, they said, and argued that though no actual remains of the body might be left there, still the tablets would remain. Therefore Necropolis it was called. I had hoped that a smiling hamlet might grow up at the gate, inhabited by those who would administer to the wants of the deposited; but I had forgot that the deposited must come first. The hamlet had not yet built itself, and round the handsome gates there was nothing at present but a desert. While land in Britannula was plenty, no one had cared to select ground so near to those awful furnaces by which the mortal clay should be transported into the air. From the gates up to the temple which stood in the middle of the grounds,—that temple in which the last scene of life was to be encountered,—there ran a broad gravel path, which was intended to become a beautiful avenue. It was at present planted alternately with eucalypti and ilexes— the gum-trees for the present generation, and the green-oaks for those to come; but even the gum-trees had not as yet done much to give a furnished appearance to the place. Some had demanded that cedars and yew-trees should be placed there, and I had been at great pains to explain to them that our object should be to make the spot cheerful, rather than sad. Round the temple, at the back of it, were the sets of chambers in which were to live the deposited during their year of probation. Some of these were very handsome, and were made so, no doubt, with a view of alluring the first comers. In preparing wisdom for babes, it is necessary to wrap up its precepts in candied sweets. But, though handsome, they were at present anything but pleasant abodes. Not one of them had as yet been inhabited. As I looked at them, knowing Crasweller as well as I did, I almost ceased to wonder at his timidity. A hero was wanted; but Crasweller was no hero. Then further off, but still in the circle round the temple, there were smaller abodes, less luxurious, but still comfortable, all of which would in a few short years be inhabited,—if the Fixed Period could be carried out in accordance with my project. And foundations had been made for others still smaller,—for a whole township of old men and women, as in the course of the next thirty years they might come hurrying on to find their last abode in the college. I had already selected one, not by any means the finest or the largest, for myself and my wife, in which we might prepare ourselves for the grand departure. But as for Mrs Neverbend, nothing would bring her to set foot within the precincts of the college ground. 'Before those next ten years are gone,' she would say, 'common-sense will have interfered to let folks live out their lives properly.' It had been quite useless for me to attempt to make her understand how unfitting was such a speech for the wife of the President of the Republic. My wife's opposition had been an annoyance to me from the first, but I had consoled myself by thinking how impossible it always is to imbue a woman's mind with a logical idea. And though, in all respects of domestic life, Mrs Neverbend is the best of women, even among women she is the most illogical.

I now inspected the buildings in a sad frame of mind, asking myself whether it would ever come to pass that they should be inhabited for their intended purpose. When the Assembly, in compliance with my advice, had first enacted the law of the Fixed Period, a large sum had been voted for these buildings. As the enthusiasm had worn off, men had asked themselves whether the money had not been wasted, and had said that for so small a community the college had been planned on an absurdly grand scale. Still I had gone on, and had watched them as they grew from day to day, and had allowed no shilling to be spared in perfecting them. In my earlier years I had been very successful in the wool trade, and had amassed what men called a large fortune. During the last two or three years I had devoted a great portion of this to the external adornment of the college, not without many words on the matter from Mrs Neverbend. 'Jack is to be ruined,' she had said, 'in order that all the old men and women may be killed artistically.' This and other remarks of the kind I was doomed to bear. It was a part of the difficulty which, as a great reformer, I must endure. But now, as I walked mournfully among the disconsolate and half-finished buildings, I could not but ask myself as to the purpose to which my money had been devoted. And I could not but tell myself that if in coming years these tenements should be left tenantless, my country would look back upon me as one who had wasted the produce of her young energies. But again I bethought me of Columbus and Galileo, and swore that I would go on or perish in the attempt.

As these painful thoughts were agitating my mind, a slow decrepit old gentleman came up to me and greeted me as Mr President. He linked his arm familiarly through mine, and remarked that the time seemed to be very long before the college received any of its inhabitants. This was Mr Graybody, the curator, who had been specially appointed to occupy a certain residence, to look after the grounds, and to keep the books of the establishment. Graybody and I had come as young men to Britannula together, and whereas I had succeeded in all my own individual attempts, he had unfortunately failed. He was exactly of my age, as was also his wife. But under the stress of misfortune they had both become unnaturally old, and had at last been left ruined and hopeless, without a shilling on which to depend. I had always been a sincere friend to Graybody, though he was, indeed, a man very difficult to befriend. On most subjects he thought as I did, if he can be said to have thought at all. At any rate he had agreed with me as to the Fixed Period, saying how good it would be if he could be deposited at fifty-eight, and had always declared how blessed must be the time when it should have come for himself and his old wife. I do not think that he ever looked much to the principle which I had in view. He had no great ideas as to the imbecility and weakness of human life when protracted beyond its fitting limits. He only felt that it would be good to give up; and that if he did so, others might be made to do so too. As soon as a residence at the college was completed, I asked him to fill it; and now he had been living there, he and his wife together, with an attendant, and drawing his salary as curator for the last three years. I thought that it would be the very place for him. He was usually melancholy, disheartened, and impoverished; but he was always glad to see me, and I was accustomed to go frequently to the college, in order to find a sympathetic soul with whom to converse about the future of the establishment. 'Well, Graybody,' I said, 'I suppose we are nearly ready for the first comer.'

'Oh yes; we're always ready; but then the first comer is not.' I had not said much to him during the latter months as to Crasweller, in particular. His name used formerly to be very ready in all my conversations with Graybody, but of late I had talked to him in a more general tone. 'You can't tell me yet when it's to be, Mr President? We do find it a little dull here.'

Now he knew as well as I did the day and the year of Crasweller's birth. I had intended to speak to him about Crasweller, but I wished our friend's name to come first from him. 'I suppose it will be some time about mid-winter,' I said.

'Oh, I didn't know whether it might not have been postponed'.

'How can it be postponed? As years creep on, you cannot postpone their step. If there might be postponement such as that, I doubt whether we should ever find the time for our inhabitants to come. No, Graybody; there can be no postponement for the Fixed Period.'

'It might have been made sixty-nine or seventy,' said he.

'Originally, no doubt. But the wisdom of the Assembly has

settled all that. The Assembly has declared that they in Britannula who are left alive at sixty-seven shall on that day be brought into the college. You yourself have, I think, ten years to run, and you will not be much longer left to pass them in solitude.'

'It is weary being here all alone, I must confess. Mrs G. says that she could not bear it for another twelve months. The girl we have has given us notice, and she is the ninth within a year. No followers will come after them here, because they say they'll smell the dead bodies.'

'Rubbish!' I exclaimed, angrily; 'positive rubbish! The actual clay will evaporate into the air, without leaving a trace either for the eye to see or the nose to smell.'

'They all say that when you tried the furnaces there was a savour of burnt pork.'* Now great trouble was taken in that matter of cremation; and having obtained from Europe and the States all the best machinery for the purpose, I had supplied four immense hogs, in order that the system might be fairly tested, and I had fattened them for the purpose, as old men are not unusually very stout. These we consumed in the furnaces all at the same time, and the four bodies had been dissolved into their original atoms without leaving a trace behind them by which their former condition of life might be recognised. But a trap-door in certain of the chimneys had been left open by accident,—either that or by an enemy on purpose,—and undoubtedly some slight flavour of the pig had been allowed to escape. I had been there on the spot, knowing that I could trust only my own senses, and was able to declare that the scent which had escaped was very slight, and by no means disagreeable. And I was able to show that the trap-door had been left open either by chance or by design,—the very trap-door which was intended to prevent any such escape during the moments of full cremation,—so that there need be no fear of a repetition of the accident. I ought, indeed, to have supplied four other hogs, and to have tried the experiment again. But the theme was disagreeable, and I thought that the trial had been so far successful as to make it unnecessary that the expense should be again incurred. 'They say that men and women would not have quite the same smell,' said he.

'How do they know that?' I exclaimed, in my anger. 'How do they know what men and women will smell like? They haven't tried. There won't be any smell at all—not the least; and the smoke will all consume itself, so that even you, living just where you are, will not know when cremation is going on. We might consume all Gladstonopolis, as I hope we shall some day, and not a living soul would know anything about it. But the prejudices of the citizens are ever the stumbling-blocks of civilisation.'

'At any rate, Mrs G. tells me that Jemima is going, because none of the young men will come up and see her.'

This was another difficulty, but a small one, and I made up my mind that it should be overcome. 'The shrubs seem to grow very well,' I said, resolved to appear as cheerful as possible.

'They're pretty nearly all alive,' said Graybody; 'and they do give the place just an appearance like the cemetery at Old Christchurch.' He meant the capital in the province of Canterbury.

'In the course of a few years you will be quite—cheerful here.'

'I don't know much about that, Mr President. I'm not sure that for myself I want to be cheerful anywhere. If I've only got somebody just to speak to sometimes, that will be quite enough for me. I suppose old Crasweller will be the first?'

'I suppose so.'

'It will be a gruesome time when I have to go to bed early, so as not to see the smoke come out of his chimney.'

'I tell you there will be nothing of the kind. I don't suppose you will even know when they're going to cremate him.'

'He will be the first, Mr President; and no doubt he will be looked closely after. Old Barnes will be here by that time, won't he, sir?'

'Barnes is the second, and he will come just three months before Crasweller's departure. But Tallowax, the grocer in

High Street, will be up here by that time. And then they will come so quickly, that we must soon see to get other lodgings finished. Exors, the lawyer, will be the fourth; but he will not come in till a day or two after Craswellerʼs departure.'

'They all will come; won't they, sir?' asked Graybody.

'Will come! Why, they must. It is the law.'

'Tallowax swears he'll have himself strapped to his own kitchen table, and defend himself to the last gasp with a carving-knife. Exors says that the law is bad, and you can't touch him. As for Barnes, he has gone out of what little wits he ever had with the fright of it, and people seem to think that you couldn't touch a lunatic.'

'Barnes is no more a lunatic than I am.'

'I only tell you what folk tell me. I suppose you'll try it on by force, if necessary. You never expected that people would come and deposit themselves of their own accord.'

'The National Assembly expects that the citizens of Britannula will obey the law.'

'But there was one question I was going to ask, Mr President. Of course I am altogether on your side, and do not wish to raise difficulties. But what shall I do suppose they take to running away after they have been deposited? If old Crasweller goes off in his steam-carriage, how am I to go after him, and whom am I to ask to help to bring him back again?'

I was puzzled, but I did not care to show it. No doubt a hundred little arrangements would be necessary before the affairs of the institution could be got into a groove so as to run steadily. But our first object must be to deposit Crasweller and Barnes and Tallowax, so that the citizens should be accustomed to the fashion of depositing the aged. There were, as I knew, two or three old women living in various parts of the island, who would, in due course, come in towards the end of Craswellerʼs year. But it had been rumoured that they had already begun to invent falsehoods as to their age, and I was aware that we might be led astray by them. This I had been prepared to accept as being unavoidable; but now, as the time grew nearer, I could not but see how difficult it would be to enforce the law against well-known men, and how easy to allow the women to escape by the help of falsehood. Exors, the lawyer, would say at once that we did not even attempt to carry out the law; and Barnes, lunatic as he pretended to be, would by very hard to manage. My mind misgave me as I thought of all these obstructions, and I felt that I could so willingly deposit myself at once, and then depart without waiting for my year of probation. But it was necessary that I should show a determined front to old Graybody, and make him feel that I at any rate was determined to remain firm to my purpose. 'Mr Crasweller will give you no such trouble as you suggest,' said I.

'Perhaps he has come round.'

'He is a gentleman whom we have both known intimately for many years, and he has always been a friend to the Fixed Period. I believe that he is so still, although there is some little hitch as to the exact time at which he should be deposited.'

'Just twelve months, he says.'

'Of course,' I replied, 'the difference would be sure to be that of one year. He seems to think that there are only nine years between him and me.'

'Ten, Mr President; ten. I know the time well.'

'I had always thought so; but I should be willing to abandon a year if I could make things run smooth by doing so. But all that is a detail with which up here we need not, perhaps, concern ourselves.'

'Only the time is getting very short, Mr President, and my old woman will break down altogether if she's told that she's to live another year all alone. Crasweller won't be a bit readier next year than he is this; and of course if he is let off, you must let off Barnes and Tallowax. And there are a lot of old women about who are beginning to tell terrible lies about their ages. Do think of it all, Mr President.'

I never thought of anything else, so full was my mind of the subject. When I woke in the morning, before I could face the light of day, it was necessary that I should fortify myself with Columbus and Galileo. I began to fancy, as the danger became nearer and still nearer, that neither of those great men had been surrounded by obstructions such as encompassed me. To plough on across the waves, and either to be drowned or succeed; to tell a new truth about the heavens, and either to perish or become great for ever!—either was within the compass of a man who had only his own life to risk. My life,—how willingly could I run any risk, did but the question arise of risking it! How often I felt, in these days, that there is a fortitude needed by man much greater than that of jeopardising his life! Life! what is it? Here was that poor Crasweller, belying himself and all his convictions just to gain one year more of it, and then when the year was gone he would still have his deposition before him! Is it not so with us all? For me I feel,—have felt for years,—tempted to rush on, and pass through the gates of death. That man should shudder at the thought of it does not appear amiss to me. The unknown future is always awful; and the unknown future of another world, to be approached by so great a change of circumstances,—by the loss of our very flesh and blood and body itself,—has in it something so fearful to the imagination that the man who thinks of it cannot but be struck with horror as he acknowledges that by himself too it has to be encountered. But it has to be encountered; and though the change be awful, it should not therefore, by the sane judgment, be taken as a change necessarily for the worst. Knowing the great goodness of the Almighty, should we not be prepared to accept it as a change probably for the better; as an alteration of our circumstances, by which our condition may be immeasurably improved? Then one is driven back to consider the circumstances by which such change may be effected. To me it seems rational to suppose that as we leave this body so shall we enter that new phase of life in which we are destined to live;—but with all our higher resolves somewhat sharpened, and with our lower passions, alas! made stronger also. That theory by which a human being shall jump at once to a perfection of bliss, or fall to an eternity of evil and misery, has never found credence with me. For myself, I have to say that, while acknowledging my many drawbacks, I have so lived as to endeavour to do good to others, rather than evil, and that therefore I look to my departure from this world with awe indeed, but still with satisfaction. But I cannot look with satisfaction to a condition of life in which, from my own imbecility, I must necessarily retrograde into selfishness. It may be that He who judges of us with a wisdom which I cannot approach, shall take all this into account, and that He shall so mould my future being as to fit it to the best at which I had arrived in this world; still I cannot but fear that a taint of that selfishness which I have hitherto avoided, but which will come if I allow myself to become old, may remain, and that it will be better for me that I should go hence while as yet my own poor wants are not altogether uppermost in my mind. But then, in arranging this matter, I am arranging it for my fellow-citizens, and not for myself. I have to endeavour to think how Craswceller's mind may be affected rather than my own. He dreads his departure with a trembling, currish fear; and I should hardly be doing good to him were I to force him to depart in a frame of mind so poor and piteous. But then, again, neither is it altogether of Craswceller that I must think,—not of Craswceller or of myself. How will the coming ages of men be affected by such a change as I propose, should such a change become the normal condition of Death? Can it not be brought about that men should arrange for their own departure, so as to fall into no senile weakness, no slippered selfishness, no ugly whinings of undefined want, before they shall go hence, and be no more thought of? These are the ideas that have actuated me, and to them I have been brought by seeing the conduct of those around me. Not for Craswceller, or Barnes, or Tallowax, will this thing be good,—nor for those old women who are already lying about their ages in their cottages,—nor for myself, who am, I know, too apt to boast of myself, that even though old age should come upon me, I may be able to avoid the worst of its effects; but for those untold generations to come, whose lives may be modelled for them under the knowledge that at a certain Fixed Period they shall depart hence with all circumstances of honour and glory.

I was, however, quite aware that it would be useless to spend my energy in dilating on this to Mr Graybody. He simply was willing to shuffle off his mortal coil, because he found it uncomfortable in the wearing. In all likelihood, had his time come as nigh as that of Crasweller, he too, like Crasweller, would impotently implore the grace of another year. He would ape madness like Barnes, or arm himself with a carving-knife like Tallowax, or swear that there was a flaw in the law, as Exors was disposed to do. He too would clamorously swear that he was much younger, as did the old women. Was not the world peopled by Craswellers, Tallowaxes, Exorses, and old women? Had I a right to hope to alter the feelings which nature herself had implanted in the minds of men? But still it might be done by practice,— by practice; if only we could arrive at the time in which practice should have become practice. Then, as I was about to depart from the door of Graybody's house, I whispered to myself again the names of Galileo and Columbus.

'You think that he will come on the thirtieth?' said Graybody, as he took my hand at parting.

'I think,' replied I, 'that you and I, as loyal citizens of the Republic, are bound to suppose that he will do his duty as a citizen.' Then I went, leaving him standing in doubt at his door.

## CHAPTER VII
### Columbus and Galileo

I HAD left Graybody with a lie on my tongue. I said that I was bound to suppose that Crasweller would do his duty as a citizen,—by which I had meant Graybody to understand that I expected my old friend to submit to deposition. Now I expected nothing of the kind, and it grieved me to think that I should be driven to such false excuses. I began to doubt whether my mind would hold its proper bent under the strain thus laid upon it, and to ask myself whether I was in all respects sane in entertaining the ideas which filled my mind. Galileo and Columbus,—Galileo and Columbus! I endeavoured to comfort myself with these names,—but in a vain, delusive manner; and though I used them constantly, I was beginning absolutely to hate them. Why could I not return to my wool-shed, and be contented among my bales, and my ships, and my credits, as I was of yore, before this theory took total possession of me? I was doing good then. I robbed no one. I assisted very many in their walks of life. I was happy in the praises of all my fellow-citizens. My health was good, and I had ample scope for my energies then, even as now. But there came on me a day of success,—a day, shall I say, of glory or of wretchedness? or shall I not most truly say of both?—and I persuaded my fellow-citizens to undertake this sad work of the Fixed Period. From that moment all quiet had left me, and all happiness. Still, it is not necessary that a man should be happy. I doubt whether Cæsar was happy with all those enemies around him,— Gauls, and Britons, and Romans. If a man be doing his duty, let him not think too much of that condition of mind which he calls happiness. Let him despise happiness and do his duty, and he will in one sense be happy. But if there creep upon him a doubt as to his duty, if he once begin to feel that he may perhaps be wrong, then farewell all peace of mind,— then will come that condition in which a man is tempted to ask himself whether he be in truth of sane mind.

What should I do next? The cricketing Englishmen, I knew, were going. Two or three days more would see their gallant ship steam out of the harbour. As I returned in my cab to the city, I could see the English colours fluttering from her topmast, and the flag of the English cricket-club waving from her stern. But I knew well that they had discussed the question of the Fixed Period among them, and that there was still time for them to go home and send back some English mandate which ought to be inoperative, but which we should be unable to disobey. And letters might have been written before this,—treacherous letters, calling for the assistance of another country in opposition to the councils of their own.

But what should I do next? I could not enforce the law *vi et armis** against Crasweller. I had sadly but surely acknowledged so much as that to myself. But I thought that I had seen signs of relenting about the man,—some symptoms of sadness which seemed to bespeak a yielding spirit. He only asked for a year. He was still in theory a supporter of the Fixed Period,—pleading his own little cause, however, by a direct falsehood. Could I not talk him into a generous assent? There would still be a year for him. And in old days there had been a spice of manliness in his bosom, to which it might be possible that I should bring him back. Though the hope was poor, it seemed at present to be my only hope.

As I returned, I came round by the quays, dropping my cab at the corner of the street. There was the crowd of Englishmen, all going off to the vessel to see their bats and bicycles disposed of, and among them was Jack the hero. They were standing at the water's-edge, while three long-boats were being prepared to take them off. 'Here's the President,' said Sir Kennington Oval; 'he has not seen our yacht yet: let him come on board with us.' They were very gracious; so I got into one boat, and Jack into another, and old Crasweller, who had come with his guests from Little Christchurch, into the third; and we were pulled off to the yacht. Jack, I perceived, was quite at home there. He had dined there frequently, and had slept on board; but to me and Crasweller it was altogether new. 'Yes,' said Lord Marylebone; 'if a fellow is to make his home for a month upon the seas, it is as well to make it as comfortable as possible. Each of us has his own crib, with a bath to himself, and all the et-ceteras. This is where we feed. It is not altogether a bad shop for grubbing.' As I looked round I thought that I had never seen anything more palatial and beautiful. 'This is where we pretend to sit,' continued the lord; 'where we are supposed to write our letters and read our books. And this,' he said, opening another door, 'is where we really sit, and smoke our pipes, and drink our brandy-and-water. We came out under the rule of that tyrant King MacNuffery. We mean to go back as a republic. And I, as being the only lord, mean to elect myself president. You couldn't give me any wrinkles as to a pleasant mode of governing? Everybody is to be allowed to do exactly what he pleases, and nobody is to be interfered with unless he interferes with somebody else. We mean to take a wrinkle from you fellows in Britannula, where everybody seems, under your presidency, to be as happy as the day is long.'

'We have no Upper House with us, my lord,' said I.

'You have got rid, at any rate, of one terrible bother. I daresay we shall drop it before long in England. I don't see why we should continue to sit merely to register the edicts of the House of Commons, and be told that we're a pack of fools when we hesitate.' I told him that it was the unfortunate destiny of a House of Lords to be made to see her own unfitness for legislative work.

'But if we were abolished,' continued he, 'then I might get into the other place and do something. You have to be elected a Peer of Parliament, or you can sit nowhere. A ship can only be a ship, after all; but if we must live in a ship, we are not so bad here. Come and take some tiffin.' An Englishman, when he comes to our side of the globe, always calls his lunch tiffin.

I went back to the other room with Lord Marylebone; and as I took my place at the table, I heard that the assembled cricketers were all discussing the Fixed Period.

'I'd be shot,' said Mr Puddlebrane, 'if they should deposit me, and bleed me to death, and cremate me like a big pig.' Then he perceived that I had entered the saloon, and there came a sudden silence across the table.

'What sort of wind will be blowing next Friday at two o'clock?' asked Sir Lords Longstop.

It was evident that Sir Lords had only endeavoured to change the conversation because of my presence; and it did not suit me to allow them to think that I was afraid to talk of the Fixed Period. 'Why should you object to be cremated, Mr Puddlebrane,' said I, 'whether like a big pig or otherwise? It has not been suggested that any one shall cremate you while alive.'

'Because my father and mother were buried. And all the Puddlebranes were always buried. There are they, all to be seen in Puddlebrane Church, and I should like to appear among them.'

'I suppose it's only their names that appear, and not their bodies, Mr Puddlebrane. And a cremated man may have as big a tombstone as though he had been allowed to become rotten in the orthodox fashion.'

'What Puddlebrane means is,' said another, 'that he'd like to have the same chance of living as his ancestors.'

'If he will look back to his family records he will find that they very generally died before sixty-eight. But we have no idea of invading your Parliament and forcing our laws upon you.'

'Take a glass of wine, Mr President,' said Lord Marylebone, 'and leave Puddlebrane to his ancestors. He's a very good Slip, though he didn't catch Jack when he got a chance. Allow me to recommend you a bit of ice-pudding. The mangoes came from Jamaica, and are as fresh as the day they were picked.' I ate my mango-pudding, but I did not enjoy it, for I was sure that the whole crew were returning to England laden with prejudices against the Fixed Period. As soon as I could escape, I got back to the shore, leaving Jack among my enemies. It was impossible not to feel that they were my enemies, as I was sure that they were about to oppose the cherished conviction of my very heart and soul. Crasweller had sat there perfectly silent while Mr Puddlebrane had spoken of his own possible cremation. And yet Crasweller was a declared Fixed-Periodist.

On the Friday, at two o'clock, the vessel sailed amidst all the plaudits which could be given by mingled kettle-drums and trumpets, and by a salvo of artillery. They were as good a set of fellows as ever wore pink-flannel clothing, and as generous as any that there are born to live upon *pâté* and champagne. I doubt whether there was one among them who could have earned his bread in a counting-house, unless it was Stumps the professional. When we had paid all honour to the departing vessel, I went at once to Little Christchurch, and there I found my friend in the verandah with Eva. During the last month or two he seemed to be much older than I had ever before known him, and was now seated with his daughter's hand within his own. I had not seen him since the day on board the yacht, and he now seemed to be greyer and more haggard than he was then. 'Crasweller,' said I, taking him by the hand, 'it is a sad thing that you and I should quarrel after so many years of perfect friendship.'

'So it is; so it is. I don't want to quarrel, Mr President.'

'There shall be no quarrel. Well, Eva, how do you bear the loss of all your English friends?'

'The loss of my English friends won't hurt me if I can only keep those which I used to have in Britannula.' I doubted whether she alluded to me or to Jack. It might be only to me, but I thought she looked as if she were thinking of Jack.

'Eva, my dear,' said Mr Crasweller, 'you had better leave us. The President, I think, wishes to speak to me on business.' Then she came up and looked me in the face, and pressed my hand, and I knew that she was asking for mercy for her father. The feeling was not pleasant, seeing that I was bound by the strongest oath which the mind can conceive not to show him mercy.

I sat for a few minutes in silence, thinking that as Mr Crasweller had banished Eva, he would begin. But he said nothing, and would have remained silent had I allowed him to do so. 'Crasweller,' I said, 'it is certainly not well that you and I should quarrel on this matter. In your company I first learned to entertain this project, and for years we have agreed that in it is to be found the best means for remedying the condition of mankind.'

'I had not felt then what it is to be treated as one who was already dead.'

'Does Eva treat you so?'

'Yes; with all her tenderness and all her sweet love, Eva feels that my days are numbered unless I will boldly declare myself opposed to your theory. She already regards me as though I were a visitant from the other world. Her very gentleness is intolerable.'

'But, Crasweller, the convictions of your mind cannot be changed.'

'I do not know. I will not say that any change has taken place. But it is certain that convictions become vague when they operate against one's self. The desire to live is human, and therefore God-like. When the hand of God is felt to have struck one with coming death, the sufferer, knowing the blow to be inevitable, can reconcile himself; but it is very hard to walk away to one's long rest while health, and work, and means of happiness yet remain.'

There was something in this which seemed to me to imply that he had abandoned the weak assertion as to his age, and no longer intended to ask for a year of grace by the use of that falsehood. But it was necessary that I should be sure of this. 'As to your exact age, I've been looking at the records,' I began.

'The records are right enough,' he said; 'you need trouble yourself no longer about the records. Eva and I have discussed all that.' From this I became aware that Eva had convinced him of the baseness of the falsehood.

'Then there is the law,' said I, with, as I felt, unflinching hardness.

'Yes, there is the law,—if it be a law. Mr Exors is prepared to dispute it, and says that he will ask permission to argue the case out with the executive.'

'He would argue about anything. You know what Exors is.'

'And there is that poor man Barnes has gone altogether out of his mind, and has become a drivelling idiot.'

'They told me yesterday that he was a raging lunatic; but I learn from really good authority that whether he takes one part or the other, he is only acting.'

'And Tallowax is prepared to run amuck against those who come to fetch him. He swears that no one shall lead him up to the college.'

'And you?' Then there was a pause, and Crasweller sat silent with his face buried in his hands. He was, at any rate, in a far better condition of mind for persuasion than that in which I had last found him. He had given up the fictitious year, and had acknowledged that he had assented to the doctrine with which he was now asked to comply. But it was a hard task that of having to press him under such circumstances. I thought of Eva and her despair, and of himself with all that natural desire for life eager at his heart. I looked round and saw the beauty of the scenery, and thought how much worse to such a man would be the melancholy shades of the college than even departure itself. And I am not by nature hard-hearted. I have none of that steel and fibre which will enable a really strong man to stand firm by convictions even when opposed by his affections. To have liberated Crasweller at this moment, I would have walked off myself, oh, so willingly, to the college! I was tearing my own heart to pieces;—but I remembered Columbus and Galileo. Neither of them was surely ever tried as I was at this moment. But it had to be done, or I must yield, and for ever. If I could not be strong to prevail with my own friend and fellow-labourer,—with Crasweller, who was the first to come, and who should have entered the college with an heroic grandeur,—how could I even desire any other to immure himself? how persuade such men as Barnes, or Tallowax, or that pettifogger Exors, to be led quietly up through the streets of the city? 'And you?' I asked again.

'It is for you to decide.'

The agony of that moment! But I think that I did right. Though my very heart was bleeding, I know that I did right. 'For the sake of the benefits which are to accrue to unknown thousands of your fellow-creatures, it is your duty to obey the law.' This I said in a low voice, still holding him by the hand. I felt at the moment a great love for him,—and in a certain sense admiration, because he had so far conquered his fear of an unknown future as to promise to do this thing simply because he had said that he would do it. There was no high feeling as to future generations of his fellow-creatures, no grand idea that he was about to perform a great duty for the benefit of mankind in general, but simply the notion that as he had always advocated my theory as my friend, he would not now depart from it, let the cost to himself be what it might. He answered me only by drawing away his hand. But I felt that in his heart he accused me of cruelty, and of mad adherence to a theory. 'Should it not be so, Crasweller?'

'As you please, President.'

'But should it not be so?' Then, at great length, I went over once again all my favourite arguments, and endeavoured with the whole strength of my eloquence to reach his mind. But I knew, as I was doing so, that that was all in vain. I had succeeded,—or perhaps Eva had done so,—in inducing him to repudiate the falsehood by which he had endeavoured to escape. But I had not in the least succeeded in making him see the good which would come from his deposition. He was ready to become a martyr, because in years back he had said that he would do so. He had now left it for me to decide whether he should be called upon to perform his promise; and I, with an unfeeling pertinacity, had given the case against him. That was the light in which Mr Crasweller looked at it. 'You do not think that I am cruel?' I asked.

'I do,' said Crasweller. 'You ask the question, and I answer you. I do think that you are cruel. It concerns life and death,—that is a matter of course,—and it is the life and death of your most intimate friend, of Eva's father, of him who years since came hither with you from another country, and has lived with you through all the struggles and all the successes of a long career. But you have my word, and I will not depart from it, even to save my life. In a moment of weakness I was tempted to a weak lie. I will not lie. I will not demean myself to claim a poor year of life by such means, though I do not lack evidence to support the statement. I am ready to go with you;' and he rose up from his seat as though intending to walk away and be deposited at once.

'Not now, Crasweller.'

'I shall be ready when you may come for me. I shall not again leave my home till I have to leave it for the last time. Days and weeks mean nothing with me now. The bitterness of death has fallen upon me.'

'Crasweller, I will come and live with you, and be a brother to you, during the entire twelve months.'

'No; it will not be needed. Eva will be with me, and perhaps Jack may come and see me,—though I must not allow Jack to express the warmth of his indignation in Eva's hearing. Jack had perhaps better leave Britannula for a time, and not come back till all shall be over. Then he may enjoy the lawns of Little Christchurch in peace,—unless, per-chance, an idea should disturb him, that he has been put into their immediate possession by his father's act.' Then he got up from his chair and went from the verandah back into the house.

As I rose and returned to the city, I almost repented myself of what I had done. I had it in my heart to go back and yield, and to tell him that I would assent to the aban-donment of my whole project. It was not for me to say that I would spare my own friend, and execute the law against Barnes and Tallowax; nor was it for me to declare that the victims of the first year should be forgiven. I could easily let the law die away, but it was not in my power to decide that it should fall into partial abeyance. This I almost did. But when I had turned on my road to Little Christchurch, and was prepared to throw myself into Crasweller's arms, the idea of Galileo and Columbus, and their ultimate success, again filled my bosom. The moment had now come in which I might succeed. The first man was ready to go to the stake, and I had felt all along that the great difficulty would be in obtaining the willing assent of the first martyr. It might well be that these accusations of cruelty were a part of the suffering without which my great reform could not be carried to success. Though I should live to be accounted as cruel as Cæsar, what would that be if I too could reduce my Gaul to civilisation? 'Dear Craasweller,' I murmured to myself as I turned again towards Gladstonopolis, and hurrying back, buried myself in the obscurity of the executive chambers.

The following day occurred a most disagreeable scene in my own house at dinner. Jack came in and took his chair at the table in grim silence. It might be that he was lamenting for his English friends who were gone, and therefore would not speak. Mrs Neverbend, too, ate her dinner without a word. I began to fear that presently there would be something to be said,—some cause for a quarrel; and as is customary on such occasions, I endeavoured to become specially gracious and communicative. I talked about the ship that had started on its homeward journey, and praised Lord Marylebone, and laughed at Mr Puddlebrane; but it was to no effect. Neither would Jack nor Mrs Neverbend say anything, and they ate their dinner gloomily till the attendant left the room. Then Jack began. 'I think it right to tell you, sir, that there's going to be a public meeting on the Town Flags the day after to-morrow.' The Town Flags was an open unenclosed place, over which, supported by arches, was erected the Town Hall. It was here that the people were accustomed to hold those outside assemblies which too often guided the responsible Assembly in the Senate-house.

'And what are you all going to talk about there?'

'There is only one subject,' said Jack, 'which at present occupies the mind of Gladstonopolis. The people don't intend to allow you to deposit Mr Craasweller.'

'Considering your age and experience, Jack, don't you think that you're taking too much upon yourself to say whether people will allow or will not allow the executive of the country to perform their duty?'

'If Jack isn't old,' said Mrs Neverbend, 'I, at any rate, am older, and I say the same thing.'

'Of course I only said what I thought,' continued Jack.

'What I want to explain is, that I shall be there myself, and shall do all that I can to support the meeting.'

'In opposition to your father?' said I.

'Well;—yes, I am afraid so. You see it's a public subject on a public matter, and I don't see that father and son have anything to do with it. If I were in the Assembly, I don't suppose I should be bound to support my father.'

'But you're not in the Assembly.'

'I have my own convictions all the same, and I find myself called upon to take a part.'

'Good gracious—yes! and to save poor old Mr Crasweller's life from this most inhuman law. He's just as fit to live as are you and I.'

'The only question is, whether he be fit to die,—or rather to be deposited, I mean. But I'm not going to argue the subject here. It has been decided by the law; and that should be enough for you two, as it is enough for me. As for Jack, I will not have him attend any such meeting. Were he to do so, he would incur my grave displeasure,—and consequent punishment.'

'What do you mean to do to the boy?' asked Mrs Neverbend.

'If he ceases to behave to me like a son, I shall cease to treat him like a father. If he attends this meeting he must leave my house, and I shall see him no more.'

'Leave the house!' shrieked Mrs Neverbend.

'Jack,' said I, with the kindest voice which I was able to assume, 'you will pack up your portmanteau and go to New Zealand the day after to-morrow. I have business for you to transact with Macmurdo and Brown of some importance. I will give you the particulars when I see you in the office.'

'Of course he won't go, Mr Neverbend,' cried my wife. But, though the words were determined, there was a certain vacillation in the tone of her voice which did not escape me.

'We shall see. If Jack intends to remain as my son, he must obey his father. I have been kind, and perhaps too indulgent, to him. I now require that he shall proceed to

New Zealand the day after to-morrow. The boat sails at eight. I shall be happy to go down with him and see him on board.'

Jack only shook his head,—by which I understood that he meant rebellion. I had been a most generous father to him, and loved him as the very apple of my eye; but I was determined that I would be stern. 'You have heard my order,' I said, 'and you can have to-morrow to think about it. I advise you not to throw over, and for ever, the affection, the fostering care, and all the comforts, pecuniary as well as others, which you have hitherto had from an indulgent father.'

'You do not mean to say that you will disinherit the boy?' said Mrs Neverbend.

I knew that it was utterly out of my power to do so. I could not disinherit him. I could not even rob him of a single luxury without an amount of suffering much greater than he would feel. Was I not thinking of him day and night as I arranged my worldly affairs? That moment when he knocked down Sir Kennington Oval's wicket, had I not been as proud as he was? When the trumpet sounded, did not I feel the honour more than he? When he made his last triumphant run, and I threw my hat in the air, was it not to me sweeter than if I had done it myself? Did I not even love him the better for swearing that he would make this fight for Crasweller? But yet it was necessary that I should command obedience, and, if possible, frighten him into subservience. We talk of a father's power, and know that the old Romans could punish filial disobedience by death; but a Britannulan father has a heart in his bosom which is more powerful than law or even custom, and I believe that the Roman was much the same. 'My dear, I will not discuss my future intentions before the boy. It would be unseemly. I command him to start for New Zealand the day after to-morrow, and I shall see whether he will obey me. I strongly advise him to be governed in this matter by his father.' Jack only shook his head, and left the room. I became aware afterwards that he slept that night at Little Christchurch.

That night I received such a lecture from Mrs Neverbend in our bedroom as might have shamed that Mrs Caudle* of whom we read in English history. I hate these lectures, not as thinking them unbecoming, but as being peculiarly disagreeable. I always find myself absolutely impotent during their progress. I am aware that it is quite useless to speak a word, and that I can only allow the clock to run itself down. What Mrs Neverbend says at such moments has always in it a great deal of good sense; but it is altogether wasted, because I knew it all beforehand, and with pen and ink could have written down the lecture which she delivered at that peculiar moment. And I fear no evil results from her anger for the future, because her conduct to me will, I know by experience, be as careful and as kind as ever. Were another to use harsh language to me, she would rise in wrath to defend me. And she does not, in truth, mean a tenth of what she says. But I am for the time as though I were within the clapper of a mill; and her passion goes on increasing because she can never get a word from me. 'Mr Neverbend, I tell you this,—you are going to make a fool of yourself. I think it my duty to tell you so, as your wife. Everybody else will think it. Who are you, to liken yourself to Galileo?—an old fellow of that kind who lived a thousand years ago, before Christianity had ever been invented. You have got nasty murderous thoughts in your mind, and want to kill poor Mr Crasweller, just out of pride, because you have said you would. Now, Jack is determined that you shan't, and I say that he is right. There is no reason why Jack shouldn't obey me as well as you. You will never be able to deposit Mr Crasweller,—not if you try it for a hundred years. The city won't let you do it; and if you have a grain of sense left in your head, you won't attempt it. Jack is determined to meet the men on the Town Flags the day after to-morrow, and I say that he is right. As for your disinheriting him, and spending all your money on machinery to roast pigs,—I say you can't do it. There will be a commission to inquire into you if you do not mind yourself, and then you will remember what I told you. Poor Mr Crasweller, whom you have known for forty years! I wonder how you can bring yourself to think of killing the poor man, whose bread you have so often eaten! And if you think you are going to frighten Jack, you are very much mistaken. Jack would do twice more for Eva Crasweller than for you or me, and it's natural he should. You may be sure he will not give up; and the end will be, that he will get Eva for his own. I do believe he has gone to sleep.' Then I gave myself infinite credit for the pertinacity of my silence, and for the manner in which I had put on an appearance of somnolency without overacting the part. Mrs Neverbend did in truth go to sleep, but I lay awake during the whole night thinking of the troubles before me.

# CHAPTER VIII

## The 'John Bright'

JACK, of course, did not go to New Zealand, and I was bound to quarrel with him,—temporarily. They held the meeting on the Town Flags, and many eloquent words were, no doubt, spoken. I did not go, of course, nor did I think it well to read the reports. Mrs Neverbend took it into her head at this time to speak to me only respecting the material wants of life. 'Will you have another lump of sugar in your tea, Mr President?' Or, 'If you want a second blanket on your bed, Mr Neverbend, and will say the word, it shall be supplied.' I took her in the same mood, and was dignified, cautious, and silent. With Jack I was supposed to have quarrelled altogether, and very grievous it was to me not to be able to speak to the lad of a morning or an evening. But he did not seem to be much the worse for it. As for turning him out of the house or stopping his pocket-money, that would be carrying the joke further than I could do it. Indeed it seemed to me that he was peculiarly happy at this time, for he did not go to his office. He spent his mornings in making speeches, and then went down in the afternoon on his bicycle to Little Christchurch.

So the time passed on, and the day absolutely came on which Crasweller was to be deposited. I had seen him constantly during the last few weeks, but he had not spoken to me on the subject. He had said that he would not leave Little Christchurch, and he did not do so. I do not think that he had been outside his own grounds once during these six weeks. He was always courteous to me, and would offer me tea and toast when I came, with a stately civility, as though there had been no subject of burning discord between us. Eva I rarely saw. That she was there I was aware,—but she never came into my presence till the evening before the appointed day, as I shall presently have to tell. Once or twice I did endeavour to lead him on to the subject; but he showed a disinclination to discuss it so invincible, that I was silenced. As I left him on the day before that on which he was to be deposited, I assured him that I would call for him on the morrow.

'Do not trouble yourself,' he said, repeating the words twice over. 'It will be just the same whether you are here or not.' Then I shook my head by way of showing him that I would come, and I took my leave.

I must explain that during these last few weeks things had not gone quietly in Gladstonopolis, but there had been nothing like a serious riot. I was glad to find that, in spite of Jack's speechifying, the younger part of the population was still true to me, and I did not doubt that I should still have got the majority of votes in the Assembly. A rumour was spread abroad that the twelve months of Crasweller's period of probation were to be devoted to discussing the question, and I was told that my theory as to the Fixed Period would not in truth have been carried out merely because Mr Crasweller had changed his residence from Little Christchurch to the college. I had ordered an open barouche to be prepared for the occasion, and had got a pair of splendid horses fit for a triumphal march. With these I intended to call at Little Christchurch at noon, and to accompany Mr Craswell up to the college, sitting on his left hand. On all other occasions, the President of the Republic sat in his carriage on the right side, and I had ever stood up for the dignities of my position. But this occasion was to be an exception to all rule.

On the evening before, as I was sitting in my library at home mournfully thinking of the occasion, telling myself that after all I could not devote my friend to what some might think a premature death, the door was opened, and Eva Craswell was announced. She had on one of those round, close-fitting men's hats which ladies now wear, but under it was a veil which quite hid her face. 'I am taking a liberty, Mr Neverbend,' she said, 'in troubling you at the present moment.'

'Eva, my dear, how can anything you do be called a liberty?'

'I do not know, Mr Neverbend. I have come to you because I am very unhappy.'

'I thought you had shunned me of late.'

'So I have. How could I help it, when you have been so anxious to deposit poor papa in that horrid place?'

'He was equally anxious a few years since.'

'Never! He agreed to it because you told him, and because you were a man able to persuade. It was not that he ever had his heart in it, even when it was not near enough to alarm himself. And he is not a man fearful of death in the ordinary way. Papa is a brave man.'

'My darling child, it is beautiful to hear you say so of him.'

'He is going with you to-morrow simply because he has made you a promise, and does not choose to have it said of him that he broke his word even to save his own life. Is not that courage? It is not with him as it is with you, who have your heart in matter, because you think of some great thing that you will do, so that your name may be remembered to future generations.'

'It is not for that, Eva. I care not at all whether my name be remembered. It is for the good of many that I act.'

'He believes in no good, but is willing to go because of his promise. Is it fair to keep him to such a promise under such circumstances?'

'But the law——'

'I will hear nothing of the law. The law means you and your influences. Papa is to be sacrificed to the law to suit your pleasure. Papa is to be destroyed, not because the law wishes it, but to suit the taste of Mr Neverbend.'

'Oh, Eva!'

'It is true.'

'To suit my taste?'

'Well—what else? You have got the idea into your head, and you will not drop it. And you have persuaded him because he is your friend. Oh, a most fatal friendship! He is to be sacrificed because, when thinking of other things, he did not care to differ with you.' Then she paused, as though to see whether I might not yield to her words. And if the words of any one would have availed to make me yield, I think it would have been hers as now spoken. 'Do you know what people will say of you, Mr Neverbend?' she continued.

'What will they say?'

'If I only knew how best I could tell you! Your son has asked me—to be his wife.'

'I have long known that he has loved you well.'

'But it can never be,' she said, 'if my father is to be carried away to this fearful place. People would say that you had hurried him off in order that Jack——'

'Would you believe it, Eva?' said I, with indignation.

'It does not matter what I would believe. Mr Grundle is saying it already, and is accusing me too. And Mr Exors, the lawyer, is spreading it about. It has become quite the common report in Gladstonopolis that Jack is to become at once the owner of Little Christchurch.'

'Perish Little Christchurch!' I exclaimed. 'My son would marry no man's daughter for his money.'

'I do not believe it of Jack,' she said, 'for I know that he is generous and good. There! I do love him better than any one in the world. But as things are, I can never marry him if papa is to be shut up in that wretched City of the Dead.'

'Not City of the Dead, my dear.'

'Oh, I cannot bear to think of it!—all alone with no one but me with him to watch him as day after day passes away, as the ghastly hour comes nearer and still nearer, when he is to be burned in those fearful furnaces!'

'The cremation, my dear, has nothing in truth to do with the Fixed Period.'

'To wait till the fatal day shall have arrived, and then to know that at a fixed hour he will be destroyed just because you have said so! Can you imagine what my feelings will be when that moment shall have come?'

I had not in truth thought of it. But now, when the idea was represented to my mind's eye, I acknowledged to myself that it would be impossible that she should be left there for the occasion. How or when she should be taken away, or whither, I could not at the moment think. These would form questions which it would be very hard to answer. After some score of years, say, when the community would be used to the Fixed Period, I could understand that a daughter or a wife might leave the college, and go away into such solitudes as the occasion required, a week perhaps before the hour arranged for departure had come. Custom would make it comparatively easy; as custom has arranged such a period of mourning for a widow, and such another for a widower, a son, or a daughter. But here, with Eva, there would be no custom. She would have nothing to guide her, and might remain there till the last fatal moment. I had hoped that she might have married Jack, or perhaps Grundle, during the interval,—not having foreseen that the year, which was intended to be one of honour and glory, should become a time of mourning and tribulation. 'Yes, my dear, it is very sad.'

'Sad! Was there ever a position in life so melancholy, so mournful, so unutterably miserable?' I remained there opposite, gazing into vacancy, but I could say nothing. 'What do you intend to do, Mr Neverbend?' she asked. 'It is altogether in your bosom. My father's life or death is in your hands. What is your decision?' I could only remain steadfast; but it seemed to be impossible to say so. 'Well, Mr Neverbend, will you speak?'

'It is not for me to decide. It is for the country.'

'The country!' she exclaimed, rising up; 'it is your own pride,—your vanity and cruelty combined. You will not yield in this matter to me, your friend's daughter, because your vanity tells you that when you have once said a thing, that thing shall come to pass.' Then she put the veil down over her face, and went out of the room.

I sat for some time motionless, trying to turn over in my mind all that she had said to me; but it seemed as though my faculties were utterly obliterated in despair. Eva had been to me almost as a daughter, and yet I was compelled to refuse her request for her father's life. And when she had told me that it was my pride and vanity which had made me do so, I could not explain to her that they were not the cause. And, indeed, was I sure of myself that it was not so? I had flattered myself that I did it for the public good; but was I sure that obduracy did not come from my anxiety to be counted with Columbus and Galileo? or if not that, was there not something personal to myself in my desire that I should be known as one who had benefited my species? In considering such matters, it is so hard to separate the motives,—to say how much springs from some glorious longing to assist others in their struggle upwards in humanity, and how much again from mean personal ambition. I had thought that I had done it all in order that the failing strength of old age might be relieved, and that the race might from age to age be improved. But I now doubted myself, and feared lest that vanity of which Eva had spoken to me had overcome me. With my wife and son I could still be brave,—even with Crasweller I could be constant and hard; but to be obdurate with Eva was indeed a struggle. And when she told me that I did so through pride, I found it very hard to bear. And yet it was not that I was angry with the child. I became more and more attached to her the more loudly she spoke on behalf of her father. Her very indignation endeared me to her, and made me feel how excellent she was, how noble a wife she would be for my son. But was I to give way after all? Having brought the matter to such a pitch, was I to give up everything to the prayers of a girl? I was well aware even then that my theory was true. The old and effete should go, in order that the strong and manlike might rise in their places and do the work of the world with the wealth of the world at their command. Take the average of mankind all round, and there would be but the lessening of a year or two from the life of them all. Even taking those men who had arrived at twenty-five, to how few are allotted more than forty years of life! But yet how large a proportion of the wealth of the world remains in the hands of those who have passed that age, and are unable from senile imbecility to employ that wealth as it should be used! As I thought of this, I said to myself that Eva's prayers might not avail, and I did take some comfort to myself in thinking that all was done for the sake of posterity. And then, again, when I thought of her prayers, and of those stern words which had followed her prayers,—of that charge of pride and vanity,—I did tell myself that pride and vanity were not absent.

She was gone now, and I felt that she must say and think evil things of me through all my future life. The time might perhaps come, when I too should have been taken away, and when her father should long since have been at rest, that softer thoughts would come across her mind. If it were only possible that I might go, so that Jack might be married to the girl he loved, that might be well. Then I wiped my eyes, and went forth to make arrangements for the morrow.

The morning came,—the 30th of June,—a bright, clear, winter morning, cold but still genial and pleasant as I got into the barouche and had myself driven to Little Christchurch. To say that my heart was sad within me would give no fair record of my condition. I was so crushed by grief, so obliterated by the agony of the hour, that I hardly saw what passed before my eyes. I only knew that the day had come, the terrible day for which in my ignorance I had yearned, and that I was totally unable to go through its ceremonies with dignity, or even with composure. But I observed as I was driven down the street, lying out at sea many miles to the left, a small spot of smoke on the horizon, as though it might be of some passing vessel. It did not in the least awaken my attention; but there it was, and I remembered to have thought as I passed on how blessed were they who steamed by unconscious of that terrible ordeal of the Fixed Period which I was bound to encounter.

I went to Little Christchurch, and there I found Mr Craswaller waiting for me in the hall. I came in and took his limp hand in mine, and congratulated him. Oh how vain, how wretched, sounded that congratulation in my own ears!

And it was spoken, I was aware, in a piteous tone of voice, and with meagre, bated breath. He merely shook his head, and attempted to pass on. 'Will you not take your greatcoat?' said I, seeing that he was going out into the open air without protection.

'No; why should I? It will not be wanted up there.'

'You do not know the place,' I replied. 'There are twenty acres of pleasure-ground for you to wander over.' Then he turned upon me a look,—oh, such a look!—and went on and took his place in the carriage. But Eva followed him, and spread a rug across his knees, and threw a cloak over his shoulders.

'Will not Eva come with us?' I said.

'No; my daughter will hide her face on such a day as this. It is for you and me to be carried through the city,—you because you are proud of the pageant, and me because I do not fear it.' This, too, added something to my sorrow. Then I looked and saw that Eva got into a small closed carriage in the rear, and was driven off by a circuitous route, to meet us, no doubt, at the college.

As we were driven away,—Craswaller and I,—I had not a word to say to him. And he seemed to collect himself in his fierceness, and to remain obdurately silent in his anger. In this way we drove on, till, coming to a turn of the road, the expanse of the sea appeared before us. Here again I observed a small cloud of smoke which had grown out of the spot I had before seen, and I was aware that some large ship was making its way into the harbour of Gladstonopolis. I turned my face towards it and gazed, and then a sudden thought struck me. How would it be with me if this were some great English vessel coming into our harbour on the very day of Crasweller's deposition? A year since I would have rejoiced on such an occasion, and would have assured myself that I would show to the strangers the grandeur of this ceremony, which must have been new to them. But now a creeping terror took possession of me, and I felt my heart give way within me. I wanted no Englishman, nor American, to come and see the first day of our Fixed Period.

It was evident that Crasweller did not see the smoke; but to my eyes, as we progressed, it became nearer, till at last the hull of the vast vessel became manifest. Then as the carriage passed on into the street of Gladstonopolis at the spot where one side of the street forms the quay, the vessel with extreme rapidity steamed in, and I could see across the harbour that she was a ship of war. A certain sense of relief came upon my mind just then, because I felt sure that she had come to interfere with the work which I had in hand; but how base must be my condition when I could take delight in thinking that it had been interrupted!

By this time we had been joined by some eight or ten carriages, which formed, as it were, a funeral *cortège* behind us. But I could perceive that these carriages were filled for the most part by young men, and that there was no contemporary of Crasweller to be seen at all. As we went up the town hill, I could espy Barnes gibbering on the doorstop of his house, and Tallowax brandishing a large knife in his hand, and Exors waving a paper over his head, which I well knew to be a copy of the Act of our Assembly; but I could only pretend not to see them as our carriage passed on.

The chief street of Gladstonopolis, running through the centre of the city, descends a hill to the level of the harbour. As the vessel came in we began to ascend the hill, but the horses progressed very slowly. Crasweller sat perfectly speechless by my side. I went on with a forced smile upon my face, speaking occasionally to this or the other neighbour as we met them. I was forced to be in a certain degree cheerful, but grave and solemn in my cheerfulness. I was taking this man home for that last glorious year which he was about to pass in joyful anticipation of a happier life; and therefore I must be cheerful. But this was only the thing to be acted, the play to be played, by me the player. I must be solomn too,—silent as the churchyard, mournful as the grave,—because of the truth. Why was I thus driven to act a part that was false? On the brow of the hill we met a concourse of people both young and old, and I was glad to see that the latter had come out to greet us. But by degrees the crowd became so numerous that the carriage was stopped in its progress; and rising up, I motioned to those around us to let us pass. We became, however, more firmly enveloped in the masses, and at last I had to ask aloud that they would open and let us go on. 'Mr President,' said one old gentleman to me, a tanner in the city, 'there's an English ship of war come into the harbour. I think they've got something to say to you.'

'Something to say to me! What can they have to say to me?' I replied, with all the dignity I could command.

'We'll just stay and see;—we'll just wait a few minutes,' said another elder. He was a bar-keeper with a red nose, and as he spoke he took up a place in front of the horses. It was in vain for me to press the coachman. It would have been indecent to do so at such a moment, and something at any rate was due to the position of Crasweller. He remained speechless in the carriage; but I thought that I could see, as I glanced at his face, that he took a strong interest in the proceedings. 'They're going to begin to come up the hill, Mr Bunnit,' said the bar-keeper to the tanner, 'as soon as ever they're out of their boats.'

'God bless the old flag for ever and ever!' said Mr Bunnit. 'I knew they wouldn't let us deposit any one.'

Thus their secret was declared. These old men,—the tanner and whisky-dealer, and the like,—had sent home to England to get assistance against their own Government!

There had always been a scum of the population,—the dirty, frothy, meaningless foam at the top,—men like the drunken old bar-keeper, who had still clung submissive to the old country,—men who knew nothing of progress and civilisation,—who were content with what they ate and drank, and chiefly with the latter. 'Here they come. God bless their gold bands!' said he of the red nose. Yes;— up the hill they came, three gilded British naval officers surrounded by a crowd of Britannulans.

Crasweller heard it all, but did not move from his place. But he leaned forward, and he bit his lip, and I saw that his right hand shook as it grasped the arm of the carriage. There was nothing for me but to throw myself back and remain tranquil. I was, however, well aware that an hour of despair and opposition, and of defeat, was coming upon me. Up they came, and were received with three deafening cheers by the crowd immediately round the carriage. 'I beg your pardon, sir,' said one of the three, whom I afterwards learned to be the second lieutenant; 'are you the President of this Republic?'

'I am,' replied I; 'and what may you be?'

'I am the second lieutenant on board HM's gunboat, the John Bright.'* I had heard of this vessel, which had been named from a gallant officer, who, in the beginning of the century, had seated himself on a barrel of gunpowder, and had, single-handed, quelled a mutiny. He had been made Earl Bright for what he had done on that occasion, but the vessel was still called J.B. throughout the service.

'And what may be your business with me, Mr Second Lieutenant?'

'Our captain, Captain Battleax's compliments, and he hopes you won't object to postpone this interesting ceremony for a day or two till he may come and see. He is sure that Mr Crasweller won't mind.' Then he took off his hat to my old friend. 'The captain would have come up himself, but he can't leave the ship before he sees his big gun laid on and made safe. He is very sorry to be so unceremonious, but the 250-ton steam-swiveller requires a great deal of care.'

'Laid on?' I suggested.

'Well—yes. It is always necessary, when the ship lets go her anchor, to point the gun in the most effective manner.'

'She won't go off, will she?' asked Bunnit.

'Not without provocation, I think. The captain has the exploding wire under double lock and key in his own state-room. If he only touched the spring, we about the locality here would be knocked into little bits in less time than it will take you to think about it. Indeed the whole of this side of the hill would become an instantaneous ruin without the sign of a human being anywhere.'

There was a threat in this which I could not endure. And indeed, for myself, I did not care how soon I might be annihilated. England, with unsurpassed tyranny, had sent out one of her brutal modern inventions, and threatened us all with blood and gore and murder if we did not give up our beneficent modern theory. It was the malevolent influence of the intellect applied to brute force, dominating its benevolent influence as applied to philanthropy. What was the John Bright to me that it should come there prepared to send me into eternity by its bloodthirsty mechanism? It is an evil sign of the times,—of the times that are in so many respects hopeful,—that the greatest inventions of the day should always take the shape of engines of destruction! But what could I do in the agony of the moment? I could but show the coolness of my courage by desiring the coachman to drive on.

'For God's sake, don't!' said Crasweller, jumping up.

'He shan't stir a step,' said Bunnit to the bar-keeper.

'He can't move an inch,' replied the other. 'We know what our precious lives are worth; don't we, Mr Bunnit?'

What could I do? 'Mr Second Lieutenant, I must hold you responsible for this interruption,' said I.

'Exactly so. I am responsible,—as far as stopping this carriage goes. Had all the town turned out in your favour, and had this gentleman insisted on being carried away to be buried——'

'Nothing of that kind,' said Crasweller.

'Then I think I may assume that Captain Battleax will not fire his gun. But if you will allow me, I will ask him a question.' Then he put a minute whistle up to his mouth, and I could see, for the first time, that there hung from this the thinnest possible metal wire,—a thread of silk, I would have said, only that it was much less palpable,—which had been dropped from the whistle as the lieutenant had come along, and which now communicated with the vessel. I had, of course, heard of this hair telephone, but I had never before seen it used in such perfection. I was assured afterwards that one of the ship's officers could go ten miles inland and still hold communication with his captain. He put the instrument alternately to his mouth and to his ear, and then informed me that Captain Battleax was desirous that we should all go home to our own houses.

'I decline to go to my own house,' I said. The lieutenant shrugged his shoulders. 'Coachman, as soon as the crowd has dispersed itself, you will drive on.' The coachman, who was an old assistant in my establishment, turned round and looked at me aghast. But he was soon put out of his trouble. Bunnit and the bar-keeper took out the horses and proceeded to lead them down the hill. Crasweller, as soon as he saw this, said that he presumed he might go back, as he could not possibly go on. 'It is but three miles for us to walk,' I said.

'I am forbidden to permit this gentleman to proceed either on foot or with the carriage,' said the lieutenant. 'I am to ask if he will do Captain Battleax the honour to come on board and take tiffin with him. If I could only prevail on you, Mr President.' On this I shook my head in eager denial. 'Exactly so; but he will hope to see you on another occasion soon.' I little thought then, how many long days I should have to pass with Captain Battleax and his officers, or how pleasant companions I should find them when the remembrance of the present indignity had been somewhat softened by time.

Crasweller turned upon his heel and walked down the hill with the officers,—all the crowd accompanying them; while Bunnit and the bar-keeper had gone off with the horses.

I had not descended from the carriage; but there I was, planted alone,—the President of the Republic left on the top of the hill in his carriage without means of locomotion! On looking round I saw Jack, and with Jack I saw also a lady, shrouded from head to foot in black garments, with a veil over her face, whom I knew, from the little round hat upon her head, to be Eva. Jack came up to me, but where Eva went I could not see. 'Shall we walk down to the house?' he said. I felt that his coming to me at such a moment was kind, because I had been, as it were, deserted by all the world. Then he opened the door of the carriage, and I came out. 'It was very odd that those fellows should have turned up just at this moment,' said Jack.

'When things happen very oddly, as you call it, they seem to have been premeditated.'

'Not their coming to-day. That has not been premeditated; at least not to my knowledge. Indeed I did not in the least know what the English were likely to do.'

'Do you think it right to send to the enemies of your country for aid against your country?' This I asked with much indignation, and I had refused as yet to take his arm.

'Oh but, sir, England isn't our enemy.'

'Not when she comes and interrupts the quiet execution of our laws by threats of blowing us and our city and our citizens to instant destruction!'

'She would never have done it. I don't suppose that big gun is even loaded.'

'The more contemptible is her position. She threatens us with a lie in her mouth.'

'I know nothing about it, sir. The gun may be there all right, and the gunpowder, and the twenty tons of iron shot. But I'm sure she'll not fire it off in our harbour. They say that each shot costs two thousand five hundred pounds, and that the wear and tear to the vessel is two thousand more. There are things so terrible, that if you will only create a belief in them, that will suffice without anything else. I suppose we may walk down. Crasweller has gone, and you can do nothing without him.'

This was true, and I therefore prepared to descend the hill. My position as President of the Republic did demand a certain amount of personal dignity; and how was I to uphold that in my present circumstances? 'Jack,' said I, 'it is the sign of a noble mind to bear contumely without petulance. Since our horses have gone before us, and Crasweller and the crowd have gone, we will follow them.' Then I put my arm within his, and as I walked down the hill, I almost took joy in thinking that Crasweller had been spared.

'Sir,' said Jack, as we walked on, 'I want to tell you something.'

'What is it?'

'Something of most extreme importance to me! I never thought that I should have been so fortunate as to announce to you what I've now got to say. I hardly know whether I am standing on my head or my heels. Eva Crasweller has promised to be my wife.'

'Indeed!'

'If you will make us happy by giving us your permission.'

'I should not have thought that she would have asked for that.'

'She has to ask her father, and he's all right. He did say, when I spoke to him this morning, that his permission would go for nothing, as he was about to be led away and deposited. Of course I told him that all that would amount to nothing.'

'To nothing! What right had you to say so?'

'Well, sir,—you see that a party of us were quite determined. Eva had said that she would never let me even speak to her as long as her father's life was in danger. She altogether hated that wretch Grundle for wanting to get rid of him. I swore to her that I would do the best I could, and she said that if I could succeed, then—she thought she could love me. What was a fellow to do?'

'What did you do?'

'I had it all out with Sir Kennington Oval, who is the prince of good fellows; and he telegraphed to his uncle, who is Secretary for Benevolence, or some such thing, at home.'

'England is not your home,' said I.

'It's the way we all speak of it.'

'And what did he say?'

'Well, he went to work, and the John Bright was sent out here. But it was only an accident that it should come on this very day.'

And this was the way in which things are to be managed in Britannula! Because a young boy had fallen in love with a pretty girl, the whole wealth of England was to be used for a most nefarious purpose, and a great nation was to exercise its tyranny over a small one, in which her own language was spoken and her own customs followed! In every way England had had reason to be proud of her youngest child. We Britannulans had become noted for intellect, morals, health, and prosperity. We had advanced a step upwards, and had adopted the Fixed Period. Then, at the instance of this lad, a leviathan of war was to be sent out to crush us unless we would consent to put down the cherished conviction of our hearts! As I thought of all, walking down the street hanging on Jack's arm, I had to ask myself whether the Fixed Period was the cherished conviction of our hearts. It was so of some, no doubt; and I had been able, by the intensity of my will,—and something, too, by the covetousness and hurry of the younger men,—to cause my wishes to prevail in the community. I did not find that I had reconciled myself to the use of this covetousness with the object of achieving a purpose which I believed to be thoroughly good. But the heartfelt conviction had not been strong with the people. I was forced to confess as much. Had it indeed been really strong with any but myself? Was I not in the position of a shepherd driving sheep into a pasture which was distasteful to them? Eat, O sheep, and you will love the food in good time,—you or the lambs that are coming after you! What sheep will go into unsavoury pastures, with no hopes but such as these held out to them? And yet I had been right. The pasture had been the best which the ingenuity of man had found for the maintenance of sheep.

'Jack,' said I, 'what a poor, stupid, lovelorn boy you are!'

'I daresay I am,' said Jack, meekly.

'You put the kisses of a pretty girl, who may perhaps make you a good wife,—and, again, may make you a bad one,—against all the world in arms.'

'I am quite sure about that,' said Jack.

'Sure about what?'

'That there is not a fellow in all Britannula will have such a wife as Eva.'

'That means that you are in love. And because you are in love, you are to throw over—not merely your father, because in such an affair that goes for nothing——'

'Oh, but it does; I have thought so much about it.'

'I'm much obliged to you. But you are to put yourself in opposition to the greatest movement made on behalf of the human race for centuries; you are to set yourself up against——'

'Galileo and Columbus,' he suggested, quoting my words with great cruelty.

'The modern Galileo, sir; the Columbus of this age. And you are to conquer them! I, the father, have to submit to you the son; I the President of fifty-seven, to you the schoolboy of twenty-one; I the thoughtful man, to you the thoughtless boy! I congratulate you; but I do not congratulate the world on the extreme folly which still guides its actions.' Then I left him, and going into the executive chambers, sat myself down and cried in the very agony of a broken heart.

# CHAPTER IX
## The New Governor

'So,' said I to myself, 'because of Jack and his love, all the aspirations of my life are to be crushed! The whole dream of my existence, which has come so near to the fruition of a waking moment, is to be violently dispelled because my own son and Sir Kennington Oval have settled between them that a pretty girl is to have her own way.' As I thought of it, there seemed to be a monstrous cruelty and potency in Fortune, which she never could have been allowed to exercise in a world which was not altogether given over to injustice. It was for that that I wept. I wept to think that a spirit of honesty should as yet have prevailed so little in the world. Here, in our waters, was lying a terrible engine of British power, sent out by a British Cabinet Minister,—the so-called Minister of Benevolence, by a bitter chance,—at the instance of that Minister's nephew, to put down by brute force the most absolutely benevolent project for the governance of the world which the mind of man had ever projected. It was in that that lay the agony of the blow.

I remained there alone for many hours, but I must acknowledge that before I left the chambers I had gradually brought myself to look at the matter in another light. Had Eva Crasweller not been good-looking, had Jack been still at college, had Sir Kennington Oval remained in England, had Mr Bunnit and the bar-keeper not succeeded in stopping my carriage on the hill,—should I have succeeded in arranging for the final departure of my old friend? That was the question which I ought to ask myself. And even had I succeeded in carrying my success so far as that, should I not have appeared a murderer to my fellow-citizens had not his departure been followed in regular sequence by that of all others till it had come to my turn? Had Crasweller departed, and had the system then been stopped, should I not have appeared a murderer even to myself? And what hope had there been, what reasonable expectation, that the system should have been allowed fair-play?

It must be understood that I, I myself, have never for a moment swerved. But though I have been strong enough to originate the idea, I have not been strong enough to bear the terrible harshness of the opinions of those around me when I should have exercised against those dear to me the mandates of the new law. If I could, in the spirit, have leaped over a space of thirty years and been myself deposited in due order,

I could see that my memory would have been embalmed with those who had done great things for their fellow-citizens. Columbus, and Galileo, and Newton, and Harvey, and Wilberforce, and Cobden, and that great Banting\* who has preserved us all so completely from the horrors of obesity, would not have been named with honour more resplendent than that paid to the name of Neverbend. Such had been my ambition, such had been my hope. But it is necessary that a whole age should be carried up to some proximity to the reformer before there is a space sufficiently large for his operations. Had the telegraph been invented in the days of ancient Rome, would the Romans have accepted it, or have stoned Wheatstone?\* So thinking, I resolved that I was before my age, and that I must pay the allotted penalty.

On arriving at home at my own residence, I found that our *salon* was filled with a brilliant company. We did not usually use the room; but on entering the house I heard the clatter of conversation, and went in. There was Captain Battleax seated there, beautiful with a cocked-hat, and an epaulet, and gold braid. He rose to meet me, and I saw that he was a handsome tall man about forty, with a determined face and a winning smile. 'Mr President,' said he, 'I am in command of her Majesty's gunboat, the John Bright, and I have come to pay my respects to the ladies.'

'I am sure the ladies have great pleasure in seeing you.' I looked round the room, and there, with other of our fair citizens, I saw Eva. As I spoke I made him a gracious bow, and I think I showed him by my mode of address that I did not bear any grudge as to my individual self.

'I have come to your shores, Mr President, with the purpose of seeing how things are progressing in this distant quarter of the world.'

'Things were progressing, Captain Battleax, pretty well before this morning. We have our little struggles here as elsewhere, and all things cannot be done by rose-water. But, on the whole, we are a prosperous and well-satisfied people.'

'We are quite satisfied now, Captain Battleax,' said my wife.

'Quite satisfied,' said Eva.

'I am sure we are all delighted to hear the ladies speak in so pleasant a manner,' said First-Lieutenant Crosstrees, an officer with whom I have since become particularly intimate.

Then there was a little pause in the conversation, and I felt myself bound to say something as to the violent interruption to which I had this morning been subjected. And yet that something must be playful in its nature. I must by no means show in such company as was now present the strong feeling which pervaded my own mind. 'You will perceive, Captain Battleax, that there is a little difference of opinion between us all here as to the ceremony which was to have been accomplished this morning. The ladies, in compliance with that softness of heart which is their characteristic, are on one side; and the men, by whom the world has to be managed, are on the other. No doubt, in process of time the ladies will follow——'

'Their masters,' said Mrs Neverbend. 'No doubt we shall do so when it is only ourselves that we have to sacrifice, but never when the question concerns our husbands, our fathers, and our sons.'

This was a pretty little speech enough, and received the eager compliments of the officers of the John Bright. 'I did not mean,' said Captain Battleax, 'to touch upon public subjects at such a moment as this. I am here only to pay my respects as a messenger from Great Britain to Britannula, to congratulate you all on your late victory at cricket, and to say how loud are the praises bestowed on Mr John Neverbend, junior, for his skill and gallantry. The power of his arm is already the subject discussed at all clubs and drawing-rooms at home. We had received details of the whole affair by water-telegram before the John Bright started. Mrs Neverbend, you must indeed be proud of your son.'

Jack had been standing in the far corner of the room talking to Eva, and was now reduced to silence by his praises.

'Sir Kennington Oval is a very fine player,' said my wife.

'And my Lord Marylebone behaves himself quite like

a British peer,' said the wife of the Mayor of Gladstonopolis,—a lady whom he had married in England, and who
had not moved there in quite the highest circles.

Then we began to think of the hospitality of the island,
and the officers of the John Bright were asked to dine with
us on the following day. I and my wife and son, and the two
Craswellers, and three or four others, agreed to dine on
board the ship on the next. To me personally an extreme of
courtesy was shown. It seemed as though I were treated with
almost royal honour. This, I felt, was paid to me as being
President of the republic, and I endeavoured to behave
myself with such mingled humility and dignity as might befit
the occasion; but I could not but feel that something was
wanting to the simplicity of my ordinary life. My wife, on the
spur of the moment, managed to give the gentlemen a very
good dinner. Including the chaplain and the surgeon, there
were twelve of them, and she asked twelve of the prettiest
girls in Gladstonopolis to meet them. This, she said, was
true hospitality; and I am not sure that I did not agree with
her. Then there were three or four leading men of the
community, with their wives, who were for the most part the
fathers and mothers of the young ladies. We sat down thirty-
six to dinner; and I think that we showed a great divergence
from those usual colonial banquets, at which the elders are
only invited to meet distinguished guests. The officers were
chiefly young men; and a greater babel of voices was, I'll
undertake to say, never heard from a banqueting-hall than
came from our dinner-table. Eva Crasweller was the queen
of the evening, and was as joyous, as beautiful, and as
high-spirited as a queen should ever be. I did once or twice
during the festivity glance round at old Crasweller. He was
quiet, and I might almost say silent, during the whole
evening; but I could see from the testimony of his altered
countenance how strong is the passion for life that dwells in
the human breast.

'Your promised bride seems to have it all her own way,'
said Captain Battleax to Jack, when at last the ladies had
withdrawn.

'Oh, yes,' said Jack, 'and I'm nowhere. But I mean to have my innings before long.'

Of what Mrs Neverbend had gone through in providing birds, beasts, and fishes, not to talk of tarts and jellies, for the dinner of that day, no one but myself can have any idea; but it must be admitted that she accomplished her task with thorough success. I was told, too, that after the invitations had been written, no milliner in Britannula was allowed to sleep a single moment till half an hour before the ladies were assembled in our drawing-room; but their efforts, too, were conspicuously successful.

On the next day some of us went on board the John Bright for a return dinner; and very pleasant the officers made it. The living on board the John Bright is exceedingly good, as I have had occasion to learn from many dinners eaten there since that day. I little thought when I sat down at the right hand of Captain Battleax as being the President of the republic, with my wife on his left, I should ever spend more than a month on board the ship, or write on board it this account of all my thoughts and all my troubles in regard to the Fixed Period. After dinner Captain Battleax simply proposed my health, paying to me many unmeaning compliments, in which, however, I observed that no reference was made to the special doings of my presidency; and he ended by saying, that though he had, as a matter of courtesy, and with the greatest possible alacrity, proposed my health, he would not call upon me for any reply. And immediately on his sitting down, there got up a gentleman to whom I had not been introduced before this day, and gave the health of Mrs Neverbend and the ladies of Britannula. Now in spite of what the captain said, I undoubtedly had intended to make a speech. When the President of the republic has his health drunk, it is, I conceive, his duty to do so. But here the gentleman rose with a rapidity which did at the moment seem to have been premeditated. At any rate, my eloquence was altogether stopped. The gentleman was named Sir Ferdinando Brown. He was dressed in simple black, and was clearly not one of the ship's officers; but I could not but suspect at the moment that he was in some special measure concerned in the mission on which the gunboat had been sent. He sat on Mrs Neverbend's left hand, and did seem in some respect to be the chief man on that occasion. However, he proposed Mrs Neverbend's health and the ladies, and the captain instantly called upon the band to play some favourite tune. After that there was no attempt at speaking. We sat with the officers some little time after dinner, and then went ashore. 'Sir Ferdinando and I,' said the captain, as we shook hands with him, 'will do ourselves the honour of calling on you at the executive chambers to-morrow morning.'

I went home to bed with a presentiment of evil running across my heart. A presentiment indeed! How much of evil,—of real accomplished evil,—had there not occurred to me during the last few days! Every hope for which I had lived, as I then told myself, had been brought to sudden extinction by the coming of these men to whom I had been so pleasant, and who, in their turn, had been so pleasant to me! What could I do now but just lay myself down and die? And the death of which I dreamt could not, alas! be that true benumbing death which we think may put an end, or at any rate give a change, to all our thoughts. To die would be as nothing; but to live as the late President of the republic who had fixed his aspirations so high, would indeed be very melancholy. As President I had still two years to run, but it occurred to me now that I could not possibly endure those two years of prolonged nominal power. I should be the laughing-stock of the people; and as such, it would become me to hide my head. When this captain should have taken himself and his vessel back to England, I would retire to a small farm which I possessed at the farthest side of the island, and there in seclusion would I end my days. Mrs Neverbend should come with me, or stay, if it so pleased her, in Gladstonopolis. Jack would become Eva's happy husband, and would remain amidst the hurried duties of the eager world. Craysweller, the triumphant, would live, and at last die, amidst the flocks and herds of Little Christchurch.

I, too, would have a small herd, a little flock of my own, surrounded by no such glories as those of Little Christ-church,—owing nothing to wealth, or scenery, or neigh-bourhood,—and there, till God should take me, I would spend the evening of my day. Thinking of all this, I went to sleep.

On the next morning Sir Ferdinando Brown and Captain Battleax were announced at the executive chambers. I had already been there at my work for a couple of hours; but Sir Ferdinando apologised for the earliness of his visit. It seemed to me as he entered the room and took the chair that was offered to him, that he was the greater man of the two on the occasion,—or perhaps I should say of the three. And yet he had not before come on shore to visit me, nor had he made one at our little dinner-party. 'Mr Neverbend,' began the captain,—and I observed that up to that moment he had generally addressed me as President,—'it cannot be denied that we have come here on an unpleasant mission. You have received us with all that courtesy and hospitality for which your character in England stands so high. But you must be aware that it has been our intention to interfere with that which you must regard as the performance of a duty.'

'It is a duty,' said I. 'But your power is so superior to any that I can advance, as to make us here feel that there is no disgrace in yielding to it. Therefore we can be courteous while we submit. Not a doubt but had your force been only double or treble our own, I should have found it my duty to struggle with you. But how can a little State, but a few years old, situated on a small island, far removed from all the centres of civilisation, contend on any point with the owner of the great 250-ton swiveller-gun?'

'That is all quite true, Mr Neverbend,' said Sir Ferdinando Brown.

'I can afford to smile, because I am absolutely powerless before you; but I do not the less feel that, in a matter in which the progress of the world is concerned, I, or rather we, have been put down by brute force. You have come to us threatening us with absolute destruction. Whether your gun be loaded or not matters little.'

'It is certainly loaded,' said Captain Battleax.

'Then you have wasted your powder and shot. Like a highwayman, it would have sufficed for you merely to tell the weak and cowardly that your pistol would be made to go off when wanted. To speak the truth, Captain Battleax, I do not think that you excel us more in courage than you do in thought and practical wisdom. Therefore, I feel myself quite able, as President of this republic, to receive you with a courtesy due to the servants of a friendly ally.'

'Very well put,' said Sir Ferdinando. I simply bowed to him. 'And now,' he continued, 'will you answer me one question?'

'A dozen if it suits you to ask them.'

'Captain Battleax cannot remain here long with that expensive toy which he keeps locked up somewhere among his cocked-hats and white gloves. I can assure you he has not even allowed me to see the trigger since I have been on board. But 250-ton swivellers do cost money, and the John Bright must steam away, and play its part in other quarters of the globe. What do you intend to do when he shall have taken his pocket-pistol away?'

I thought for a little what answer it would best become me to give to this question, but I paused only for a moment or two. 'I shall proceed at once to carry out the Fixed Period.' I felt that my honour demanded that to such a question I should make no other reply.

'And that in opposition to the wishes, as I understand, of a large proportion of your fellow-citizens?'

'The wishes of our fellow-citizens have been declared by repeated majorities in the Assembly.'

'You have only one House in your Constitution,' said Sir Ferdinando.

'One House I hold to be quite sufficient.'

I was proceeding to explain the theory on which the Britannulan Constitution had been formed, when Sir

Ferdinando interrupted me. 'At any rate, you will admit that a second Chamber is not there to guard against the sudden action of the first. But we need not discuss all this now. It is your purpose to carry out your Fixed Period as soon as the John Bright shall have departed?'

'Certainly.'

'And you are, I am aware, sufficiently popular with the people here to enable you to do so?'

'I think I am,' I said, with a modest acquiescence in an assertion which I felt to be so much to my credit. But I blushed for its untruth.

'Then,' said Sir Ferdinando, 'there is nothing for it but that he must take you with him.'

There came upon me a sudden shock when I heard these words, which exceeded anything which I had yet felt. Me, the President of a foreign nation, the first officer of a people with whom Great Britain was at peace,—the captain of one of her gunboats must carry me off, hurry me away a prisoner, whither I knew not, and leave the country ungoverned, with no President as yet elected to supply my place! And I, looking at the matter from my own point of view, was a husband, the head of a family, a man largely concerned in business,—I was to be carried away in bondage—I, who had done no wrong, had disobeyed no law, who had indeed been conspicuous for my adherence to my duties! No opposition ever shown to Columbus and Galileo had come near to this in audacity and oppression. I, the President of a free republic, the elected of all its people, the chosen depository of its official life,—I was to be kidnapped and carried off in a ship of war, because, forsooth, I was deemed too popular to rule the country! And this was told to me in my own room in the executive chambers, in the very sanctum of public life, by a stout florid gentleman in a black coat, of whom I hitherto knew nothing except that his name was Brown!

'Sir,' I said, after a pause, and turning to Captain Battleax and addressing him, 'I cannot believe that you, as an officer in the British navy, will commit any act of tyranny so oppressive, and of injustice so gross, as that which this gentleman has named.'

'You hear what Sir Ferdinando Brown has said,' replied Captain Battleax.

'I do not know the gentleman,—except as having been introduced to him at your hospitable table. Sir Ferdinando Brown is to me—simply Sir Ferdinando Brown.'

'Sir Ferdinando has lately been our British Governor in Ashantee, where he has, as I may truly say, "bought golden opinions from all sorts of people."* He has now been sent here on this delicate mission, and to no one could it be intrusted by whom it would be performed with more scrupulous honour.' This was simply the opinion of Captain Battleax, and expressed in the presence of the gentleman himself whom he so lauded.

'But what is the delicate mission?' I asked.

Then Sir Ferdinando told his whole story, which I think should have been declared before I had been asked to sit down to dinner with him in company with the captain on board the ship. I was to be taken away and carried to England or elsewhere,—or drowned upon the voyage, it mattered not which. That was the first step to be taken towards carrying out the tyrannical, illegal, and altogether injurious intention of the British Government. Then the republic of Britannula was to be declared as non-existent, and the British flag was to be exalted, and a British Governor installed in the executive chambers! That Governor was to be Sir Ferdinando Brown.

I was lost in a maze of wonderment as I attempted to look at the proceeding all round. Now, at the close of the twentieth century, could oppression be carried to such a height as this? 'Gentlemen,' I said, 'you are powerful. That little instrument which you have hidden in your cabin makes you the master of us all. It has been prepared by the ingenuity of men, able to dominate matter though altogether powerless over mind. On myself, I need hardly say that it would be inoperative. Though you should reduce me to atoms, from them would spring those opinions which would serve altogether to silence your artillery. But the dread of it is to the generality much more powerful than the fact of its possession.'

'You may be quite sure it's there,' said Captain Battleax, 'and that I can so use it as to half obliterate your town within two minutes of my return on board.'

'You propose to kidnap me,' I said. 'What would become of your gun were I to kidnap you?'

'Lieutenant Crosstrees has sealed orders, and is practically acquainted with the mechanism of the gun. Lieutenant Crosstrees is a very gallant officer. One of us always remains on board while the other is on shore. He would think nothing of blowing me up, so long as he obeyed orders.'

'I was going on to observe,' I continued, 'that though this power is in your hands, and in that of your country, the exercise of it betrays not only tyranny of disposition, but poorness and meanness of spirit.' I here bowed first to the one gentleman, and then to the other. 'It is simply a contest between brute strength and mental energy.'

'If you will look at the contests throughout the world,' said Sir Ferdinando, 'you will generally find that the highest respect is paid to the greatest battalions.'

'What world-wide iniquity such a speech as that discloses!' said I, still turning myself to the captain; for though I would have crushed them both by my words had it been possible, my dislike centred itself on Sir Ferdinando. He was a man who looked as though everything were to yield to his meagre philosophy; and it seemed to me as though he enjoyed the exercise of the tyranny which chance had put into his power.

'You will allow me to suggest,' said he, 'that that is a matter of opinion. In the meantime, my friend Captain Battleax has below a guard of fifty marines, who will pay you the respect of escorting you on board with two of the ship's cutters. Everything that can be there done for your accommodation and comfort,—every luxury which can be provided to solace the President of this late republic,—shall be afforded. But, Mr Neverbend, it is necessary that you should go to England; and allow me to assure you, that your departure can neither be prevented nor delayed by uncivil words spoken to the future Governor of this prosperous colony.'

'My words are, at any rate, less uncivil than Captain Battleax's marines; and they have, I submit, been made necessary by the conduct of your country in this matter. Were I to comply with your orders without expressing my own opinion, I should seem to have done so willingly hereafter. I say that the English Government is a tyrant, and that you are the instruments of its tyranny. Now you can proceed to do your work.'

'That having all been pleasantly settled,' said Sir Ferdinando, with a smile, 'I will ask you to read the document by which this duty has been placed in my hands.' He then took out of his pocket a letter addressed to him by the Duke of Hatfield, as Minister for the Crown Colonies, and gave it to me to read. The letter ran as follows:—

'COLONIAL OFFICE, CROWN COLONIES,
15*th May* 1980.

'SIR,—I have it in command to inform your Excellency that you have been appointed Governor of the Crown colony which is called Britannula. The peculiar circumstances of the colony are within your Excellency's knowledge. Some years since, after the separation of New Zealand, the inhabitants of Britannula requested to be allowed to manage their own affairs, and HM Minister of the day thought it expedient to grant their request. The country has since undoubtedly prospered, and in a material point of view has given us no grounds for regret. But in their selection of a Constitution the Britannulists have unfortunately allowed themselves but one deliberative assembly, and hence have sprung their present difficulties. It must be, that in such circumstances crude councils should be passed as laws without the safeguard coming from further discussion and thought. At the present moment a law has been passed which, if carried into action, would become abhorrent to mankind at large. It is contemplated to destroy all those who shall have reached a certain fixed age. The arguments put forward to justify so strange a measure I need not here explain at length. It is founded on the acknowledged weakness of those who survive that period of life at which men cease to work. This terrible doctrine has been adopted at the advice of an eloquent citizen of the republic, who is at present its President, and whose general popularity seems to be so great, that, in compliance with his views, even this measure will be carried out unless Great Britain shall interfere.

'You are desired to proceed at once to Britannula, to reannex the island, and to assume the duties of the Governor of a Crown colony. It is understood that a year of probation is to be allowed to those victims who have agreed to their own immolation. You will therefore arrive there in ample time to prevent the first bloodshed. But it is surmised that you will find difficulties in the way of your entering at once upon your government. So great is the popularity of their President, Mr Neverbend, that, if he be left on the island, your Excellency will find a dangerous rival. It is therefore desired that you should endeavour to obtain information as to his intentions; and that, if the Fixed Period be not abandoned altogether, with a clear conviction as to its cruelty on the part of the inhabitants generally, you should cause him to be carried away and brought to England.

'To enable you to effect this, Captain Battleax, of HM gunboat the John Bright, has been instructed to carry you out. The John Bright is armed with a weapon of great power, against which it is impossible that the people of Britannula should prevail. You will carry out with you 100 men of the North-north-west Birmingham regiment, which will probably suffice for your own security, as it is thought that if Mr Neverbend be withdrawn, the people will revert easily to their old habits of obedience.

'In regard to Mr Neverbend himself, it is the especial wish of HM Government that he shall be treated with all respect, and that those honours shall be paid to him which are due to the President of a friendly republic. It is to be expected that he should not allow himself to make an enforced visit to England without some opposition; but it is considered in the interests of humanity to be so essential that this scheme of the Fixed Period shall not be carried out, that HM Government consider that his absence from Britannula shall be for a time insured. You will therefore insure it; but will take care that, as far as lies in your Excellency's power, he be treated with all that respect and hospitality which would be due to him were he still the President of an allied republic.

'Captain Battleax, of the John Bright, will have received a letter to the same effect from the First Lord of the Admiralty, and you will find him ready to co-operate with your Excellency in every respect.—I have the honour to be, sir, your Excellency's most obedient servant,

HATFIELD.'

This I read with great attention, while they sat silent. 'I understand it; and that is all, I suppose, that I need say upon the subject. When do you intend that the John Bright shall start?'

'We have already lighted our fires, and our sailors are weighing the anchors. Will twelve o'clock suit you?'

'To-day!' I shouted.

'I rather think we must move to-day,' said the captain.

'If so, you must be content to take my dead body. It is now nearly eleven.'

'Half-past ten,' said the captain, looking at his watch.

'And I have no one ready to whom I can give up the archives of the Government.'

'I shall be happy to take charge of them,' said Sir Ferdinando.

'No doubt,—knowing nothing of the forms of our government, or——'

'They, of course, must all be altered.'

'Or of the habits of our people. It is quite impossible. I, too, have the complicated affairs of my entire life to arrange, and my wife and son to leave;—though I would not for a moment be supposed to put these private matters forward when the public service is concerned. But the time you name is so unreasonable as to create a feeling of horror at your tyranny.'

'A feeling of horror would be created on the other side of the water,' said Sir Ferdinando, 'at the idea of what you may do if you escape us. I should not consider my head to be safe on my own shoulders were it to come to pass that while I am on the island an old man were executed in compliance with your system.'

Alas! I could not but feel how little he knew of the sentiment which prevailed in Britannula; how false was his idea of my power; and how potent was that love of life which had been evinced in the city when the hour for deposition had become nigh. All this I could hardly explain to him, as I should thus be giving to him the strongest evidence against my own philosophy. And yet it was necessary that I should say something to make him understand that this sudden deportation was not necessary. And then during that moment there came to me suddenly an idea that it might be well that I should take this journey to England, and there begin again my career,—as Columbus, after various obstructions, had recommenced his,—and that I should endeavour to carry with me the people of Great Britain, as I had already carried the more quickly intelligent inhabitants of Britannula. And in order that I may do so, I have now prepared these pages, writing them on board HM gunboat, the John Bright.

'Your power is sufficient,' I said.

'We are not sure of that,' said Sir Ferdinando. 'It is always well to be on the safe side.'

'Are you so afraid of what a single old man can do,—you with your 250-ton swivellers, and your guard of marines, and your North-north-west Birmingham soldiery?'

'That depends on who and what the old man may be.' This was the first complimentary speech which Sir Ferdinando had made, and I must confess that it was efficacious. I did not after that feel so strong a dislike to the man as I had done before. 'We do not wish to make ourselves disagreeable to you, Mr Neverbend.' I shrugged my shoulders. 'Unnecessarily disagreeable, I should have said. You are a man of your word.' Here I bowed to him. 'If you will give us your promise to meet Captain Battleax here at this time to-morrow, we will stretch a point and delay the departure of the John Bright for twenty-four hours.' To this again I objected violently; and at last, as an extreme favour, two entire days were allowed for my departure.

The craft of men versed in the affairs of the old Eastern world is notorious. I afterwards learned that the stokers on board the ship were only pretending to get up their fires, and the sailors pretending to weigh their anchors, in order that their operations might be visible, and that I might suppose that I had received a great favour from my enemies' hands. And this plan was adopted, too, in order to extract from me a promise that I would depart in peace. At any rate, I did make the promise, and gave these two gentlemen my word that I would be present there in my own room in the executive chambers at the same hour on the day but one following.

'And now,' said Sir Ferdinando, 'that this matter is settled between us, allow me most cordially to shake you by the hand, and to express my great admiration for your character. I cannot say that I agree with you in theory as to the Fixed Period,—my wife and children could not, I am sure, endure to see me led away when a certain day should come,—but I can understand that much may be said on the point, and I admire greatly the eloquence and energy which you have devoted to the matter. I shall be happy to meet you here at any hour to-morrow, and to receive the Britannulan archives from your hands. You, Mr Neverbend, will always be regarded as the father of your country—

"Roma patrem patriæ Ciceronem libera dixit."'*

With this the two gentlemen left the room.

# CHAPTER X
## The Town-hall

WHEN I went home and told them what was to be done, they were of course surprised, but apparently not very unhappy. Mrs Neverbend suggested that she should accompany me, so as to look after my linen and other personal comforts. But I told her, whether truly or not I hardly then knew, that there would be no room for her on board a ship of war such as the John Bright. Since I have lived on board her, I have become aware that they would willingly have accommodated, at my request, a very much larger family than my own. Mrs Neverbend at once went to work to provide for my enforced absence, and in the course of the day Eva Crasweller came in to help her. Eva's manner to myself had become perfectly altered since the previous morning. Nothing could be more affectionate, more gracious, or more winning, than she was now; and I envied Jack the short moments of *tête-à-tête* retreat which seemed from time to time to be necessary for carrying out the arrangements of the day.

I may as well state here, that from this time Abraham Grundle showed himself to be a declared enemy, and that the partnership was dissolved between Crasweller and himself. He at once brought an action against my old friend for the recovery of that proportion of his property to which he was held to be entitled under our marriage laws. This Mr Crasweller immediately offered to pay him; but some of our more respectable lawyers interfered, and persuaded him not to make the sacrifice. There then came on a long action, with an appeal,—all which was given against Grundle, and nearly ruined the Grundles. It seemed to me, as far as I could go into the matter, that Grundle had all the law on his side. But there arose certain quibbles and questions, all of which Jack had at his fingers'-ends, by the strength of which the unfortunate young man was trounced. As I learned by the letters which Eva wrote to me, Crasweller was all through most anxious to pay him; but the lawyers would not have it so, and therefore so much of the property of Little Christchurch was saved for the ultimate benefit of that happy fellow Jack Neverbend.

On the afternoon of the one day which, as a matter of grace, had been allowed to me, Sir Ferdinando declared his intention of making a speech to the people of Gladstonopolis. 'He was desirous,' he said, 'of explaining to the community at large the objects of HM Government in sending him to Britannula, and in requesting the inhabitants to revert to their old form of government.' 'Request indeed,' I said to Crasweller, throwing all possible scorn into the tone of my voice,—'request! with the North-north-west Birmingham regiment, and his 250-ton steam-swiveller in the harbour! That Ferdinando Brown knows how to conceal his claws beneath a velvet glove. We are to be slaves,—slaves because England so wills it. We are robbed of our constitution, our freedom of action is taken from us, and we are reduced to the lamentable condition of a British Crown colony! And all this is to be done because we had striven to rise above the prejudices of the day.' Crasweller smiled, and said not a word to oppose me, and accepted all my indignation with assent; but he certainly did not show any enthusiasm. A happier old gentleman, or one more active for his years, I had never known. It was but yesterday that I had seen him so absolutely cowed as to be hardly able to speak a word. And all this change had occurred simply because he was to be allowed to die out in the open world, instead of enjoying the honour of having been the first to depart in conformity with the new theory. He and I, however, spent thus one day longer in sweet friendship; and I do not doubt but that, when I return to Britannula, I shall find him living in great comfort at Little Christchurch.

At three o'clock we all went into our great town-hall to hear what Sir Ferdinando had to say to us. The chamber is a very spacious one, fitted up with a large organ, and all the arrangements necessary for a music-hall; but I had never seen a greater crowd than was collected there on this occasion. There was not a vacant corner to be found; and I heard that very many of the inhabitants went away greatly displeased in that they could not be accommodated. Sir Ferdinando had been very particular in asking the attendance of Captain Battleax, and as many of the ship's officers as could be spared. This, I was told, he did in order that something of the *éclat* of his oration might be taken back to England. Sir Ferdinando was a man who thought much of his own eloquence,—and much also of the advantage which he might reap from it in the opinion of his fellow-countrymen generally. I found that a place of honour had been reserved for me too at his right hand, and also one for my wife at his left. I must confess that in these last moments of my sojourn among the people over whom I had ruled, I was treated with the most distinguished courtesy. But, as I continued to say to myself, I was to be banished in a few hours as one whose intended cruelties were too abominable to allow of my remaining in my own country. On the first seat behind the chair sat Captain Battleax, with four or five of his officers behind him. 'So you have left Lieutenant Crosstrees in charge of your little toy,' I whispered to Captain Battleax.

'With a glass,' he replied, 'by which he will be able to see whether you leave the building. In that case, he will blow us all into atoms.'

Then Sir Ferdinando rose to his legs, and began his speech. I had never before heard a specimen of that special oratory to which the epithet flowery may be most appropriately applied. It has all the finished polish of England, joined to the fervid imagination of Ireland. It streams on without a pause, and without any necessary end but that which the convenience of time may dictate. It comes without the slightest effort, and it goes without producing any great effect. It is sweet at the moment. It pleases many, and can offend none. But it is hardly afterwards much remembered; and is efficacious only in smoothing somewhat the rough ways of this harsh world. But I have observed that in what I have read of British debates, those who have been eloquent after this fashion are generally firm to some purpose of self-interest. Sir Ferdinando had on this occasion dressed himself with minute care; and though he had for the hour before been very sedulous in manipulating certain notes, he now was careful to show not a scrap of paper; and I must do him the justice to declare that he spun out the words from the reel of his memory as though they all came spontaneous and pat to his tongue.

'Mr Neverbend,' he said, 'ladies and gentlemen,—I have to-day for the first time the great pleasure of addressing an intelligent concourse of citizens in Britannula. I trust that before my acquaintance with this prosperous community may be brought to an end, I may have many another opportunity afforded me of addressing you. It has been my lot in life to serve my Sovereign in various parts of the world, and humbly to represent the throne of England in every quarter of the globe. But by the admitted testimony of all people,—my fellow-countrymen at home in England, and those who are equally my fellow-countrymen in the colonies to which I have been sent,—it is acknowledged that in prosperity, intelligence, and civilisation, you are excelled by no English-speaking section of the world. And if by none who speak English, who shall then aspire to excel you? Such, as I have learned, has been the common verdict given; and as I look round this vast room, on a spot which fifty years ago the marsupial races had under their own dominion, and see the feminine beauty and manly grace which greet me on every side, I can well believe that some peculiarly kind freak of nature has been at work, and has tended to produce a people as strong as it is beautiful, and as clever in its wit as it is graceful in its actions.' Here the speaker paused, and the audience all clapped their hands and stamped their feet, which seemed to me to be a very improper mode of testifying their assent to their own praises. But Sir Ferdinando took it all in good part, and went on with his speech.

'I have been sent here, ladies and gentlemen, on a peculiar mission,—on a duty as to which, though I am desirous of explaining it to all of you in every detail, I feel a difficulty of saying a single word.' 'Fixed Period,' was shouted from one of the balconies in a voice which I recognised as that of Mr Tallowax. 'My friend in the gallery,' continued Sir Ferdinando, 'reminds me of the very word for which I should in vain have cudgelled my brain. The Fixed Period is the subject on which I am called upon to say to you a few words;—the Fixed Period, and the man who has, I believe, been among you the chief author of that system of living,—and if I may be permitted to say so, of dying also.' Here the orator allowed his voice to fade away in a melancholy cadence, while he turned his face towards me, and with a gentle motion laid his right hand upon my shoulder. 'Oh, my friends, it is, to say the least of it, a startling project.' 'Uncommon, if it was your turn next,' said Tallowax in the gallery. 'Yes, indeed,' continued Sir Ferdinando, 'if it were my turn next! I must own, that though I should consider myself to be affronted if I were told that I were faint-hearted,—though I should know myself to be maligned if it were said of me that I have a coward's fear of death,—still I should feel far from comfortable if that age came upon me which this system has defined, and were I to live in a country in which it has prevailed. Though I trust that I may be able to meet death like a brave man when it may come, still I should wish that it might come by God's hand, and not by the wisdom of a man.

'I have nothing to say against the wisdom of that man,' continued he, turning to me again. 'I know all the arguments with which he has fortified himself. They have travelled even as far as my ears; but I venture to use the experience which I have gathered in many countries, and to tell him that in accordance with God's purposes the world is not as yet ripe for his wisdom.' I could not help thinking as he spoke thus, that he was not perhaps acquainted with all the arguments on which my system of the Fixed Period was founded; and that if he would do me the honour to listen to a few words which I proposed to speak to the people of Britannula before I left them, he would have clearer ideas about it than had ever yet entered into his mind. 'Oh, my friends,' said he, rising to the altitudes of his eloquence, 'it is fitting for us that we should leave these things in the hands of the Almighty. It is fitting for us, at any rate, that we should do so till we have been brought by Him to a state of god-like knowledge infinitely superior to that which we at present possess.' Here I could perceive that Sir Ferdinando was revelling in the sounds of his own words, and that he had prepared and learnt by heart the tones of his voice, and even the motion of his hands. 'We all know that it is not allowed to us to rush into His presence by any deed of our own. You all remember what the poet says,—

> "Or that the Everlasting had not fixed
> His canon 'gainst self-slaughter!"*

Is not this self-slaughter, this theory in accordance with which a man shall devote himself to death at a certain period? And if a man may not slay himself, how shall he then, in the exercise of his poor human wit, devote a fellow-creature to certain death?' 'And he as well as ever he was in his life,' said Tallowax in the gallery.

'My friend does well to remind me. Though Mr Neverbend has named a Fixed Period for human life, and has perhaps chosen that at which its energies may usually be found to diminish, who can say that he has even approached the certainty of that death which the Lord sends upon us all at His own period? The poor fellow to whom nature has been unkind, departs from us decrepit and worn out at forty; whereas another at seventy is still hale and strong in performing the daily work of his life.'

'I am strong enough to do a'most anything for myself, and I was to be the next to go,—the very next.' This in a treble voice came from that poor fellow Barnes, who had suffered nearly the pangs of death itself from the Fixed Period.

'Yes, indeed; in answer to such an appeal as that, who shall venture to say that the Fixed Period shall be carried out with all its startling audacity? The tenacity of purpose which distinguishes our friend here is known to us all. The fame of his character in that respect had reached my ears even among the thick-lipped inhabitants of Central Africa.' I own I did wonder whether this could be true. ' "Justum et tenacem propositi virum!"* Nothing can turn him from his purpose, or induce him to change his inflexible will. You know him, and I know him, and he is well known throughout England. Persuasion can never touch him; fear has no power over him. He, as one unit, is strong against a million. He is invincible, imperturbable, and ever self-assured.'

I, as I sat there listening to this character of myself, heroic somewhat, but utterly unlike the person for whom it was intended, felt that England knew very little about me, and cared less; and I could not but be angry that my name should be used in this way to adorn the sentences of Sir Ferdinando's speech. Here in Gladstonopolis I was well known,—and well known to be neither imperturbable nor self-assured. But all the people seemed to accept what he said, and I could not very well interrupt him. He had his opportunity now, and I perhaps might have mine by-and-by.

'My friends,' continued Sir Ferdinando, 'at home in England, where, though we are powerful by reason of our wealth and numbers——' 'Just so,' said I. 'Where we are powerful, I repeat, by reason of our wealth and numbers, though perhaps less advanced than you are in the philosophical arrangements of life, it has seemed to us to be impossible that the theory should be allowed to be carried to its legitimate end. The whole country would be horrified were one life sacrificed to this theory.' 'We knew that,—we knew that,' said the voice of Tallowax. 'And yet your Assembly had gone so far as to give to the system all the stability of law. Had not the John Bright steamed into your harbour yesterday, one of your most valued citizens would have been already—deposited.' When he had so spoken, he turned round to Mr Crasweller, who was sitting on my right hand, and bowed to him. Crasweller looked straight before him, and took no notice of Sir Ferdinando. He was at the present moment rather on my side of the question, and having had his freedom secured to him, did not care for Sir Ferdinando.

'But that has been prevented, thanks to the extraordinary rapidity with which my excellent friend Captain Battleax has made his way across the ocean. And I must say that every one of these excellent fellows, his officers, has done his best to place HM ship the John Bright in her commanding position with the least possible delay.' Here he turned round and bowed to the officers, and by keen eyes might have been observed to bow through the windows also to the vessel, which lay a mile off in the harbour. 'There will not, at any rate for the present, be any Fixed Period for human life in Britannula. That dream has been dreamed,—at any rate for the present. Whether in future ages such a philosophy may prevail, who shall say? At present we must all await our death from the hands of the Almighty. "Sufficient for the day is the evil thereof."*

'And now, gentlemen, I have to request your attention for a few moments to another matter, and one which is very different from this which we have discussed. I am to say a few words of the past and the present,—of your past constitution, and of that which it is my purpose to inaugurate.' Here there arose a murmur through the room very audible, and threatening by its sounds to disturb the orator. 'I will ask your favour for a few minutes; and when you shall have heard me to-day, I will in my turn hear you to-morrow. Great Britain at your request surrendered to you the power of self-government. To so small an English-speaking community has this never before been granted. And I am bound to say that you have in many respects shown yourselves fit for the responsibility imposed upon you. You have been intelligent, industrious, and prudent. Ignorance has been expelled from your shores, and poverty has been forced to hide her diminished head.' Here the orator paused to receive that applause which he conceived to be richly his due; but the occupants of the benches before him sat sternly silent. There were many there who had been glad to see a ship of war come in to stop the Fixed Period, but hardly one who was pleased to lose his own independence. 'But though that is so,' said Sir Ferdinando, a little nettled at the want of admiration with which his words had been received, 'HM Government is under the necessity of putting an end to the contitution under which the Fixed Period can be allowed to prevail. While you have made laws for yourselves, any laws so made must have all the force of law.' 'That's not so certain,' said a voice from a distance, which I shrewdly suspect to have been that of my hopeful son, Jack Neverbend. 'As Great Britain cannot and will not permit the Fixed Period to be carried out among any English-speaking race of people——'

'How about the United States?' said a voice.

'The United States have made no such attempt; but I will proceed. It has therefore sent me out to assume the reins, and to undertake the power, and to bear the responsibility of being your governor during a short term of years. Who shall say what the future may disclose? For the present I shall rule here. But I shall rule by the aid of your laws.'

'Not the Fixed Period law,' said Exors, who was seated on the floor of the chamber immediately under the orator.

'No; that law will be specially wiped out from your statute-book. In other respects, your laws and those of Great Britain are nearly the same. There may be divergences, as in reference to the non-infliction of capital punishment. In such matters I shall endeavour to follow your wishes, and so to govern you that you may still feel that you are living under the rule of a president of your own selection.' Here I cannot but think that Sir Ferdinando was a little rash. He did not quite know the extent of my popularity, nor had he gauged the dislike which he himself would certainly encounter. He had heard a few voices in the hall, which, under fear of death, had expressed their dislike to the Fixed Period; but he had no idea of the love which the people felt for their own independence, or,—I believe I may say,—for their own president. There arose in the hall a certain amount of clamour, in the midst of which Sir Ferdinando sat down.

Then there was a shuffling of feet as of a crowd going away. Sir Ferdinando having sat down, got up again and shook me warmly by the hand. I returned his greeting with my pleasantest smile; and then, while the people were moving, I spoke to them two or three words. I told them that I should start to-morrow at noon for England, under a promise made by me to their new governor, and that I purposed to explain to them, before I went, under what circumstances I had given that promise, and what it was that I intended to do when I should reach England. Would they meet me there, in that hall, at eight o'clock that evening, and hear the last words which I should have to address to them? Then the hall was filled with a mighty shout, and there arose a great fury of exclamation. There was a waving of handkerchiefs, and a holding up of hats, and all those signs of enthusiasm which are wont to greet thĕ popular man of the hour. And in the midst of them, Sir Ferdinando Brown stood up upon his legs, and continued to bow without cessation.

At eight, the hall was again full to overflowing. I had been busy, and came down a little late, and found a difficulty in making my way to the chair which Sir Ferdinando had occupied in the morning. I had had no time to prepare my words, though the thoughts had rushed quickly,—too quickly,—into my mind. It was as though they would tumble out from my own mouth in precipitate energy. On my right hand sat the governor, as I must now call him; and in the chair on my left was placed my wife. The officers of the gunboat were not present, having occupied themselves, no doubt, in banking up their fires.

'My fellow-citizens,' I said, 'a sudden end has been brought to that self-government of which we have been proud, and by which Sir Ferdinando has told you that "ignorance has been expelled from your shores, and poverty has been forced to hide her diminished head." I trust that, under his experience, which he tells us as a governor has been very extensive, those evils may not now fall upon you. We are, however, painfully aware that they do prevail wherever the concrete power of Great Britain is found to be in full force. A man ruling us,—us and many other millions of subjects,—from the other side of the globe, cannot see our wants and watch our progress as we can do ourselves. And even Sir Ferdinando coming upon us with all his experience, can hardly be able to ascertain how we may be made happy and prosperous. He has with him, however, a company of a celebrated English regiment, with its attendant officers, who, by their red coats and long swords, will no doubt add to the cheerfulness of your social gatherings. I hope that you may not find that they shall ever interfere with you after a rougher fashion.

'But upon me, my fellow-citizens, has fallen the great disgrace of having robbed you of your independence.' Here a murmur ran through the hall, declaring that this was not so. 'So your new Governor has told you, but he has not told you the exact truth. With whom the doctrine of the Fixed Period first originated, I will not now inquire. All the responsibility I will take upon myself, though the honour and glory I must share with my fellow-countrymen.

'Your Governor has told you that he is aware of all the arguments by which the Fixed Period is maintained; but I think that he must be mistaken here, as he has not ventured to attack one of them. He has told us that it is fitting that we should leave the question of life and death in the hands of the Almighty. If so, why is all Europe bristling at this moment with arms,—prepared, as we must suppose, for shortening life,—and why is there a hangman attached to the throne of Great Britain as one of its necessary executive officers? Why in the Old Testament was Joshua commanded to slay mighty kings? And why was Pharaoh and his hosts drowned in the Red Sea? Because the Almighty so willed it, our Governor will say, taking it for granted that He willed everything of which a record is given in the Old Testament. In those battles which have ravished the North-west of India during the last half-century, did the Almighty wish that men should perish miserably by ten thousands and twenty thousands? Till any of us can learn more than we know at present of the will of the Almighty, I would, if he will allow me, advise our Governor to be silent on that head.

'Ladies and gentlemen, it would be a long task, and one

not to be accomplished before your bedtime, were I to recount to you, for his advantage, a few of the arguments which have been used in favour of the Fixed Period,—and it would be useless, as you are all acquainted with them. But Sir Ferdinando is evidently not aware that the general prolongation of life on an average, is one of the effects to be gained, and that, though he himself might not therefore live the longer if doomed to remain here in Britannula, yet would his descendants do so, and would live a life more healthy, more useful, and more sufficient for human purposes.

'As far as I can read the will of the Almighty, or rather the progress of the ways of human nature, it is for man to endeavour to improve the conditions of mankind. It would be as well to say that we would admit no fires into our establishments because a life had now and again been lost by fire, as to use such an argument as that now put forward against the Fixed Period. If you will think of the line of reasoning used by Sir Ferdinando, you will remember that he has, after all, only thrown you back upon the old prejudices of mankind. If he will tell me that he is not as yet prepared to discard them, and that I am in error in thinking that the world is so prepared, I may perhaps agree with him. The John Bright in our harbour is the strongest possible proof that such prejudices still exist. Sir Ferdinando Brown is now your Governor, a fact which in itself is strong evidence. In opposition to these witnesses I have nothing to say. The ignorance which we are told that we had expelled from our shores, has come back to us; and the poverty is about, I fear, to show its head.' Sir Ferdinando here arose and expostulated. But the people hardly heard him, and at my request he again sat down.

'I do think that I have endeavoured in this matter to advance too quickly, and that Sir Ferdinando has been sent here as the necessary reprimand for that folly. He has required that I shall be banished to England; and as his order is backed by a double file of red-coats,—an instrument which in Britannula we do not possess,—I purpose to obey him. I shall go to England, and I shall there use what little strength remains to me in my endeavour to put forward those arguments for conquering the prejudices of the people which have prevailed here, but which I am very sure would have no effect upon Sir Ferdinando Brown.

'I cannot but think that Sir Ferdinando gave himself unnecessary trouble in endeavouring to prove to us that the Fixed Period is a wicked arrangement. He was not likely to succeed in that attempt. But he was sure to succeed in telling us that he would make it impossible by means of the double file of armed men by whom he is accompanied, and the 250-ton steam-swiveller with which, as he informed me, he is able to blow us all into atoms, unless I would be ready to start with Captain Battleax to-morrow. It is not his religion but his strength that has prevailed. That Great Britain is much stronger than Britannula none of us can doubt. Till yesterday I did doubt whether she would use her strength to perpetuate her own prejudices and to put down the progress made by another people.

'But, fellow-citizens, we must look the truth in the face. In this generation probably, the Fixed Period must be allowed to be in abeyance.' When I had uttered these words there came much cheering and a loud sound of triumph, which was indorsed probably by the postponement of the system, which had its terrors; but I was enabled to accept these friendly noises as having been awarded to the system itself. 'Well, as you all love the Fixed Period, it must be delayed till Sir Ferdinando and the English have—been converted.'

'Never, never!' shouted Sir Ferdinando; 'so godless an idea shall never find a harbour in this bosom,' and he struck his chest violently.

'Sir Ferdinando is probably not aware to what ideas that bosom may some day give a shelter. If he will look back thirty years, he will find that he had hardly contemplated even the weather-watch which he now wears constantly in his waistcoat-pocket. At the command of his Sovereign he may still live to carry out the Fixed Period somewhere in the centre of Africa.'

'Never!'

'In what college among the negroes he may be deposited, it may be too curious to inquire. I, my friends, shall leave these shores to-morrow; and you may be sure of this, that while the power of labour remains to me, I shall never desist to work for the purpose that I have at heart. I trust that I may yet live to return among you, and to render you an account of what I have done for you and for the cause in Europe.' Here I sat down, and was greeted by the deafening applause of the audience; and I did feel at the moment that I had somewhat got the better of Sir Ferdinando.

I have been able to give the exact words of these two speeches, as they were both taken down by the reporting telephone-apparatus, which on the occasion was found to work with great accuracy. The words as they fell from the mouth of the speakers were composed by machinery, and my speech appeared in the London morning newspapers within an hour of the time of its utterance.

# CHAPTER XI
## Farewell!

I WENT home to my house in triumph; but I had much to do before noon on the following day, but very little time in which to do it. I had spent the morning of that day in preparing for my departure, and in so arranging matters with my clerks that the entrance of Sir Ferdinando on his new duties might be easy. I had said nothing, and had endeavoured to think as little as possible, of the Fixed Period. An old secretary of mine,—old in years of work, though not as yet in age,—had endeavoured to comfort me by saying that the college up the hill might still be used before long. But I had told him frankly that we in Britannula had all been too much in a hurry, and had foolishly endeavoured to carry out a system in opposition to the world's prejudices, which system, when successful, must pervade the entire world. 'And is nothing to be done with those beautiful buildings?' said the secretary, putting in the word beautiful by way of flattery to myself. 'The chimneys and the furnaces may perhaps be used,' I replied. 'Cremation is no part of the Fixed Period. But as for the residences, the less we think about them the better.' And so I determined to trouble my thoughts no further with the college. And I felt that there might be some consolation to me in going away to England, so that I might escape from the great vexation and eyesore which the empty college would have produced.

But I had to bid farewell to my wife and my son, and to Eva and Crasweller. The first task would be the easier, because there would be no necessity for any painful allusion to my own want of success. In what little I might say to Mrs Neverbend on the subject, I could continue that tone of sarcastic triumph in which I had replied to Sir Ferdinando. What was pathetic in the matter I might altogether ignore. And Jack was himself so happy in his nature, and so little likely to look at anything on its sorrowful side, that all would surely go well with him. But with Eva, and with Eva's father, things would be different. Words must be spoken which would be painful in the speaking, and regrets must be uttered by me which could not certainly be shared by him. 'I am broken down and trampled upon, and all the glory is departed from my name, and I have become a byword and a reproach* rather than a term of honour in which future ages may rejoice, because I have been unable to carry out my long-cherished purpose by—depositing you, and insuring at least your departure!' And then Crasweller would answer me with his general kindly feeling, and I should feel at the moment of my leaving him the hollowness of his words. I had loved him the better because I had endeavoured to commence my experiment on his body. I had felt a vicarious regard for the honour which would have been done him, almost regarding it as though I myself were to go in his place. All this had received a check when he in his weakness had pleaded for another year. But he had yielded; and though he had yielded without fortitude, he had done so to comply with my wishes, and I could not but feel for the man an extraordinary affection. I was going to England, and might probably never see him again; and I was going with aspirations in my heart so very different from those which he entertained!

From the hours intended for slumber, a few minutes could be taken for saying adieu to my wife. 'My dear,' said I, 'this is all very sudden. But a man engaged in public life has to fit himself to the public demands. Had I not promised to go to-day, I might have been taken away yesterday or the day before.'

'Oh, John,' said she, 'I think that everything has been put up to make you comfortable.'

'Thanks; yes, I'm sure of it. When you hear my name mentioned after I am gone, I hope that they'll say of me that I did my duty as President of the republic.'

'Of course they will. Every day you have been at these nasty executive chambers from nine till five, unless when you've been sitting in that wretched Assembly.'

'I shall have a holiday now, at any rate,' said I, laughing gently under the bedclothes.

'Yes; and I am sure it will do you good, if you only take your meals regular. I sometimes think that you have been encouraged to dwell upon this horrid Fixed Period by the melancholy of an empty stomach.'

It was sad to hear such words from her lips after the two speeches to which she had listened, and to feel that no trace had been left on her mind of the triumph which I had achieved over Sir Ferdinando; but I put up with that, and determined to answer her after her own heart. 'You have always provided a sandwich for me to take to the chambers.'

'Sandwiches are nothing. Do remember that. At your time of life you should always have something warm,—a frizzle* or a cutlet, and you shouldn't eat it without thinking of it. What has made me hate the Fixed Period worse than anything is, that you have never thought of your victuals. You gave more attention to the burning of these pigs than to the cooking of any food in your own kitchen.'

'Well, my dear, I'm going to England now,' said I, beginning to feel weary of her reminiscences.

'Yes, my dear, I know you are; and do remember that as you get nearer and nearer to that chilly country the weather will always be colder and colder. I have put you up four pairs of flannel drawers, and a little bag which you must wear upon your chest.* I observed that Sir Ferdinando, when he was preparing himself for his speech, showed that he had just such a little bag on. And all the time I endeavoured to spy how it was that he wore it. When I came home I immediately went to work, and I shall insist on your putting it on the first thing in the morning, in order that I may see that it sits flat. Sir Ferdinando's did not sit flat, and it looked bulgy. I thought to myself that Lady Brown did not do her duty properly by him. If you would allow me to come with you, I could see that you always put it on rightly. As it is, I know that people will say that it is all my fault when it hangs out and shows itself.' Then I went to sleep, and the parting words between me and my wife·had been spoken.

Early on the following morning I had Jack into my dressing-room, and said good-bye to him. 'Jack,' said I, 'in this little contest which there has been between us, you have got the better in everything.'

'Nobody thought so when they heard your answer to Sir Ferdinando last night.'

'Well, yes; I think I managed to answer him. But I haven't got the better of you.'

'I didn't mean anything,' said Jack, in a melancholy tone of voice. 'It was all Eva's doing. I never cared twopence whether the old fellows were deposited or not, but I do think that if your own time had come near, I shouldn't have liked it much.'

'Why not? why not? If you will only think of the matter all round, you will find that it is all a false sentiment.'

'I should not like it,' said Jack, with determination.

'Yes, you would, after you had got used to it.' Here he looked very incredulous. 'What I mean is, Jack, that when sons were accustomed to see their fathers deposited at a certain age, and were aware that they were treated with every respect, that kind of feeling which you describe would wear off. You would have the idea that a kind of honour was done to your parents.'

'When I knew that somebody was going to kill him on the next day, how would it be then?'

'You might retire for a few hours to your thoughts,— going into mourning, as it were.' Jack shook his head. 'But, at any rate, in this matter of Mr Crasweller you have got the better of me.'

'That was for Eva's sake.'

'I suppose so. But I wish to make you understand, now that I am going to England, and may possibly never return to these shores again——'

'Don't say that, father.'

'Well, yes; I shall have much to do there, and of course it may be that I shall not come back, and I wish you to understand that I do not part from you in the least in anger. What you have done shows a high spirit, and great devotion to the girl.'

'It was not quite altogether for Eva either.'

'What then?' I demanded.

'Well, I don't know. The two things went together, as it were. If there had been no question about the Fixed Period, I do think I could have cut out Abraham Grundle. And as for Sir Kennington Oval, I am beginning to believe that that was all Eva's pretence. I like Sir Kennington, but Eva never cared a button for him. She had taken to me because I had shown myself an anti-Fixed-Period man. I did it at first simply because I hated Grundle. Grundle wanted to fix-period old Crasweller for the sake of the property; and therefore I belonged naturally to the other side. It wasn't that I liked opposing you. If it had been Tallowax that you were to begin with, or Exors, you might have burnt 'em up without a word from me.'

'I am gratified at hearing that.'

'Though the Fixed Period does seem to be horrible, I would have swallowed all that at your bidding. But you can see how I tumbled into it, and how Eva egged me on, and how the nearer the thing came the more I was bound to fight. Will you believe it?—Eva swore a most solemn oath, that if her father was put into that college she would never marry a human being. And up to that moment when the lieutenant met us at the top of the hill, she was always as cold as snow.'

'And now the snow is melted?'

'Yes,—that is to say, it is beginning to thaw!' As he said this I remembered the kiss behind the parlour-door which had been given to her by another suitor before these troubles began, and my impression that Jack had seen it also; but on that subject I said nothing. 'Of course it has all been very happy for me,' Jack continued; 'but I wish to say to you before you go, how unhappy it makes me to think that I have opposed you.'

'All right, Jack; all right. I will not say that I should not have done the same at your age, if Eva had asked me. I wish you always to remember that we parted as friends. It will not be long before you are married now.'

'Three months,' said Jack, in a melancholy tone.

'In an affair of importance of this kind, that is the same as to-morrow. I shall not be here to wish you joy at your wedding.'

'Why are you to go if you don't wish it?'

'I promised that I would go when Captain Battleax talked of carrying me off the day before yesterday. With a hundred soldiers, no doubt he could get me on board.'

'There are a great many more than a hundred men in Britannula as good as their soldiers. To take a man away by force, and he the President of the republic! Such a thing was never heard of. I would not stir if I were you. Say the word to me, and I will undertake that not one of these men shall touch you.'

I thought of his proposition; and the more I thought of it,

the more unreasonable it did appear that I, who had committed no offence against any law, should be forced on board the John Bright. And I had no doubt that Jack would be as good as his word. But there were two causes which persuaded me that I had better go. I had pledged my word. When it had been suggested that I should at the moment be carried on board,—which might no doubt then have been done by the soldiers,—I had said that if a certain time were allowed me I would again be found in the same place. If I were simply there, and were surrounded by a crowd of Britannulans ready to fight for me, I should hardly have kept my promise. But a stronger reason than this perhaps actuated me. It would be better for me for a while to be in England than in Britannula. Here in Britannula I should be the ex-President of an abolished republic, and as such subject to the notice of all men; whereas in England I should be nobody, and should escape the constant mortification of seeing Sir Ferdinando Brown. And then in England I could do more for the Fixed Period than at home in Britannula. Here the battle was over, and I had been beaten. I began to perceive that the place was too small for making the primary efforts in so great a cause. The very facility which had existed for the passing of the law through the Assembly had made it impossible for us to carry out the law; and therefore, with the sense of failure strong upon me, I should be better elsewhere than at home. And the desire of publishing a book in which I should declare my theory,—this very book which I have so nearly brought to a close,—made me desire to go. What could I do by publishing anything in Britannula? And though the manuscript might have been sent home, who would see it through the press with any chance of success? Now I have my hopes, which I own seem high, and I shall be able to watch from day to day the way in which my arguments in favour of the Fixed Period are received by the British public. Therefore it was that I rejected Jack's kind offer. 'No, my boy,' said I, after a pause, 'I do not know but that on the whole I shall prefer to go.'

'Of course if you wish it.'

'I shall be taken there at the expense of the British public, which is in itself a triumph, and shall, I presume, be sent back in the same way. If not, I shall have a grievance in their parsimony, which in itself will be a comfort to me; and I am sure that I shall be treated well on board. Sir Ferdinando with his eloquence will not be there, and the officers are, all of them, good fellows. I have made up my mind, and I will go. The next that you will hear of your father will be the publication of a little book that I shall write on the journey, advocating the Fixed Period. The matter has never been explained to them in England, and perhaps my words may prevail.' Jack, by shaking his head mournfully, seemed to indicate his idea that this would not be the case; but Jack is resolute, and will never yield on any point. Had he been in my place, and had entertained my convictions, I believe that he would have deposited Crasweller in spite of Sir Ferdinando Brown and Captain Battleax. 'You will come and see me on board, Jack, when I start.'

'They won't take me off, will they?'

'I should have thought you would have liked to have seen England.'

'And leave Eva! They'd have to look very sharp before they could do that. But of course I'll come.' Then I gave him my blessing, told him what arrangements I had made for his income, and went down to my breakfast, which was to be my last meal in Britannula.

When that was over, I was told that Eva was in my study waiting to see me. I had intended to have gone out to Little Christchurch, and should still do so, to bid farewell to her father. But I was not sorry to have Eva here in my own house, as she was about to become my daughter-in-law. 'Eva has come to bid you good-bye,' said Jack, who was already in the room, as I entered it.

'Eva, my dear,' said I.

'I'll leave you,' said Jack. 'But I've told her that she must be very fond of you. Bygones have to be bygones,— particularly as no harm has been done.' Then he left the room.

She still had on the little round hat, but as Jack went she laid it aside. 'Oh, Mr Neverbend,' she said, 'I hope you do not think that I have been unkind.'

'It is I, my dear, who should express that hope.'

'I have always known how well you have loved my dear father. I have been quite sure of it. And he has always said so. But——'

'Well, Eva, it is all over now.'

'Oh yes, and I am so happy! I have got to tell you how happy I am.'

'I hope you love Jack.'

'Oh!' she exclaimed, and in a moment she was in my arms and I was kissing her. 'If you knew how I hate that Mr Grundle; and Jack is all,—all that he ought to be. One of the things that makes me like him best is his great affection for you. There is nothing that he would not do for you.'

'He is a very good young man,' said I, thinking of the manner in which he had spoken against me on the Town Flags.

'Nothing!' said Eva.

'And nothing that he would not do for you, my dear. But that is all as it should be. He is a high-spirited, good boy; and if he will think a little more of the business and a little less of cricket, he will make an excellent husband.'

'Of course he had to think a little of the match when the Englishmen were here; and he did play well, did he not? He beat them all there.' I could perceive that Eva was quite as intent upon cricket as was her lover, and probably thought just as little about the business. 'But, Mr Neverbend, must you really go?'

'I think so. It is not only that they are determined to take me, but that I am myself anxious to be in England.'

'You wish to—to preach the Fixed Period?'

'Well, my dear, I have got my own notions, which at my time of life I cannot lay aside. I shall endeavour to ventilate them in England, and see what the people there may say about them.'

'You are not angry with me?'

'My child, how could I be angry with you? What you did, you did for your father's sake.'

'And papa? You will not be angry with papa because he didn't want to give up Little Christchurch, and to leave the pretty place which he has made himself, and to go into the college,—and be killed!'

I could not quite answer her at the moment, because in truth I was somewhat angry with him. I thought that he should have understood that there was something higher to be achieved than an extra year or two among the prettinesses of Little Christchurch. I could not but be grieved because he had proved himself to be less of a man than I had expected. But as I remained silent for a few moments, Eva held my hand in hers, and looked up into my face with beseeching eyes. Then my anger went, and I remembered that I had no reason to expect heroism from Crasweller, simply because he had been my friend. 'No, dear, no; all feeling of anger is at an end. It was natural that he should wish to remain at Little Christchurch; and it was better than natural, it was beautiful, that you should wish to save him by the use of the only feminine weapon at your command.'

'Oh, but I did love Jack,' she said.

'I have still an hour or two before I depart, and I shall run down to Little Christchurch to take your father by the hand once more. You may be sure that what I shall say to him will not be ill-natured. And now good-bye, my darling child. My time here in Britannula is but short, and I cannot give up more of it even to my chosen daughter.' Then again she kissed me, and putting on her little hat, went away to Mrs Neverbend,—or to Jack.

It was now nearly ten o'clock, and I had out my tricycle in order to go down as quickly as possible to Little Christchurch. At the door of my house I found a dozen of the English soldiers with a sergeant. He touched his hat, and asked me very civilly where I was going. When I told him that it was but five or six miles out of town, he requested my permission to accompany me. I told him that he certainly might if he had a vehicle ready, and was ready to use it. But as at that moment my luggage was brought out of the house with the view of being taken on board ship, the man thought that it would be as well and much easier to follow the luggage; and the twelve soldiers marched off to see my portmanteaus put safely on board the John Bright.

And I was again,—and I could not but say to myself, probably for the last time,—once again on the road to Little Christchurch. During the twenty minutes which were taken in going down there, I could not but think of the walks I had had up and down with Crasweller in old times, talking as we went of the glories of a Fixed Period, and of the absolute need which the human race had for such a step in civilisation. Probably on such occasions the majority of the words spoken had come from my own mouth; but it had seemed to me then that Crasweller had been as energetic as myself. The period which we had then contemplated at a distance had come round, and Crasweller had seceded woefully. I could not but feel that had he been staunch to me, and allowed himself to be deposited not only willingly but joyfully, he would have set an example which could not but have been efficacious. Barnes and Tallowax would probably have followed as a matter of course, and the thing would have been done. My name would have gone down to posterity with those of Columbus and Galileo, and Britannula would have been noted as the most prominent among the nations of the earth, instead of having become a by-word among countries as a deprived republic and reannexed Crown colony. But all that on the present occasion had to be forgotten, and I was to greet my old friend with true affection, as though I had received from his hands no such ruthless ruin of all my hopes.

'Oh, Mr President,' he said, as he met me coming up the drive towards the house, 'this is kind of you. And you who must be so busy just before your departure!'

'I could not go without a word of farewell to you.' I had not spoken with him since we had parted on the top of the hill on our way out to the college, when the horses had been taken from the carriage, and he had walked back to life and

Little Christchurch instead of making his way to his last home, and to find deposition with all the glory of a great name.

'It is very kind of you. Come in. Eva is not at home.'

'I have just parted with her at my own house. So she and Jack are to make a match of it. I need not tell you how more than contented I shall be that my son should have such a wife. Eva to me has been always dear, almost as a daughter. Now she is like my own child.'

'I am sure that I can say the same of Jack.'

'Yes; Jack is a good lad too. I hope he will stick to the business.'

'He need not trouble himself about that. He will have Little Christchurch and all that belongs to it as soon as I am gone. I had made up my mind only to allow Eva an income out of it while she was thinking of that fellow Grundle. That man is a knave.'

I could not but remember that Grundle had been a Fixed-Periodist, and that it would not become me to abuse him; and I was aware that though Crasweller was my sincere friend, he had come to entertain of late an absolute hatred of all those, beyond myself, who had advocated his own deposition.

'Jack, at any rate, is happy,' said I, 'and Eva. You and I, Crasweller have had our little troubles to imbitter the evenings of our life.'

'You are yet in the full daylight.'

'My ambition has been disappointed. I cannot conceal the fact from myself,—nor from you. It has come to pass that during the last year or two we have lived with different hopes. And these hopes have been founded altogether on the position which you might occupy.'

'I should have gone mad up in that college, Neverbend.'

'I would have been with you.'

'I should have gone mad all the same. I should have committed suicide.'

'To save yourself from an honourable—deposition!'

'The fixed day, coming at a certain known hour; the

feeling that it must come, though it came at the same time so slowly and yet so fast; every day growing shorter day by day, and every season month by month; the sight of these chimneys——'

'That was a mistake, Crasweller; that was a mistake. The cremation should have been elsewhere.'

'A man should have been an angel to endure it,—or so much less than a man. I struggled,—for your sake. Who else would have struggled as I did to oblige a friend in such a matter?'

'I know it—I know it.'

'But life under such a weight became impossible to me. You do not know what I endured even for the last year. Believe me that man is not so constituted as to be able to make such efforts.'

'He would get used to it. Mankind would get used to it.'

'The first man will never get used to it. That college will become a madhouse. You must think of some other mode of letting them pass their last year. Make them drunk, so that they shall not know what they are doing. Drug them and make them senseless; or, better still, come down upon them with absolute power, and carry them away to instant death. Let the veil of annihilation fall upon them before they know where they are. The Fixed Period, with all its damnable certainty, is a mistake. I have tried it and I know it. When I look back at the last year, which was to be the last, not of my absolute life but of my true existence, I shudder as I think what I went through. I am astonished at the strength of my own mind in that I did not go mad. No one would have made such an effort for you as I made. Those other men had determined to rebel since the feeling of the Fixed Period came near to them. It is impossible that human nature should endure such a struggle and not rebel. I have been saved now by these Englishmen, who have come here in their horror, and have used their strength to prevent the barbarity of your benevolence. But I can hardly keep myself quiet as I think of the sufferings which I have endured during the last month.'

'But, Crasweller, you had assented.'

'True; I did assent. But it was before the feeling of my fate had come near to me. You may be strong enough to bear it. There is nothing so hard but that enthusiasm will make it tolerable. But you will hardly find another who will not succumb. Who would do more for you than I have done? Who would make a greater struggle? What honester man is there whom you know in this community of ours? And yet even me you drove to be a liar. Think how strong must have been the facts against you when they have had this effect. To have died at your behest at the instant would have been as nothing. Any danger,—any immediate certainty,—would have been child's-play; but to have gone up into that frightful college, and there to have remained through that year, which would have wasted itself so slowly, and yet so fast,—that would have required a heroism which, as I think, no Greek, no Roman, no Englishman ever possessed.'

Then he paused, and I was aware that I had overstayed my time. 'Think of it,' he continued; 'think of it on board that vessel, and try to bring home to yourself what such a phase of living would mean.' Then he grasped me by the hand, and taking me out, put me upon my tricycle, and returned into the house.

As I went back to Gladstonopolis, I did think of it, and for a moment or two my mind wavered. He had convinced me that there was something wrong in the details of my system; but not,—when I came to argue the matter with myself,— that the system itself was at fault. But now at the present moment I had hardly time for meditation. I had been surprised at Crasweller's earnestness, and also at his eloquence, and I was in truth more full of his words than of his reasons. But the time would soon come when I should be able to devote tranquil hours to the consideration of the points which he had raised. The long hours of enforced idleness on board ship would suffice to enable me to sift his objections, which seemed at the spur of the moment to resolve themselves into the impatience necessary to a year's quiescence. Crasweller had declared that human nature could not endure it. Was it not the case that human nature had never endeavoured to train itself? As I got back to Gladstonopolis, I had already a glimmering of an idea that we must begin with human nature somewhat earlier, and teach men from their very infancy to prepare themselves for the undoubted blessings of the Fixed Period. But certain aids must be given, and the cremating furnace must be removed, so as to be seen by no eye and smelt by no nose.

As I rode up to my house there was that eternal guard of soldiers,—a dozen men, with abominable guns and ungainly military hats or helmets on their heads. I was so angered by their watchfulness, that I was half minded to turn my tricycle, and allow them to pursue me about the island. They could never have caught me had I chosen to avoid them; but such an escape would have been below my dignity. And moreover, I certainly did wish to go. I therefore took no notice of them when they shouldered their arms, but went into the house to give my wife her last kiss. 'Now, Neverbend, remember you wear the flannel drawers I put up for you, as soon as ever you get out of the opposite tropics. Remember it becomes frightfully cold almost at once; and whatever you do, don't forget the little bag.' These were Mrs Neverbend's last words to me. I there found Jack waiting for me, and we together walked down to the quay. 'Mother would like to have gone too,' said Jack.

'It would not have suited. There are so many things here that will want her eye.'

'All the same, she would like to have gone.' I had felt that it was so, but yet she had never pressed her request.

On board I found Sir Ferdinando, and all the ship's officers with him, in full dress. He had come, as I supposed, to see that I really went; but he assured me, taking off his hat as he addressed me, that his object had been to pay his last respects to the late President of the republic. Nothing could now be more courteous than his conduct, or less like the bully that he had appeared to be when he had first claimed to represent the British sovereign in Britannula. And I must confess that there was absent all that tone of

domineering ascendancy which had marked his speech as
to the Fixed Period. The Fixed Period was not again mentioned while he was on board; but he devoted himself to
assuring me that I should be received in England with every
distinction, and that I should certainly be invited to Windsor
Castle. I did not myself care very much about Windsor
Castle; but to such civil speeches I could do no other than
make civil replies; and there I stood for half an hour gri-
macing and paying compliments, anxious for the moment
when Sir Ferdinando would get into the six-oared gig which
was waiting for him, and return to the shore. To me it was of
all half-hours the weariest, but to him it seemed as though to
grimace and to pay compliments were his second nature. At
last the moment came when one of the junior officers came
up to Captain Battleax and told him that the vessel was ready
to start. 'Now, Sir Ferdinando,' said the captain, 'I am afraid
that the John Bright must leave you to the kindness of the
Britannulists.'

'I could not be left in more generous hands,' said Sir
Ferdinando, 'nor in those of warmer friends. The Britannulists speak English as well as I do, and will, I am sure,
admit that we boast of a common country.'

'But not a common Government,' said I, determined to
fire a parting shot. 'But Sir Ferdinando is quite right in
expecting that he personally will receive every courtesy from
the Britannulists. Nor will his rule be in any respect disobeyed until the island shall, with the agreement of England,
again have resumed its own republican position.' Here I
bowed, and he bowed, and we all bowed. Then he departed,
taking Jack with him, leaning on whose arm he stepped
down into the boat; and as the men put their oars into the
water, I jumped with a sudden start at the sudden explosion
of a subsidiary cannon, which went on firing some dozens of
times till the proper number had been completed supposed
to be due to an officer of such magnitude.

# CHAPTER XII
## Our Voyage To England

THE boat had gone ashore and returned before the John Bright had steamed out of the harbour. Then everything seemed to change, and Captain Battleax bade me make myself quite at home. 'He trusted,' he said, 'that I should always dine with him during the voyage, but that I should be left undisturbed during all other periods of the day. He dined at seven o'clock, but I could give my own orders as to breakfast and tiffin. He was sure that Lieutenant Crosstrees would have pleasure in showing me my cabins, and that if there was anything on board which I did not feel to be comfortable, it should be at once altered. Lieutenant Crosstrees would tell my servant to wait upon me, and would show me all the comforts,—and discomforts,—of the vessel.' With that I left him, and was taken below under the guidance of the lieutenant. As Mr Crosstrees became my personal friend during the voyage,—more peculiarly than any of the other officers, all of whom were my friends,—I will give some short description of him. He was a young man, perhaps eight-and-twenty years old, whose great gift in the eyes of all those on board was his personal courage. Stories were told to me by the junior officers of marvellous things which he had done, which, though never mentioned in his own presence, either by himself or by others, seemed to constitute for him a special character,—so that had it been necessary that any one should jump overboard to attack a shark, all on board would have thought that the duty as a matter of course belonged to Lieutenant Crosstrees. Indeed, as I learnt afterwards, he had quite a peculiar name in the British navy. He was a small fair-haired man, with a pallid face and a bright eye, whose idiosyncrasy it was to conceive that life afloat was infinitely superior in all its attributes to life on shore. If there ever was a man entirely devoted to his profession, it was Lieutenant Crosstrees. For women he seemed to care nothing, nor for bishops, nor for judges, nor for members of Parliament. They were all as children skipping about the world in their foolish playful ignorance, whom it was the sailor's duty to protect. Next to the sailor came the soldier, as having some kindred employment; but at a very long interval. Among sailors the British sailor,— that is, the British fighting sailor,—was the only one really worthy of honour; and among British sailors the officers on board HM gunboat the John Bright were the happy few who had climbed to the top of the tree. Captain Battleax he regarded as the sultan of the world; but he was the sultan's vizier, and having the discipline of the ship altogether in his own hands, was, to my thinking, its very master. I should have said beforehand that a man of such sentiments and feelings was not at all to my taste. Everything that he loved I have always hated, and all that he despised I have revered. Nevertheless I became very fond of him, and found in him an opponent to the Fixed Period that has done more to shake my opinion than Crasweller with all his feelings, or Sir Ferdinando with all his arguments. And this he effected by a few curt words which I have found almost impossible to resist. 'Come this way, Mr President,' he said. 'Here is where you are to sleep; and considering that it is only a ship, I think you'll find it fairly comfortable.' Anything more luxurious than the place assigned to me, I could not have imagined on board ship. I afterwards learned that the cabins had been designed for the use of a travelling admiral, and I gathered from the fact that they were allotted to me an idea that England intended to atone for the injury done to the country by personal respect shown to the late President of the republic.

'I, at any rate, shall be comfortable while I am here. That in itself is something. Nevertheless I have to feel that I am a prisoner.'

'Not more so than anybody else on board,' said the lieutenant.

'A guard of soldiers came up this morning to look after

me. What would that guard of soldiers have done supposing that I had run away?'

'We should have had to wait till they had caught you. But nobody conceived that to be possible. The President of a republic never runs away in his own person. There will be a cup of tea in the officers' mess-room at five o'clock. I will leave you till then, as you may wish to employ yourself.' I went up immediately afterwards on deck, and looking back over the tafferel, could only just see the glittering spires of Gladstonopolis in the distance.

Now was the time for thought. I found an easy seat on the stern of the vessel, and sat myself down to consider all that Crasweller had said to me. He and I had parted,—perhaps for ever. I had not been in England since I was a little child, and I could not but feel now that I might be detained there by circumstances, or die there, or that Crasweller, who was ten years my senior, might be dead before I should have come back. And yet no ordinary farewell had been spoken between us. In those last words of his he had confined himself to the Fixed Period, so full had his heart been of the subject, and so intent had he felt himself to be on convincing me. And what was the upshot of what he had said? Not that the doctrine of the Fixed Period was in itself wrong, but that it was impracticable because of the horrors attending its last moments. These were the solitude in which should be passed the one last year; the sight of things which would remind the old man of coming death; and the general feeling that the business and pleasures of life were over, and that the stillness of the grave had been commenced. To this was to be added a certainty that death would come on some prearranged day. These all referred manifestly to the condition of him who was to go, and in no degree affected the welfare of those who were to remain. He had not attempted to say that for the benefit of the world at large the system was a bad system. That these evils would have befallen Crasweller himself, there could be no doubt. Though a dozen companions might have visited him daily, he would have felt the college to be a solitude, because he would not have been allowed to choose his promiscuous comrades as in the outer world. But custom would no doubt produce a cure for that evil. When a man knew that it was to be so, the dozen visitors would suffice for him. The young man of thirty travels over all the world, but the old man of seventy is contented with the comparative confinement of his own town, or perhaps of his own house. As to the ghastliness of things to be seen, they could no doubt be removed out of sight; but even that would be cured by custom. The business and pleasures of life at the prescribed time were in general but a pretence at business and a reminiscence of pleasure. The man would know that the fated day was coming, and would prepare for it with infinitely less of the anxious pain of uncertainty than in the outer world. The fact that death must come at the settled day, would no doubt have its horror as long as the man were able habitually to contrast his position with that of the few favoured ones who had, within his own memory, lived happily to a more advanced age; but when the time should come that no such old man had so existed, I could not but think that a frame of mind would be created not indisposed to contentment. Sitting there, and turning it all over in my mind, while my eyes rested on the bright expanse of the glass-clear sea, I did perceive that the Fixed Period, with all its advantages, was of such a nature that it must necessarily be postponed to an age prepared for it. Crasweller's eloquence had had that effect upon me. I did see that it would be impossible to induce, in the present generation, a feeling of satisfaction in the system. I should have declared that it would not commence but with those who were at present unborn; or, indeed, to allay the natural fears of mothers, not with those who should be born for the next dozen years. It might have been well to postpone it for another century. I admitted so much to myself, with the full understanding that a theory delayed so long must be endangered by its own postponement. How was I to answer for the zeal of those who were to come so long after me? I sometimes thought of a more immediate date in which I myself might be the first to be deposited, and that I might thus be allowed to set an example of a happy final year passed within the college. But then, how far would the Tallowaxes, and Barneses, and Exors of the day be led by my example?

I must on my arrival in England remodel altogether the Fixed Period, and name a day so far removed that even Jack's children would not be able to see it. It was with sad grief of heart that I so determined. All my dreams of a personal ambition were at once shivered to the ground. Nothing would remain of me but the name of the man who had caused the republic of Britannula to be destroyed, and her government to be resumed by her old mistress. I must go to work, and with pen, ink, and paper, with long written arguments and studied logic, endeavour to prove to mankind that the world should not allow itself to endure the indignities, and weakness, and selfish misery of extreme old age. I confess that my belief in the efficacy of spoken words, of words running like an electric spark from the lips of the speaker right into the heart of him who heard them, was stronger far than my trust in written arguments. They must lack a warmth which the others possess; and they enter only on the minds of the studious, whereas the others touch the feelings of the world at large. I had already overcome in the breasts of many listeners the difficulties which I now myself experienced. I would again attempt to do so with a British audience. I would again enlarge on the meanness of the man who could not make so small a sacrifice of his latter years for the benefit of the rising generation. But even spoken words would come cold to me, and would fall unnoticed on the hearts of others, when it was felt that the doctrine advocated could not possibly affect any living man. Thinking of all this, I was very melancholy when I was summoned down to tea by one of the stewards who attended the officers' mess.

'Mr President, will you take tea, coffee, cocoa, chocolate, or preserved dates? There are muffins and crumpets, dry toast, buttered toast, plum-cake, seed-cake, peach-fritters, apple-marmalade, and bread and butter. There are put-up fruits of all kinds, of which you really wouldn't know that they hadn't come this moment from graperies and orchard-houses; but we don't put them on the table, because we think that we can't eat quite so much dinner after them.' This was the invitation which came from a young naval lad who seemed to be about fifteen years old.

'Hold your tongue, Percy,' said an elder officer. 'The fruits are not here because Lord Alfred gorged himself so tremendously that we were afraid his mother, the duchess, would withdraw him from the service when she heard that he had made himself sick.'

'There are curaçoa, chartreuse, pepperwick, mangostino,* and Russian brandy on the sideboard,' suggested a third.

'I shall have a glass of madeira—just a thimbleful,' said another, who seemed to be a few years older than Lord Alfred Percy. Then one of the stewards brought the madeira, which the young man drank with great satisfaction. 'This wine has been seven times round the world,' he said, 'and the only time for drinking it is five-o'clock tea,—that is, if you understand what good living means.' I asked simply for a cup of tea, which I found to be peculiarly good, partly because of the cream which accompanied it. I then went upstairs to take a constitutional walk with Mr Crosstrees on the deck. 'I saw you sitting there for a couple of hours very thoughtful,' said he, 'and I wouldn't disturb you. I hope it doesn't make you unhappy that you are carried away to England?'

'Had it done so, I don't know whether I should have gone—alive.'

'They said that when it was suggested, you promised to be ready in two days.'

'I did say so—because it suited me. But I can hardly imagine that they would have carried me on board with violence, or that they would have put all Gladstonopolis to the sword because I declined to go on board.'

'Brown had told us that we were to bring you off dead or alive; and dead or alive, I think we should have had you. If the soldiers had not succeeded, the sailors would have taken you in hand.' When I asked him why there was this great necessity for kidnapping me, he assured me that feeling in England had run very high on the matter, and that sundry bishops had declared that anything so barbarous could not be permitted in the twentieth century. 'It would be as bad, they said, as the cannibals of New Zealand.'

'That shows the absolute ignorance of the bishops on the subject.'

'I daresay; but there is a prejudice about killing an old man, or a woman. Young men don't matter.'

'Allow me to assure you, Mr Crosstrees,' said I, 'that your sentiment is carrying you far away from reason. To the State the life of a woman should be just the same as that of a man. The State cannot allow itself to indulge in romance.'

'You get a sailor, and tell him to strike a woman, and see what he'll say.'

'The sailor is irrational. Of course, we are supposing that it is for the public benefit that the woman should be struck. It is the same with an old man. The good of the common-wealth,—and his own,—requires that, beyond a certain age, he shall not be allowed to exist. He does not work, and he cannot enjoy living. He wastes more than his share of the necessaries of life, and becomes, on the aggregate, an intolerable burden. Read Shakespeare's description of man in his last stage—

> "Second childishness, and mere oblivion,
> Sans teeth, sans eyes, sans taste, sans everything;"*

and the stage before is merely that of the 'lean and slippered pantaloon.' For his own sake, would you not save mankind from having to encounter such miseries as these?'

'You can't do it, Mr President.'

'I very nearly did do it. The Britannulist Assembly, in the majesty of its wisdom, passed a law to that effect.' I was sorry afterwards that I had spoken of the majesty of the Assembly's wisdom, because it savoured of buncombe. Our Assembly's wisdom was not particularly majestic; but I had intended to allude to the presumed majesty attached to the highest council in the State.

'Your Assembly in the majesty of its wisdom could do nothing of the kind. It might pass a law, but the law could be carried out only by men. The Parliament in England, which is, I take it, quite as majestic as the Assembly in Britannula——'

'I apologise for the word, Mr Crosstrees, which savours of the ridiculous. I did not quite explain my idea at the moment.'

'It is forgotten,' he said; and I must acknowledge that he never used the word against me again. 'The Parliament in England might order a three-months-old baby to be slain, but could not possibly get the deed done.'

'Not if it were for the welfare of Great Britain?'

'Not to save Great Britain from destruction. Strength is very strong, but it is not half so powerful as weakness. I could, with the greatest alacrity in the world, fire that big gun in among battalions of armed men, so as to scatter them all to the winds, but I could not point it in the direction of a single girl.' We went on discussing the matter at considerable length, and his convictions were quite as strong as mine. He was sure that under no circumstances would an old man ever be deprived of his life under the Fixed Period. I was as confident as he on the other side,—or, at any rate, pretended to be so,—and told him that he made no allowance for the progressive wisdom of mankind. But we parted as friends, and soon after went to dinner.

I was astonished to find how very little the captain had to do with his officers. On board ship he lived nearly alone, having his first lieutenant with him for a quarter of an hour every morning. On the occasion of this my first day on board, he had a dinner-party in honour of my coming among them; and two or three days before we reached England, he had another. I dined with him regularly every day except twice, when I was invited to the officers' mess. I breakfasted alone in my own cabin, where everything was provided for me that I could desire, and always lunched and took five-o'clock tea with the officers. I remained alone till one o'clock, and spent four hours every morning during our entire journey in composing this volume as it is now printed. I have put it into the shape of a story, because I think that I may so best depict the feelings of the people around me as I made my great endeavour to carry out the Fixed Period in Britannula, and because I may so describe the kind of opposition which was shown by the expression of those sentiments on which Lieutenant Crosstrees depended. I do not at this minute doubt but that Crasweller would have been deposited had not the John Bright appeared. Whether Barnes and Tallowax would have followed peaceably, may be doubted. They, however, are not men of great weight in Britannula, and the officers of the law might possibly have constrained them to have followed the example which Crasweller had set. But I do confess that I doubt whether I should have been able to proceed to carry out the arrangements for the final departure of Crasweller. Looking forward, I could see Eva kneeling at my feet, and could acknowledge the invincible strength of that weakness to which Crosstrees had alluded. A godlike heroism would have been demanded,—a heroism which must have submitted to have been called brutal,—and of such I knew myself not to be the owner. Had the British Parliament ordered the three-months-old baby to be slaughtered, I was not the man to slaughter it, even though I were the sworn servant of the British Parliament. Upon the whole, I was glad that the John Bright had come into our waters, and had taken me away on its return to England. It was a way out of my immediate trouble against which I was able to expostulate, and to show with some truth on my side that I was an injured man. All this I am willing to admit in the form of a tale, which I have adopted for my present work, and for which I may hope to obtain some popularity in England. Once on shore there, I shall go to work on a volume of altogether a different nature, and endeavour to be argumentative and statistical, as I have here been fanciful, though true to details.

During the whole course of my journey to England, Captain Battleax never said a word to me about the Fixed Period. He was no doubt a gallant officer, and possessed of all necessary gifts for the management of a 250-ton steam swivel-gun; but he seemed to me to be somewhat heavy. He never even in conversation alluded to Britannula, and spoke always of the dockyard at Devonport as though I had been familiar with its every corner. He was very particular about his clothes, and I was told by Lieutenant Crosstrees on the first day that he would resent it as a bitter offence had I come down to dinner without a white cravat. 'He's right, you know; those things do tell,' Crosstrees had said to me when I had attempted to be jocose about these punctilios. I took care, however, always to put on a white cravat both with the captain and with the officers. After dinner with the captain, a cup of coffee was always brought in on a silver tray, in a silver coffee-pot. This was leisurely consumed; and then, as I soon understood, the captain expected that I should depart. I learnt afterwards that he immediately put his feet up on the sofa and slept for the remainder of the evening. I retired to the lieutenant's cabin, and there discussed the whole history of Britannula over many a prolonged cigar.

'Did you really mean to kill the old men?' said Lord Alfred Percy to me one day; 'regularly to cut their throats, you know, and carry them out and burn them.'

'I did not mean it, but the law did.'

'Every poor old fellow would have been put an end to without the slightest mercy?'

'Not without mercy,' I rejoined.

'Now, there's my governor's father,' said Lord Alfred; 'you know who he is?'

'The Duke of Northumberland, I'm informed.'

'He's a terrible swell. He owns three castles, and half a county, and has half a million a-year. I can hardly tell you what sort of an old fellow he is at home. There isn't any one who doesn't pay him the most profound respect, and he's always doing good to everybody. Do you mean to say that some constable or cremator,—some sort of first hangman,—would have come to him and taken him by the nape of his neck, and cut his throat, just because he was sixty-eight years old? I can't believe that anybody would have done it.'

'But the duke is a man.'

'Yes, he's a man, no doubt.'

'If he committed murder, he would be hanged in spite of his dukedom.'

'I don't know how that would be,' said Lord Alfred, hesitating. 'I cannot imagine that my grandfather should commit a murder.'

'But he would be hanged; I can tell you that. Though it be very improbable,—impossible, as you and I may think it,—the law is the same for him as for others. Why should not all other laws be the same also?'

'But it would be murder.'

'What is your idea of murder?'

'Killing people.'

'Then you are murderers who go about with this great gun of yours for the sake of killing many people.'

'We've never killed anybody with it yet.'

'You are not the less murderers if you have the intent to murder. Are soldiers murderers who kill other soldiers in battle? The murderer is the man who illegally kills. Now, in accordance with us, everything would have been done legally; and I'm afraid that if your grandfather were living among us, he would have to be deposited like the rest.'

'Not if Sir Ferdinando were there,' said the boy. I could not go on to explain to him that he thus ran away from his old argument about the duke. But I did feel that a new difficulty would arise from the extreme veneration paid to certain characters. In England how would it be with the Royal Family? Would it be necessary to exempt them down to the extremest cousins; and if so, how large a body of cousins would be generated! I feared that the Fixed Period could only be good for a republic in which there were no classes violently distinguished from their inferior brethren. If so, it might be well that I should go to the United States, and there begin to teach my doctrine. No other republic would be strong enough to stand against those hydra-headed prejudices with which the ignorance of the world at large is fortified. 'I don't believe,' continued the boy, bringing the conversation to an end, 'that all the men in this ship could take my grandfather and kill him in cold blood.'

I was somewhat annoyed, on my way to England, by finding that the men on board,—the sailors, the stokers, and stewards,—regarded me as a most cruel person. The prejudices of people of this class are so strong as to be absolutely invincible. It is necessary that a new race should come up before the prejudices are eradicated. They were civil enough in their demeanour to me personally, but they had all been taught that I was devoted to the slaughter of old men; and they regarded me with all that horror which the modern nations have entertained for cannibalism. I heard a whisper one day between two of the stewards. 'He'd have killed that old fellow that came on board as sure as eggs if we hadn't got there just in time to prevent him.'

'Not with his own hands,' said a listening junior.

'Yes; with his own hands. That was just the thing. He wouldn't allow it to be done by anybody else.' It was thus that they regarded the sacrifice that I had thought to make of my own feelings in regard to Crasweller. I had no doubt suggested that I myself would use the lancet in order to save him from any less friendly touch. I believed afterwards, that when the time had come I should have found myself incapacitated for the operation. The natural weakness incidental to my feelings would have prevailed. But now that promise,—once so painfully made, and since that, as I had thought, forgotten by all but myself,—was remembered against me as a proof of the diabolical inhumanity of my disposition.

'I believe that they think that we mean to eat them,' I said one day to Crosstrees. He had gradually become my confidential friend, and to him I made known all the sorrows which fell upon me during the voyage from the ignorance of the men around me. I cannot boast that I had in the least affected his opinion by my arguments; but he at any rate had sense enough to perceive that I was not a bloody-minded cannibal, but one actuated by a true feeling of philanthropy. He knew that my object was to do good, though he did not believe in the good to be done.

'You've got to endure that,' said he.

'Do you mean to say, that when I get to England I shall be regarded with personal feelings of the same kind?'

'Yes; so I imagine.' There was an honesty about Crosstrees which would never allow him to soften anything.

'That will be hard to bear.'

'The first reformers had to bear such hardships. I don't exactly remember what it was that Socrates wanted to do for his ungrateful fellow-mortals; but they thought so badly of him, that they made him swallow poison. Your Galileo had a hard time when he said that the sun stood still. Why should we go further than Jesus Christ for an example? If you are not able to bear the incidents, you should not undertake the business.'

But in England I should not have a single disciple! There would not be one to solace or to encourage me! Would it not be well that I should throw myself into the ocean, and have done with a world so ungrateful? In Britannula they had known my true disposition. There I had received the credit due to a tender heart and loving feelings. No one thought there that I wanted to eat up my victims, or that I would take a pleasure in spilling their blood with my own hands. And tidings so misrepresenting me would have reached England before me, and I should there have no friend. Even Lieutenant Crosstrees would be seen no more after I had gone ashore. Then came upon me for the first time an idea that I was not wanted in England at all,—that I was simply to be brought away from my own home to avoid the supposed mischief I might do there, and that for all British purposes it would be well that I should be dropped into the sea, or left ashore on some desert island. I had been taken from the place where, as governing officer, I had undoubtedly been of use,—and now could be of use no longer. Nobody in England would want me or would care for me, and I should be utterly friendless there, and alone. For aught I knew, they might put me in prison and keep me there, so as to be sure that I should not return to my own people. If I asked for my liberty, I might be told that because of my bloodthirstiness it would be for the general welfare that I should be deprived of it. When Sir Ferdinando Brown had told me that I should certainly be asked down to Windsor, I had taken his flowery promises as being worth nothing. I had no wish to go to Windsor. But what should I do with myself immediately on my arrival? Would it not be best to return at once to my own country,—if only I might be allowed to do so. All this made me very melancholy, but especially the feeling that I should be regarded by all around as a monster of cruelty. I could not but think of the words which Lieutenant Crosstrees had spoken to me. The Saviour of the world had His disciples who believed in Him, and the one dear youth who loved Him so well. I almost doubted my own energy as a teacher of progress to carry me through the misery which I saw in store for me.

'I shall not have a very bright time when I arrive in England,' I said to my friend Crosstrees, two days before our expected arrival.

'It will be all new, and there will be plenty for you to see.'

'You will go upon some other voyage?'

'Yes; we shall be wanted up in the Baltic at once. We are very good friends with Russia; but no dog is really respected in this world unless he shows that he can bite as well as bark.'

'I shall not be respected, because I can neither bark nor bite. What will they do with me?'

'We shall put you on shore at Plymouth, and send you up to London—with a guard of honour.'

'And what will the guard of honour do with me?'

'Ah! for that I cannot answer. He will treat you with all kind of respect, no doubt.'

'It has not occurred to you to think,' said I, 'where he will deposit me? Why should it do so? But to me the question is one of some moment. No one there will want me; nobody knows me. They to whom I must be the cause of some little trouble will simply wish me out of the way; and the world at large, if it hears of me at all, will simply have been informed of my cruelty and malignity. I do not mean to destroy myself.'

'Don't do that,' said the lieutenant, in a piteous tone.

'But it would be best, were it not that certain scruples prevent one. What would you advise me to do with myself, to begin with?' He paused before he replied, and looked painfully into my face. 'You will excuse my asking you, because, little as my acquaintance is with you, it is with you alone of all Englishmen that I have any acquaintance.'

'I thought that you were intent about your book.'

'What shall I do with my book? Who will publish it? How shall I create an interest for it? Is there one who will believe, at any rate, that I believe in the Fixed Period?'

'I do,' said the lieutenant.

'That is because you first knew me in Britannula, and have since passed a month with me at sea. You are my one and only friend, and you are about to leave me,—and you also disbelieve in me. You must acknowledge to yourself that you have never known one whose position in the world was more piteous, or whose difficulties were more trying.' Then I left him, and went down to complete my manuscript.

# EXPLANATORY NOTES

6   *if by reason of strength . . . labour and sorrow*: Psalm 90: 10.

8   *that word*: the following passage, which occurs in the manu-
    script at this point, was omitted from serial and first-edition
    texts: And then we were told that it was opposed to Gods [*sic*]
    ordinance. What ordinance? How? When? Where? Quote
    the words. Show us even by deduction that the Lord has
    intended that we should keep our old men alive in these
    miseries. (See R. H. Super (ed.) *The Fixed Period* (Ann
    Arbor, Mich., 1990), 175.)

    *as spoken of in Genesis*: according to Genesis 5: 27, Methuselah
    lived 'nine hundred sixty and nine years'.

9   *cremation*: see Introduction.

10  *we named our metropolis after him*: the capital of Britannula is
    Gladstonopolis, a reference to the town of Gladstone in
    Queensland, which when Trollope visited Australia in 1871
    was intended to become the state capital. See Introduction.

    *his grandfather*: Lord Salisbury (1830–1903), Conservative
    politician, whose grandson's title derives from the family seat,
    Hatfield House. Salisbury was Foreign Secretary, 1878–80,
    leader of the Opposition in the House of Lords, 1881–2,
    and later Prime Minister from 1885.

11  *the coming races*: a glance at Bulwer Lytton's science fiction
    novel *The Coming Race* (1871). See Introduction.

17  *his lines had fallen in pleasant places*: Psalm 16: 6: 'The lines
    are fallen unto me in pleasant places.'

18  *mousometor . . . melpomeneon*: imaginary instruments, whose
    names (indicating that they are respectively the mother of the
    Muse and an instrument dedicated to the Muse of Tragedy)
    are imitations of the names given to many musical inventions
    during the nineteenth century, such as the apollonicon, the
    melophone, and the euphonion.

23  *didascalion*: place of instruction, or school (Greek).

27  *grey hairs . . . with sorrow to the grave*: Genesis 42: 38: 'then

shall ye bring down my gray hairs with sorrow to the grave'.

28  *mizzle*: run away (slang).

    *ne exeant regno*: let them not leave the realm (Latin).

32  *it won't teach anyone . . . functions of life*: as it occurs in the
    serial text and in the first edition, this sentence is confused,
    and the insertion of 'not' is the present editor's conjectural
    emendation: 'It won't teach any one [not] to think it better to
    live than to die while he is fit to perform all the functions of
    life.'

36  *Cato and Brutus*: Roman republicans and famous instances of
    honourable suicides.

    *the Everlasting . . . his canon 'gainst self-slaughter*: Hamlet, I. ii.
    131–2.

38  *flocks and herds*: the phrase occurs frequently in the Old
    Testament.

45  *the sun could not have stood still upon Gibeon*: at Joshua's
    command the sun stood still upon Gibeon—Joshua 10:
    12–13. The serial text and the first edition both read
    'Gideon'.

51  *were it not better done as others use*: Milton, 'Lycidas', 67–8:
    'Were it not better done as others use, / To sport with
    Amaryllis in the shade'.

52  *Hampden*: John Hampden (1594–1643), statesman most
    famous for resisting payment of 'Ship Money' to Charles I.

70  *now drinks the king to Hamlet*: Hamlet, v. ii. 267–70. It is
    not clear whether there is any significance in Neverbend's
    mistake in fancying himself Hamlet's father instead of his
    uncle Claudius.

82  *Aditus*: entrance or opportunity (Latin).

86  *a savour of burnt pork*: early advocates of cremation in England
    also tested their furnaces with pig carcasses, with similar
    results. See Introduction.

94  *vi et armis*: by force of arms (Latin).

105 *Mrs Caudle*: Douglas Jerrold's *Mrs Caudle's Curtain Lectures*,
    which appeared in *Punch* during 1846, show Job Caudle
    berated by his wife every night in bed.

116 *John Bright*: presumably a descendant of the radical MP and

orator of that name, 1811–89.

124 *Harvey, and Wilberforce, and Cobden, and that great Banting*: William Harvey (1578–1657) discovered the circulation of the bood; William Wilberforce (1759–1833) was parliamentary leader of the movement to abolish slavery; Richard Cobden (1804–65) was a leading pacifist and advocate of free trade; William Banting (1797–1878), a cabinet-maker and undertaker from Clerkenwell, wrote a pamphlet entitled *Letter on Corpulence* (1863) outlining a method of losing weight through diet.
*Wheatstone*: Sir Charles Wheatstone (1802–75) constructed one of the first electric telegraphs in 1837, and developed submarine telegraphy.

132 *bought golden opinions from all sorts of people*: slightly misquoted from *Macbeth*, I. vii. 32–3.

138 *Roma patrem patriae Ciceronem libera dixit*: Juvenal, *Satires*, viii. 244: 'Free Rome styled Cicero the father of his country.'

144 *or that the Everlasting . . . his canon 'gainst self-slaughter*: see note to p. 36.

145 *justum et tenacem propositi virum*: Horace, *Odes*, III. iii. 1: 'the man righteous and firm of purpose'.

146 *sufficient for the day is the evil thereof*: Matthew 6: 34: 'Take therefore no thought for the morrow: for the morrow shall take thought for the things of itself. Sufficient unto the day is the evil thereof.'

153 *all the glory is departed from my name, and I have become a byword and a reproach*: this passage contains echoes of 1 Samuel 4: 21, Job 17: 6 and 30: 9, and the books of Jeremiah and Ezekiel.

154 *frizzle*: something fried.

155 *a little bag which you must wear upon your chest*: Trollope is presumably making fun of some version of the Victorian chest-protector, which was often made from flannel and chamois leather. Sir Ferdinando's 'little bag' seems to resemble the 'Sternophylon' which the firm of Moses and Son created in 1851, and which consisted of a double layer of heart-shaped fabric fastened with elastic. (I am grateful to Miss Avril Hart of the Victoria and Albert Museum for advice on this subject.)

173   *curaçoa ... pepperwick, mangostino*: 'curaçoa' was a frequent
       English misspelling of 'curaçao'; 'pepperwick' and 'mango-
       stino' must either be real liqueurs or Trollope's inventions,
       the latter presumably derived from the Malaysian fruit, the
       mangosteen.

174   *second childishness ... sans everything*: *As You Like It*, II. vii.
       165–6.

# THE WORLD'S CLASSICS

### A Select List

JOCELIN OF BRAKELOND:
Chronicle of the Abbey of Bury St. Edmunds
*Translated by Diana Greenway and Jane Sayers*

BEN JONSON: Five Plays
*Edited by G. A. Wilkes*

LEONARDO DA VINCI: Notebooks
*Edited by Irma A. Richter*

HERMAN MELVILLE: The Confidence-Man
*Edited by Tony Tanner*

PROSPER MÉRIMÉE: Carmen and Other Stories
*Translated by Nicholas Jotcham*

EDGAR ALLAN POE: Selected Tales
*Edited by Julian Symons*

MARY SHELLEY: Frankenstein
*Edited by M. K. Joseph*

BRAM STOKER: Dracula
*Edited by A. N. Wilson*

ANTHONY TROLLOPE: The American Senator
*Edited by John Halperin*

OSCAR WILDE: Complete Shorter Fiction
*Edited by Isobel Murray*

A complete list of Oxford Paperbacks, including The World's Classics, OPUS, Past Masters, Oxford Authors, Oxford Shakespeare, and Oxford Paperback Reference, is available in the UK from the Arts and Reference Publicity Department (RS), Oxford University Press, Walton Street, Oxford OX2 6DP.

In the USA, complete lists are available from the Paperbacks Marketing Manager, Oxford University Press, 200 Madison Avenue, New York, NY 10016.

Oxford Paperbacks are available from all good bookshops. In case of difficulty, customers in the UK can order direct from Oxford University Press Bookshop, Freepost, 116 High Street, Oxford, OX1 4BR, enclosing full payment. Please add 10 per cent of published price for postage and packing.